AF610236

# THE BERLIN CONSPIRACY

DIVISION SERIES #4

ANGUS MCLEAN

Published 2018 by Smoking Gun Publications

ISBN 978 0 473 56087 4

Copyright © **Angus McLean** 2018

The right of **Angus McLean** to be identified as the author of this work has been asserted by the author in accordance with the Copyright Act 1994.

The story contained within this book is a work of fiction. Names and characters are the product of the author's imagination and any resemblance to actual persons, living or dead, is entirely coincidental.

All rights reserved. No part of this book may be reproduced, stored in or introduced into a retrieval system, or transmitted in any form, or by any means (electronic, electrostatic, magnetic tape, mechanical, photocopying, recording or otherwise) without the prior written permission of the publisher. Any person who does any unauthorised act in relation to this publication may be liable to criminal prosecution and civil claims for damages.

## ALSO BY ANGUS MCLEAN

**Chase Investigations Series**

*Old Friends*

*Honey Trap*

*Sleeping Dogs*

*Tangled Webs*

*Dirty Deeds*

*Red Mist*

*Fallen Angel*

*Holy Orders*

*Deal Breaker*

**The Division Series**

*Smoke and Mirrors*

*Call to Arms*

*The Shadow Dancers*

*The Berlin Conspiracy*

*No Second Chance*

**Nicki Cooper Mystery Series**

*The Country Club Caper*

**Early Warning Series**

*Martial Law*

*Getting Home*

*Stand Fast*

# THE BERLIN CONSPIRACY

BY ANGUS MCLEAN

# 1

Archer sat on his arse and wondered if anybody would survive when the plane went down.

The plane was a Boeing 777-300ER, the standard aircraft used by the national carrier on flights across the Pacific. It was a comfortable, reliable beast, pretty good on gas and could carry 396 passengers plus a full crew to a maximum of 13,560 kilometres.

None of that really mattered much to Craig Archer. Sure, it was good to be comfortable, but years in special ops had removed his need for constant comfort. Sure, among those 396 passengers – and it was a full flight today – there were bound to be at least a couple of lovelies. There were, and he'd clocked them earlier.

No, his main concern tonight was making sure the bastard didn't go down. No innocents were going to die on his watch.

The intel had come through late from GCSB, resulting in a mad scramble in Auckland. The intel was solid, presenting a credible threat to Air New Zealand Flight 6 from Auckland to Los Angeles.

A credible threat meant one that could realistically be achieved and that there was a strong likelihood of it actually happening. Archer didn't know where the intel had come from. There hadn't been time for that. His focus was all about getting a team together, getting on board, and making sure no fucker took it down.

The team had been easy, once they got the green light from the Director. The green light had officially been given at 16.15hrs, by which time the team was in the international terminal of Auckland Airport, queueing at check-in. It had taken the Director more than two hours to get the sign-off from above. It took that long to convince the fish-heads that something needed to be done, now, and to argue why his team should be deployed rather than the Police or Army.

Eventually common sense had prevailed. Division 5 of the Security Intelligence Service was staffed predominantly by former Special Forces guys, they were available now, and amazingly, they were actually at the airport already, good to go. There were going to be some mighty pissed-off operators when word of this op got out, there was no doubt about that.

Archer shifted in his seat, stretching his legs and crossing his ankles. Business Premier Class was certainly comfortable. He felt a smile cross his lips. Here he was flying first class in seat 5B, dressed in Country Road casuals, heading to LA with a Plan B in mind if the job didn't go down. It was a long way from years in the Green Machine.

He didn't need to look around to see the rest of the team. He knew where they were, every position imprinted on his brain, along with their plan. It was a simple plan, as far as plans went. They didn't know who the bad guys were, or even if they were actually on board, so the brief was simple; react to any threat, take the bad guys down hard and fast, and save the plane.

He turned over the intel in his mind for the millionth time. A cell of Islamic terrorists, flying from Auckland to Los Angeles, would hijack the aircraft and demand a ransom. It was old-fashioned and not easy to pull off, but remarkably effective when successful. The oddity seemed to be the ransom demand rather than a suicide flight into a high profile target. There was always the possibility that the intel was slightly off on that point, but it didn't change the fact that a hijack was a real and imminent threat.

Traditionally Islamic terrorists had preferred the mass casualties over monetary gain. They had no intel – or at least, none that the team was aware of – about the identity or nationality of the terrorists, nor of their affiliation. Al-Qaeda were the classic plane hijackers, so they naturally went straight to the top of the list.

Whoever the group was didn't really matter to Archer right now. He just needed eyes on any likely candidates, regardless of their race, colour or creed.

He turned his mind to the team for a moment.

Big Brad Travis was alone at the front of Premium Economy, his right leg encased in a full brace, his leg straight out in the extra room afforded by Seat 23K. Jack Travis and Susie Quinn had drawn the short straw and were further back, straddling the aisle in 43C and D.

Archer moved on to the likely candidates he had pinged earlier. It was near impossible to ID a cell – and they didn't know how many were in the cell – among nearly 400 passengers, but he had a short list of possibles.

Top of the list was a pair of seemingly-studious Pakistani males travelling together. They were back in Economy somewhere, with their shifty eyes and nervous dispositions. There was a fat Middle Eastern man, possibly Iraqi, sitting in Economy with his nose in a travel magazine. Something about him seemed off, and Archer had signalled him to Jack Travis back at the boarding gate.

Up in Archer's own section were a couple of well-heeled Arabs, apparently husband and wife, who were both engrossed in paperbacks. He had them pegged as Iraqis as well, but all they seemed to care about was getting comfortable and reading a few pages. Regardless, he had no doubt they would get a hard time from the Immigration agents at LAX.

Archer closed his eyes for a moment, part of him wishing he could just get some shut-eye. It had been a busy time lately, with several flights to the UK and Europe over the last few months for jobs. He had not long been back from a mission in France, involving a retired DGSE operative who had been involved in the Rainbow Warrior bombing back in '85. A debrief, a training refresher, and then straight off to this job.

No rest for the wicked, he thought wryly.

The first sign of trouble was four hours out from LA. Archer had got up and taken a walk, used the toilet at the front of the aircraft, just behind the flight deck, and carried on to do a loop down to the galley at the rear of Business Premier to stretch his legs. He paused there for a few minutes, chatting quietly to a flight attendant named Erika while she fetched him a bottle of water.

She was maybe late twenties, slim and toned with immaculate make-up and golden hair pinned up tightly. She had an engaging white smile and twinkling green eyes. She steadfastly batted off his inquiry about how long she had on the ground in LA, and smiled politely when he asked which hotel the crew were staying at.

Pointedly checking her watch, she suggested he may like to return to his seat, and busied herself checking a list of who-knew-what. Feeling suitably rebuffed, Archer took his bottle of water and began to turn away.

As he did so, the curtain between Business and Economy opened and a passenger slipped in, passing behind Erika as he headed towards the front of the aircraft.

Archer's head snapped round, pinged the guy as one of the Pakistani boys he'd noticed earlier, and sensed movement behind him at the same time. He whirled, seeing the back of a second person going past the other side of the galley.

The second Pakistani boy, surely.

Archer put his bottle aside and grabbed Erika by the arm as he drew his weapon. Her eyes went like saucers as she saw the gun.

'Special Forces,' he hissed, 'get on the PA now, announce "Six-two, six-two." Do it now.'

He spun on his heel just as the curtain behind her opened again and big Brad Travis burst through. His leg brace was gone and he had his weapon in his hand.

Their eyes met and an unspoken message passed between them.

Archer moved fast. He took the left aisle, Brad stayed on the right.

Ahead of them were the two figures, and Archer realised he was right – it was the two Pakistani boys. The books were gone but they were both still in their ill-fitting jackets. They were moving up the aisle with purpose, the flight deck only metres away. All around them in the dim light, passengers slumbered. Some with mouths open, some with eye masks, all of them oblivious.

Or maybe not all of them.

Archer spotted the well-heeled Iraqi couple, wide awake, paperbacks lowered now, watching. His eyes met the man's face, and the man's eyes narrowed.

Archer kept the Sig in his hand, a compact P228 that he favoured, tucked against his hip. The chamber was loaded, the safety off, the magazine carrying another eleven Glaser safety slugs. His left elbow touched at the ASP extendable baton on his hip, the touch a comforting reminder that it was there should it be needed.

The man ahead of him reached the end of the aisle and glanced to his associate over to the right. He spotted Brad following behind and opened his mouth to call a warning.

At the same time, the PA sounded with Erika's voice. 'Six-two,' she said calmly, 'six-two.'

The man's head snapped that way, hesitant, and he clocked Archer closing in on him. His eyes widened with surprise. The other man on the right looked towards Archer as well, his right hand going beneath his suit jacket.

There was no doubt now.

Archer closed on the first man. He was a smallish build, mid-twenties, with curly black hair and a short beard. His shirt was white, his suit a dark blue, no tie.

'Security!' Archer barked, levelling the Sig at the guy's chest, 'hands up!'

The guy ignored him and brought his right hand round in a sweeping slash. In his hand was what looked like a white plastic knife of some sort. It arced towards Archer's face as the man started to shout something in Arabic.

Brad closed up on his own target, smashing the butt of the Sig down on the guy's temple and dropping him to his knees. The guy still managed to draw a weapon from beneath his jacket. Brad saw the pistol, grabbed the guy's hair and wrenched his head straight up, jabbed the barrel of his Sig against the guy's neck and fired.

There is no safer backdrop for a loose shot than the surrounds of the flight deck, with its bomb- and bullet-proof walls. The .357 SIG Glaser slug blasted through the guy's neck, the projectile fragmenting immediately upon entry and unloading its content of #12 birdshot into the man's neck.

The neck literally blew apart, spraying blood across the wall, the sound of the shot horrendously loud in the confined space.

Archer's target wasn't as close when he fired, but the effect was no less fatal. The single round blasted into the man's chest from a metre away, dead centre over the heart, the barrel spurting orange flame.

The Glaser punched into the chest cavity, fragmented and ripped the man's heart to shreds with birdshot. He was dead before he hit the floor, his white shirt now saturated with blood and bearing a large hole. There was no exit wound at the back, the entire projectile having done its job inside the body.

People were stirring, someone screamed, someone else leaped up and went for Brad.

'Look out!' shouted Archer.

It was the Iraqi woman, the wife of the well-heeled man. She charged at Brad, shrieking, her hands flapping in the air hysterically. He sized her up, held his gun away from her, and jabbed her fair in the face with a left fist the size of a Christmas ham.

She went down like a sack of spuds, out cold, and he caught her before she touched the carpet. He straightened up again, scanning the cabin, backing up to the flight deck door. His job was to protect the pilots at all costs.

Archer quickly frisked the man he'd killed, finding no further weapons on him. No explosives, no trigger. He left the knife in the man's hand and scanned the passengers around him. Terrified eyes stared back at him. Hands went up in the air.

'Everybody, heads down,' he barked, 'hands on your heads, heads between your knees! Don't look up! Don't look up!'

There was immediate compliance, even the Iraqi husband

complying and leaving his unconscious wife to her own devices. Seeing the fear in the man's face and the hysterical reaction of the wife, Archer was reasonably confident they were no threat.

He moved fast to the galley. Erika was gone.

He threw the curtain open and moved into the next cabin. Down the back he could see Travis wrestling with a woman, both with their arms windmilling as they wrestled for something in the woman's hand.

Archer moved that way, the Sig up and his eyes scanning. He heard a flight attendant's voice over the PA again, not as calm as Erika had been but remarkably in control.

'Heads down please everyone, assume the crash position with your head between your knees.'

He half expected a polite "Air New Zealand thanks for you for your co-operation," but she was doing well enough without it. Another flight attendant, a shaven-headed guy, was in the other aisle, moving towards the front and speaking to passengers, quiet and calm as he tried to reassure them that everything was under control.

Archer moved forward, halfway down the Premium Economy aisle before he saw the door to the toilet ahead open and someone stumble out. It was Erika, her hands grabbing at the arm around her throat, a man holding her from behind with a pistol to her head. Her eyes were wide open, fixed on Archer.

The man holding her was screaming in Farsi, so fast Archer had no clue what he was saying, although his intentions were clear.

The PA sounded again, overriding the confusion around them.

'Ladies and gentlemen, this is Captain Nelson speaking,' a man said coolly. 'Please remain in your seats while we deal with an issue on board. Do not panic and do not interfere. Please remain seated and we will have this matter dealt with as soon as we can.'

From beyond Erika and the man, Archer heard a shot followed by hysterical screaming and another shot. He saw passengers turning in their seats to look behind them.

The man in front of him was still bellowing like a madman, sweat pouring off his face and dripping into Erika's hair. The hammer was back on the pistol in his hand. Archer recognised it as an old Browning, not in great nick.

He levelled the Sig at the guy's head, straight between his eyes, at the same time speaking low and confident.

'Erika, on two, you drop. On two, you drop.'

He saw the recognition in her eyes as she absorbed the instruction. The Sig was steady in his grip.

'One,' he said calmly, 'two.'

Erika seemed to push back against the terrorist holding her, twisting as she tried to break free and drop to the ground. The man was too strong for her to get free and he yanked at her, both of them pirouetting like a couple of drunks on a dance floor. The man was still screaming and Archer could hear other voices around him, but his complete focus was on the terrorist.

As Erika twisted to her right, it allowed Archer a side profile of the man. He fired without hesitation.

The Glaser blasted into the man's back ribs and the shot blew his insides apart. Blood sprayed, Erika screamed and fell, and the man fell back against the toilet door. The door folded inwards beneath his weight and he collapsed backwards onto the toilet, dropping the Walther to the floor. His eyes were open and he was still breathing.

The blood dribbling from his mouth indicated that his state was about to change.

Archer reached in, snatched him by the hair and jerked him out onto the floor, face down. He quickly frisked him for weapons, finding a knife in his pocket. He pinned the guy to the floor with a knee on his back, scanning down the aisle ahead of him.

Travis was further down, a dead female terrorist at his feet. He gave a thumbs up and Archer nodded.

He glanced down at the guy beneath him. He was no longer breathing. The pool of blood soaking into the carpet getting larger.

No more shots sounded.

He could see Susie standing over the body of a dead terrorist, the body half-fallen onto an empty seat. Her pistol was in her hands and she was talking to the passengers around her, calming them.

Erika was getting to her feet. Travis approached down the aisle, his Sig still in his hand.

'We got two X-rays,' he said, 'both down. No casualties.'

'We got three,' Archer replied. He got to his feet. 'Stay here, I'll clear from the back forwards.'

He moved down the back, stepping over the body of the female terrorist. She'd been shot in the chest and lay on her back. A woman sitting in the seat beside her was sobbing loudly. A man beside just stared at the body, ashen-faced.

'Heads down,' Archer reminded them, 'don't look up.'

The man complied immediately, too shocked to do anything else. The woman continued sobbing.

It was a long, slow process to clear every seat and every passenger until they were satisfied there no further threats. They took their time and worked methodically.

A squadron of US F-18s escorted them all the way, ready to blow the airliner out of the sky if it presented a threat to LAX.

By the time the aircraft began its descent to Los Angeles International Airport, some semblance of order had been restored. The bodies of the terrorists had been removed to a galley and secured. The crew served drinks and attended to the passengers who were suffering shock, of which there were a number, along with the Iraqi woman Brad had KO'd.

There would be a huge inquisition into the incident, of that Archer had no doubt. Skyjackings were not commonplace.

There should also, all things being equal, be a few pats on the back for a job well done. That was about as much as they could expect in the world they operated in.

But all he wanted right now, he decided, taking a crew seat beside Erika, was a good strong drink. He ran an appreciative eye over her toned calves and reconsidered that.

Maybe not just a drink, he decided.

# 2

The only window in the room was made of one-way glass, and Archer assumed they were being watched from the other side.

The air-con was cool on his skin but the atmosphere still felt heavy. No surprise, considering the number of people gathering around the conference table. Aside from himself, Travis, Susie Q and Brad, the others were all American.

The only one to identify himself properly was a tall, lean man in his early fifties. What little hair he had remaining was clipped short and mostly grey. He had a weathered complexion. To Archer he resembled a Marine Corps drill sergeant, an impression that was strengthened by the bone-crushing handshake he received.

'Rawlins, CIA,' the man said, ushering them into the room.

Archer nodded and said nothing. He spied four empty seats around the end of the table. The rest of them were occupied and, he noticed, angled towards the empty chairs. He led the way and took a seat.

As he looked around now, he counted fourteen attendees at the table. All in business attire aside from two men in casuals. Beards, diving watches, tanned. Obviously operators. Delta, he guessed. The others were probably CIA too, maybe DIA or FBI thrown in for good measure. A regular alphabet soup, he thought wryly. Hopefully no STDs though.

He glanced at Travis who took the seat beside him. Travis' face was expressionless. The people facing them were all silent. Rawlins moved to the head of the table. The table was polished pine.

A glass of water sat in front of each of them. Archer picked his up and took a sip. It was tepid. He drained the glass and put it back down.

He heard a clunk as Brad did likewise and glanced to his left. The silence was broken when Brad spoke.

'Don't suppose there's any chance of a beer,' he rasped. 'I'm pretty parched, to be fair.'

Archer saw the two Delta guys crack grins but everyone else remained stony silent.

'Perhaps later,' Rawlins said, taking his seat at the opposite end of the table. He had a large notepad in front of him.

Beside him sat a woman with jet black hair and a serious expression. Her suit was charcoal and looked expensive. She had light green eyes and her lipstick was a subtle deep red. He felt her eyes running across him. She reached his face and Archer met her gaze. It was cool and appraising.

He looked away when Rawlins began to speak.

'Before we go any further, ladies and gentlemen, I just need to highlight two things right now. Firstly, this meeting is being recorded, audio and visual. Secondly, what happens in this room stays in this room. Everybody here has the appropriate clearance and we all need to be singing from the same hymn sheet. Am I clear on this?'

There were nods all round. Archer first glanced to his colleagues then looked back to Rawlins.

'Just a question on that,' he said, 'if it all stays in this room, why is it being recorded?'

There was a low murmuring among the assembled crowd and all eyes went to Rawlins. He cleared his throat and looked bemused. Archer guessed he probably wasn't used to being questioned.

'For the purposes of today,' he said, 'we will call you Officer A.'

Archer nodded and waited.

'This,' Rawlins said, 'is how we do it, Officer A. I don't know if you've had dealings with our agency before?'

'I have.' Archer gestured towards the other people at the table. 'Are you all the same firm?'

Rawlins gave a slight frown. 'No,' he said, 'we have representatives here from various other agencies; FBI, DIA, FAMS. I can assure, Officer A, we are all on the same page, if that's what you're concerned about.'

Archer was quietly pleased that he'd been right with his assessment of the other attendees, although he should've guessed the Federal Air Marshal Service would want to be involved too. He turned to his colleagues and raised a questioning eyebrow. They each shook their heads in turn.

He turned back to Rawlins.

'With respect,' he said, 'we've just been involved in an international incident where terrorists have been killed. It would seem a bit soon to be discussing that with a room full of people.'

He saw Rawlins frown harder. The woman beside him looked faintly amused.

One of the guys that Archer had pegged as Delta turned in his chair and looked at Rawlins, interrupting as the spook began to speak.

'He's kinda gotta point there, Chuck,' he drawled, before looking back to Archer. 'I suggest we hold fire just yet, at least until these guys've had a chance to talk to their boss, right?'

The guy was nearly as wide as Brad but shorter. He had curly dark hair and wore a faded yellow T-shirt.

Rawlins was silent for a long moment as he weighed this up. The Delta operator glanced back to him.

'Their boss is on the way, is he not?'

Rawlins gave a short nod. He leaned in and whispered to the woman beside him. They nodded in agreement with each other before Rawlins looked around the table.

'Take five, people,' he said. 'Stay close and we'll call you back in shortly.'

There were murmurings and looks between the people as they filed back out.

'I think you just made some new friends, Arch,' Travis remarked, stretching and yawning.

Archer shrugged. 'Oh well,' he said.

He didn't really care; he wasn't going to be railroaded into something just to keep others happy. He saw Rawlins and the woman still huddled together, deep in conversation.

The two operators stood and approached them.

'Come with us,' said the one who had spoken to Rawlins. 'You could probably do with a cup, am I right?'

'You're right.' Archer stood and extended his hand. 'Craig.'

'EJ.' The man's shake was firm and dry. He jerked a thumb at his compadre. 'This is Rico.'

The other man nodded a greeting.

The two men led the team of New Zealanders out a side door into a hallway, past a small kitchen where most of the other meeting attendees seemed to be gathered, and down a narrow set of back stairs. The door at the bottom of the stairs led them into a meal room with a kitchenette, tables and a variety of snack machines.

'The coffee sucks,' Rico commented, 'but it's better than hanging with those square-heads upstairs.'

While the others busied themselves getting hot drinks, Archer cornered the operator who'd taken the lead.

'So you guys know who we are?' he asked.

'Close enough.' EJ had clear blue eyes in a tanned face. He ran them over Archer, quickly appraising him. 'I'm guessing either the Group or the Division.'

Archer gave a small smile. 'And you guys would be either Delta or SOG?'

The Special Activities Division of the CIA was the clandestine service's paramilitary arm. One of its two units was the Special Operations Group, or SOG, which was tasked with deniable military operations.

It was EJ's turn to grin. 'I think it'd be safe to say that we both have served on one before moving to the other.'

Archer nodded. It was always good to know exactly who you were dealing with.

EJ gave a frown and lowered his voice. 'Who's the girl though? She one of yours?'

Archer was about to reply when his iPhone dinged with an incoming message. It was Ingoe.

*Stay where you are. I'll get this sorted.*

He put the device away and turned back to his companion. 'Sorry about that, just the boss. Yeah, she's one of ours. You guys have female operators don't you?'

EJ put his hands up defensively. 'No offense, buddy, it's just unusual is all. I meant nothing by it.' He looked over at Susie again, watching her as she passed a coffee to Travis. 'I can see she's spoken for.'

Archer smiled but didn't reply. Travis and Susie Q's business was their business. He got himself a coffee while they waited.

Rico was right, the coffee did suck, but at least it was something in his belly. The adrenaline high of the incident was wearing off and he was beginning to sag. He took a seat at a table beside Brad, who had barely spoken since his crack in the boardroom.

'Alright mate?'

The big man nodded firmly. 'Yep. Could do with a feed though. I thought the Yanks always had plenty of supplies.'

'Hmm.' Archer took a sip of his coffee and checked another incoming message from Ingoe.

*On my way to you.*

He put the device away again and waited in silence.

Less than a minute later the door opened and three people entered. Book-ended by Rawlins and the brunette was Jed Ingoe – known as Jedi to those who dared use his nickname – the Operations Manager of Division 5. Average height and wiry with a buzz cut and hard eyes, he was a former Regimental Sergeant-Major of the NZSAS. After losing a leg to an IED in Afghanistan he had moved over to the shadowy special ops unit.

Rawlins waited until the woman had closed the door before he spoke.

'My apologies for keeping you all waiting,' he said. 'We had a few things to check before we go any further. What we propose to do is for you guys to break off for an internal debrief before we reconvene upstairs. And I promise…' he gave Archer a smooth smile, 'the circus will be trimmed to a more efficient number, alright?'

Archer nodded his acknowledgement, and Ingoe stepped forward.

'Team,' he said coolly, giving a curt nod to his staff. 'Well done today.' He turned to the two SOG guys. 'Thanks fellas, we'll catch you upstairs no doubt.'

Archer could tell by the look on EJ's and Rico's faces that they weren't used to being dismissed, but they filed out behind their two colleagues without further ado.

'I'm assured this room is secure,' Ingoe said, taking a seat at one of the tables. 'So hit me with it.'

In ten minutes they had briefed him on the events of the hijack. It was a succinct and unemotional telling of what, Archer had no doubt, was already major international news.

When they were finished Ingoe took a further two minutes to bring them up to speed on other developments.

'They all appear to be New Zealand citizens but originate from Syria,' he said. 'Our friends upstairs have more intel on that and hopefully they'll feel like sharing it.'

Brad grunted. 'So how long're we gunna be sitting round here for?' he wanted to know.

'With any luck, not long,' Ingoe said, indicating Travis, Susie and Brad. 'You three have another job to get on with.'

Archer glanced at his colleagues. He wondered what he would be doing while they got to go and play. Hopefully not debriefs and meetings. He hated meetings.

In the next moment his unspoken question was answered.

'You and I will be staying here for a while,' Ingoe told him. 'See what shakes out of this.'

Archer nodded. 'What's been given to the media?' he asked.

'Not a lot as yet,' Ingoe replied, 'however the jump has already been made to it being an op by Delta and/or the Sky Marshals.' His cool eyes flickered with what may have been amusement. 'It's not being discouraged. Either way, our Government is happy to keep schtum on our involvement. Worst case scenario is the credit will go to the Group, but there'll be no mention of us.'

'Fair enough.' It was a good call, as far as Archer was concerned. The fewer people who knew the Division even existed, the better.

Even with Ingoe's involvement it was still another hour before the wheels started to turn. Finally the two SOG men, EJ and Rico, came and escorted Archer's companions back through the door to begin the next leg of their journey. Where that was and what exactly it involved, Archer had no idea.

He settled for a quick handshake with each of them and a wave as they disappeared through the door, before turning to Ingoe.

'Indonesia,' Ingoe said without prompting.

Archer nodded and said nothing. It didn't bother him; he didn't need to know. He began to make himself another coffee, feeling fatigued now. He wasn't sure how long it was since he'd slept, and he could have done with some food.

*First things first*, he decided as he added a token slosh of cream to his mug. *Get this shit done and dusted, then sort yourself out.* He glanced over to Ingoe as he took the first sip. The former warrior was pacing quietly on the far side of the room, talking quietly into his phone. Probably to the Director, Archer figured. Way over his pay grade. The Yanks always seemed to have good coffee.

The door opened and the woman stood there, one hand holding the door open, the other cocked expectantly on her hip. She looked at him coolly, her thin eyebrows arched.

'They're ready for you,' she said.

# 3

Fatigue had hit Archer suddenly.

The "hot debrief", when it finally happened, was more tepid than hot, but it was exhaustive and, all things considered, it had been a long day. He made his excuses to retire early from dinner. Not that it was fine dining that he was ducking out on.

A steak that overlapped the plate it was on, a large bowl of thick-cut beer-battered fries, and a trio of Budweisers. It reminded him why he never drank Bud anymore and was nearly enough to put him to sleep in the steak house Ingoe had chosen.

His colleague had smiled wolfishly as he forked another slab of steak into his mouth, dripping meat juices onto the plate as Archer pushed back from the cheap Formica table. Blood dribbled down Ingoe's chin as he chewed, and he paused to wipe it carefully on a napkin.

It occurred to Archer that his colleague was a beast in more ways than one. He gave a rueful grin and dug in his pocket for his wallet.

'Sorry,' he said, 'I'm gassed.'

Ingoe waved away the money and took a belt of Bud. At least he was enjoying it. 'I'll see you in the morning,' he said. 'I'll come and get you about eight.'

'A sleep in?' Archer said, his eyebrows raised in surprise. Ingoe was known for surviving on very little sleep.

'I've got shit to do before I worry about you,' Ingoe said bluntly. He stabbed his steak and sawed off another chunk. 'Go get your head down.'

With that Archer was dismissed and he weaved his way through the tables of fat people chugging beer and meat to get to the door. The air outside was refreshingly normal after the air-conditioned atmosphere of the steak house. Archer ignored the cab lurking by the kerb and tucked his hands into his pockets, putting on a stride to get back to the hotel, thankful for the chance to stretch his legs and work off the meal that sat heavy in his gut.

He was halfway there, maybe a mile to go, when he felt his guts rumble. A swirl, a surge, churning over like the wash behind an outboard. It was on before he knew it, and he had just enough time to step off the footpath into a side alley before he lost it. Bracing himself against the brick wall with one hand, Archer emptied his guts down the side of a building, not even enough time to make it to a trash can.

He steadied himself, heaved again, spat, and sucked down a shuddering breath. Maybe... no, not yet. Another heave, deep and strong, and the wall took another dose of the steak house's dinner special.

He spat, wiped his mouth, and straightened up gingerly. He spat again, emptied his nostrils with two sharp blasts, and sucked in some air.

Not as bad as it had been, but it still pissed him off. He never knew when it was going to happen. His first contact had been the worst, just a rookie officer in Timor Leste, face to face with a militia man with an AK. Archer had dropped him first, but he was so close the guy's blood and brain matter had splattered back in his face.

Since then he'd had numerous contacts, killed a lot of bad guys, and sometimes – most times – it was fine. A debrief, some quiet time to get his head together, and it was sorted. Other times it was like this.

'Fuck it,' he muttered. He spat again, turned, and continued on his way. His gut felt tender and hollow and his mouth tasted like acidic hops.

The hotel was a standard Marriott with standard décor and standard facilities. Archer crossed the lobby, ignoring the punters in the hotel bar off to the side. He clocked a couple of familiar faces at the bar there – EJ and Rico. They were deep in conversation but spotted him as he went by.

At a table against the wall were two more faces – Rawlins and the female agent. They both had drinks before them but appeared to be sitting in silence. Spooks were always a bit weird like that. He ignored them all and crossed to the stairs, making his way up to the fifth floor.

He fetched himself some ice on the way to his room, secured the door and shucked off his jacket, tossing it on the plain-wrapped queen bed. He half-filled a tumbler and cracked a bottle from the mini bar. He poured a decent measure of bourbon over the ice, let it sit for a minute and watched the ice start to melt.

He lifted the tumbler, inhaled the earthy aroma, and took a good slug. The burn in his throat was welcome, cutting through the foul-tasting acid on its way down. The tumbler was drained in no time at all, and he refilled it, not bothering with more ice this time. There was nothing in his gut to soak up the booze and he quickly got a warm buzz coursing through his veins. He stood in the pool of light thrown by a side lamp, taking his time on the second drink, shadows hanging in the darkened corners of the room like ghouls waiting to take a lost soul.

'No lost souls here,' Archer muttered grimly to himself. No, he knew what he was, alright. No doubt at all.

But knowing didn't mean there were no strings attached. Archer knew soldiers who could kill another man without batting an eyelid – think no more of it than choosing a pair of socks for the day – even enjoy it. Armies the world over had such warriors, cold-blooded killers who lived for more than the thrill of combat, more than the rush of beating the odds. They lived for the thrill of the kill itself. Psychopaths, maybe. But necessary.

Archer knew he was not one of those men. No, the weight of taking another life was something he had to adjust until it sat comfortably enough for him to carry. Like a heavy pack on his back, it was always there and occasionally it caused a niggle, but he could carry it forward as he moved on.

And so it would be again. He knew this within himself, on a level deeper than even his subconscious. It was a part of him. He had no regrets over killing the hijackers, none at all. They brought it, they ran to the fight, and they lost. That was the deal, and they knew it. He was satisfied, proud even, of his actions. Innocent lives had been saved, many of them.

Innocent lives. Innocent people. People ill-equipped to protect themselves in a world foreign to their life of 9-5, mortgage payments, daily commutes, weekend football games and domestic chores. Sheep trying to get through their day without crossing paths with the wolves that hunted them.

The world needed men prepared to hunt the wolves.

Archer took a slow sip of the bourbon. It always seemed to taste better in the States. He let it sit on his tongue before easing down his throat. The drapes were open and beyond the net curtain he could see the lights of LAX, burning bright, welcoming travellers to the City of Angels. No fires there tonight, no twisted, smoking wreckage.

His gut had settled now, his aches were easing and his mind was at ease. His earlier annoyance at his physical reaction was gone now. It was just a process that had to happen.

He knew what he was.

# 4

The gym was nearly deserted at five a.m. Nearly, aside from a pair of middle-aged businessmen who were talking more than lifting.

They looked up in surprise when Archer entered, and he gave them a polite nod before dropping his towel and access card beside a treadmill and stepping up. He punched in the settings he wanted, turned up the volume on his iPod and got to it. He disliked using machines but it served a purpose, and soon he was pounding along at a steady pace, his heart pumping and his muscles getting warm and loose.

The two businessmen decided to crack on and spotted each other on a leg press as they heaved at weights Archer hadn't lifted since he was in his teens. Fair do's though, he figured, at least they were in there. They probably hadn't chugged half a cow and a barrel of ale last night.

He gave it twenty minutes on the treadmill, working up a good sweat before cracking on with the free weights. Not being a nine-to-five worker with regular gym times, he didn't have the luxury of planning out routines over a week. Instead he went for maximum effort in the minimum amount of time, working as much of his body as he could any time he could.

The G-Shock told him he'd been at it for forty minutes by the time he got onto the rowing machine for his warm-down. Five minutes at a steady pace followed by stretching – more and more important as he got older, he had come to realise – and he was good to go. His T-shirt was drenched and his muscles were pinging, but he felt alive and ready to face the world.

The two businessmen were long gone and the gym was silent. Archer flicked off the iPod, killing Jimmy Barnes halfway through *Driving Wheels*.

He paused by the water cooler while he drained another cup, feeling his heart rate steadily coming down and his breathing getting back to normal. He refilled the cup and straightened up. It was always a bit of déjà vu being in a hotel gym, he thought. Another faceless gym in another faceless hotel, where he was just another anonymous traveller passing through; the other guests and hotel staff almost oblivious to his presence.

Except not so much this time. The TV news he'd caught earlier was full of the hijacking, with plenty of old footage being shown of special forces in action. Comparisons were being made to the GSG9 assault in Mogadishu back in 1977, where the German unit – supported by two British SAS men – had stormed a hijacked plane on the tarmac and rescued the hostages. Archer was okay with that. The Germans had, in their usual efficient way, executed a textbook operation.

He only hoped that the Yanks would keep the lid of secrecy on the operation and he would remain unidentified. If they wanted to take the credit – and it appeared that they did – then that was okay too. He just wanted to slip back to New Zealand and get on with the next job.

There were no medals dished out for these sorts of things, there would no celebrations or ticker-tape parades, no exclusive interviews with women's magazines. There would never be a "*Secret Soldier Reveals All*" feature on Craig Archer, that was for sure.

The door swung open behind him and his head snapped up to

the floor to ceiling mirror opposite him. He saw the reflected image of the door opening and a woman step through, pausing with the door open as she appraised him from behind.

It was the spook from yesterday. Gone was the corporate attire and she was now clad in black Lycra tights and work-out singlet, with crisp white trainers. Her hair was pulled back in a pony-tail. She was long and lean.

Archer turned, taking a long sip as he faced the woman.

'Good morning,' he said cordially.

'Good morning yourself.' She was softly spoken, her accent difficult to pin down. She ran an eye over his torso again. 'Finished already?'

Archer crooked a grin. 'I find it's more about quality than quantity, Miss...?'

She ignored the inquiry and smiled, her pink tongue flicking over lips that shone with gloss.

'Some guys do say that,' she responded, a devilish glint in her eye. 'I have to say I'm not entirely convinced.' Her gaze ran over him again, unabashedly taking him in. 'But I think it's safe to say you've got the quantity okay.'

Archer felt himself taken aback by her brashness, but couldn't hide a grin anyway. 'One does what one can,' he said, with as much humility as he could manage.

What was it with this woman? So cold and business-like yesterday and now here she was, giving him as blatant a come-on as he'd ever had. No harm, no foul, he figured. There was nothing wrong with making her intentions clear.

'Well.' She looked, one eyebrow arched, holding the door open. 'Don't let me keep you.'

Archer emptied his cup and tossed it in the trash can beside the cooler. He wiped his mouth with the back of his hand and reached for the door. The woman didn't move and they ended up face to face. She was a few inches shorter than him and looked up at him. Her eyes were so light the green was almost grey. He could smell her perfume, something fruity and sweet.

She inhaled deeply before letting go of the door.

Archer brushed past her.

'It's Jessika,' she said suddenly. 'With a k.'

Archer paused, holding her gaze.

'Craig,' he said.

She cocked her head to the side and gave him a look. 'I know.'

'Okay then,' he said, '*Jessika* with a k.'

With that he left her there, but he knew as he strode down the hallway that she was watching him.

IT WASN'T until the next day that he saw her again, and by then she had transformed back into her business attire and it was all formalities again with not a hint of the earlier flirtatiousness.

Archer had spent the intervening time drifting around the hotel under virtual house arrest. There were a couple of CIA guys on stag, doing a pretty good job of blending into the background, but wherever he went, there they were. The gym, the restaurant, the bar, the pool. He wouldn't have been surprised if they'd even wired up his room, but despite his best efforts he failed to find any sign of a hidden camera or audio device.

Ingoe came and went and they managed another meal together, but that was it. By the end of the second day Archer was getting serious cabin fever, and was about ready to break out past the guards when Ingoe collared him for a drink.

They took stools at the bar downstairs and ordered from the rail-thin barman with slicked back hair. His skin was so sallow it was almost translucent.

'Jameson's on the rocks,' Ingoe told him.

The barman nodded and looked to Archer. He reminded Archer of a vampire with his pale complexion and black eyes.

'JD and cola thanks,' he said.

The vampire nodded again and drifted away.

'So what's the go?' Archer said, turning to his colleague.

Ingoe rubbed his face. He looked tired and Archer noticed that he had more grey creeping into his fair hair than he'd seen previously. He wondered how old the former RSM was. Somewhere close to either side of fifty, maybe. It was hard to tell – he'd lived a lot, however long it was for.

'We're not getting much from our friends,' he said. 'But they have confirmed what we already knew about these peoples' origins.'

They paused while the vampire delivered their drinks. He didn't speak. Once he had drifted off again, Ingoe continued.

'Motivation?' Archer inquired.

'Nothing.'

'Affiliations?'

'Zip.'

Archer took a sip of his drink. It was weaker than he would have liked, but that seemed standard for hotel bars.

'End game?'

Ingoe savoured his Jameson's for a long moment before answering.

'Not a hundy,' he said quietly, 'but something spectacular.'

Archer gave a slow nod. 'Not ransom then?'

'No. Int seems to have been off on that.'

A "spectacular" was a reference to a major incident, on the scale of the 9/11 or 7/7 attacks. It was something intended to cause significant death and destruction, widespread panic and garner massive attention for "the cause", whatever cause it happened to be.

Currently it was Islamic fundamentalists; in the past it had been others. Timothy McVeigh in Oklahoma was a recent classic with a different ideology.

'LAX?' he suggested quietly.

Ingoe gave a sombre nod. 'Seems to be the common thought.'

'And we're sure they're Syrians on NZ docs?'

'Yup.' Ingoe took a small sip, barely wetting his lips.

'Kinda puts the ball in our court then,' Archer said, feeling his pulse give a kick as he sensed a mission in the offing. Attacks like that couldn't be let go; looking weak made governments more vulnerable.

The conspirators would have to be tracked down and dealt with appropriately.

Ingoe eyed him over the rim of his tumbler. He gave nothing away.

'Doesn't it?' Archer prodded. 'We were attacked as much as our friends, and if they're our residents...'

Ingoe put the tumbler down on a coaster already marked with wet rings.

'Maybe,' he allowed.

Archer's sense of frustration was growing. He was itching to crack on and do it, but there seemed to be a real sense of reluctance coming from Ingoe, a sense he was not used to. He bit his tongue and fought to stay quiet. He took a hefty draft instead, the alcohol burning down his throat and into his gut. His cheeks felt hot and he couldn't look Ingoe in the eye.

'Oi.' Ingoe's voice was a whisper. 'Look at me.'

Archer reluctantly turned back to him, his face still burning.

'We're hoping to get something off the ground,' Ingoe said in a voice that was barely audible, 'but it seems our friends are already kicking into something they're keeping to themselves. If we knew what it was then maybe we could help. But if they block us out, like they tend to do, then we're gunna be the wallflowers at the school dance – ready and willing but left out in the cold.'

Well at least that meant the Director wanted to play, Archer figured. It was a start, if nothing else.

'The boss is hitting them up direct,' Ingoe continued, 'but your guess is as good as mine how that will go. All we need is a starting point.'

Archer nodded, ignoring his drink now, his focus entirely on the task at hand.

'So you want me to get back to Auckland and start digging into the backgrounds of these dudes?' he asked.

Ingoe gave a curt shake of the head. 'No, we've got plenty of people on that. You need to stick around here. I don't want to muck around having to bring you back over here when and if something does actually kick off.'

'So I'm back to solitary confinement,' Archer growled.

'Maybe not solitary.' Ingoe cracked a small grin. 'Maybe you could make friends with our friends, see if anything's forthcoming on a more...*informal* basis.'

Archer cocked an eyebrow, not sure if he was reading that correctly. Ingoe gave him a look that told him he was.

'Roger that,' Archer muttered, 'message received.'

He reached for his glass and took a slug. It was almost like pure cola now, watered down with melted ice. It didn't matter; his mind was turning over, and he knew exactly where he was going to start.

As if by an act of God, the CIA woman chose that moment to enter the bar with Rawlins in tow. She had ditched the jacket and her arms were bare under a cream blouse. Her breasts were straining at the fabric and her hair was tousled.

Yes, Archer decided, he knew exactly where he was going to start. It was time for what the politicos called a special relationship.

# 5

It had taken a one-minute conversation with a maid and twenty bucks for Archer to get Jessika's room number.

Another hundred to the vampire/barman gave him a chilled bottle of three-year-old Dom Perignon, which he was pretty sure wasn't going through the till. It didn't matter to Archer. The bottle was accompanied by a bucket of ice and two glasses, with no further questions asked.

The corridor was deserted when Archer tapped on the door. She answered within a few seconds, cautiously opening the door on the security chain.

'Why, hello there.'

Archer gave his best attempt at a charming smile and lifted the ice bucket for her to see.

'Can I interest you in a drink between friends?'

She closed the door to unhook the chain before reopening it. She was dressed in a slinky, silver gown that reached her mid-thighs. Her hair tumbled loose to her shoulders.

'And to what do I owe this honour?' she asked. 'It's not every day I get a visit from a strange man bearing champagne.'

Archer shrugged modestly. 'I like to think I'm not the average man,' he replied, 'and there's no point in being strangers, is there?'

She looked him up and down. 'You'd better come in then.'

He kicked the door closed behind him as she crossed the room to turn the TV down. He noticed she had a larger suite than his, nicely furnished, and the lights were lowered. He also noticed the sway of her hips under the short gown. He liked that better than the suite.

He placed the bucket and glasses on the sideboard, while she busied herself tidying up some papers on the table. She quickly closed down a laptop and shoved everything into a laptop bag, which she zipped up and put on the floor.

'So you've been a busy boy,' Jessika said, lowering herself into an armchair. Her gown rode up as she sat, crossing her legs and tucking it between her thighs.

Archer noticed her thighs were toned and lean. He popped the cork without losing anything, and began to pour the first glass.

'I'm at a loose end here,' he replied, 'and what better way to spend an evening than sharing bubbles with a beautiful woman?'

She smiled and her eyes twinkled. She accepted the glass he handed her. 'Well in that case, Mr Archer, make yourself comfortable.'

He poured himself a glass and settled the bottle back into the ice. He shucked off his jacket and tossed it over the back of the other chair, before clinking glasses with her. They each took a sip before she reached for the phone. Archer took a seat and waited while she dialled a single number. She watched him while she spoke.

'Yes,' she said, 'can I have a cheese platter sent up thanks...as soon as possible...for two. Caviar? No, I can't stand the stuff, but thank you.'

She clicked the receiver back into place and took a slow sip, watching him over the rim of her glass.

'I hope you're not one of these guys who are only in this game for the image,' she told him. 'All mouth, no action.'

Archer lowered his glass and looked at her. 'Oh no,' he said, 'not at all.' He ran his eyes from her ankles to her face, wanting her to know he was looking. The slinky gown was loose across her chest but he could still see the swell of her breasts, her nipples pushing at the thin fabric. 'I'm all about the action.'

'Good.' She smoothly re-crossed her legs, her gown slipping aside momentarily to reveal a glimpse of black panties. 'I was hoping you'd say that.'

THE LIGHTS of the City of Angels were shut out by the heavy drapes, with only ambient light from the lounge giving Archer some visibility as he gently eased himself from the bed. Jessika remained still, naked and deeply asleep on her side, as he padded silently towards the door.

He reached the lounge and scooped up his pants from the floor, recovering his iPhone and a small device similar to a compact USB stick. Double-checking to ensure his new friend was still asleep, Archer crouched beside her laptop bag and slid the computer out onto the floor. Opening it up, he used his body to shield the screen's glow and hopefully not be seen from the bedroom.

The USB device was a commercially available device which doubled as a keystroke logger and as spyware. It was the latest piece of kit apparently, and Archer had no idea of the technical side of its performance. He plugged it into one of the USB ports, depressed the button at the end of the device, and waited while a tiny LED flickered red on the device.

The laptop was ready, waiting for a password to be entered. It had been locked but not shut down, which made it almost child's play to crack into. That didn't do his nerves much good though. Jessika was still a CIA intelligence officer, and they were right up there in the pecking order. Getting caught cracking into her computer would do the SIS no favours with their Five Eyes partners, and there was no doubt the Yanks in particular would be less than forgiving to him personally. A robust interrogation would be the least of his concerns.

It seemed to take an age for the USB's light to go green, and as soon as it did he jumped into the apps on his iPhone. The two devices connected wirelessly, and the installation began.

When Ingoe had given him the device earlier he'd stated, somewhat doubtfully, that it was supposed to only take a minute or less for the installation to take place. Archer was pleased to see he was right. It would leave no trace on the laptop for anything less than a full forensic examination.

He quickly unplugged the USB, closed the laptop again and resecured it in the bag. There was still no sound from the bedroom, so he pushed on and took another couple of minutes to photograph the papers Jessika had in the bag.

He didn't bother reading them for now – they could've been top secret plans or letters to her mother, he didn't care – but got them all snapped and tucked away again before he put his iPhone back where it had come from. The USB stick he slipped beneath the cushion of one of the armchairs, giving it some degree of separation from himself. As long as he remembered to grab it before he left, he'd be fine.

There was always the chance that she would do the same to him, but he didn't plan on giving her the opportunity. He'd barely slept since he'd been in her room, due firstly to the vigorous lovemaking, and secondly because he was waiting for Jessika to slip into a deep sleep.

He ducked into the bathroom and flushed the toilet to cover his tracks. She stirred as he climbed back into bed, and rolled onto her back.

Archer lifted the covers and slid over to her, touching her belly and pulling himself close against her. She gave a low chuckle and slipped an arm around his shoulders. Their lips met in the darkness and their mouths came alive. He rolled on top of her, feeling her legs open beneath him without protest.

'Mmm,' she breathed, 'back for more?'

Archer moved his mouth to her nipples, flicking first one then the other with his tongue. She moaned in his ear and clutched his head to her.

'The night's not over yet,' he whispered, finding her mouth with his. Their tongues met as he entered her, and the dance began again.

Dawn was creeping over the horizon when he finally dressed himself and gave her a farewell kiss. She stayed where she was, sleepily satisfied and dishevelled. She smiled and waggled her fingers at him as he paused in the doorway.

'Here's to international relations,' she chuckled. 'But this stays strictly between us, right? I'm not that kinda girl, Craig.'

It was the first time she had used his Christian name, and she pronounced it *Creg*, as Americans always seemed to.

'I wouldn't want stories floating around about me, you get my drift?' she said.

'Of course. And I'm not that kinda guy.' He grinned and blew her a kiss. 'See you around.'

He turned and left, letting himself out quietly. The USB was safely back in his pocket and he was satisfied he'd left no trace of his spyware mission behind.

He took a breath and rolled his shoulders as he headed down the corridor. The sex had been a welcome sideshow, he couldn't deny that, but the primary task had been completed.

He allowed himself a small smile of satisfaction. *For Queen and country; job done.*

## 6

'Pack your bags, you're going to Germany.'

Venice beach was as good a place as any for a private conversation, and Archer and Ingoe had thrown in enough counter-surveillance measures to be reasonably sure they were safe to talk – at least for a little while.

They stood facing the ocean with the crash of the waves and their body positioning giving sufficient cover to help drown out their talk. No doubt the team who had followed their cab from the hotel to the beach had high-tech listening gear, so there was only so much they could do to stop the eavesdropping.

'When?'

'As soon as.' Ingoe's eyes were shielded by mirrored aviators. His face was expressionless. 'The chatter that GCSB are getting is that a major player has taken a private plane to Berlin. Not sure on where or exactly when, but it's all new chatter, so presumably it's current.'

Archer nodded. He had been shopping that morning, hitting a strip mall and spending the Government's cash on some necessities. The new LA Dodgers baseball cap shielded his face from the sun and he had the peak pulled down low over his equally-new Oakleys.

'I take it our friends here don't know?'

'No. You're going via London. You have some business to take care of there, as far as they're aware.'

'Any ID on this major player?'

'No.' Ingoe glanced at him sideways. 'You know as much as I do for now.' He cracked a small grin. 'Well, mostly.'

Archer nodded again and smiled as well. 'No doubt I'll know more when I need to.'

'You will.' Ingoe gave a short nod. His mirrored lenses followed a pair of leggy girls in their early twenties as they tracked down to the surf, their bodies lean and tanned in their minimalist bikinis. One blonde, one brunette. They were smiling and laughing, the light breeze flicking their hair.

'The American dream,' Archer muttered aloud.

'I thought that was to own your own home, drive a Detroit motor and eat oranges,' Ingoe commented.

Archer looked at him. 'Maybe I'm wrong then. I thought it was to hang out at Venice Beach and nail hot chicks.'

Ingoe's lips twitched into a wry smile. 'The sooner you get on a big bird, the safer the community of LA will be,' he said.

THE FLIGHT from Los Angeles to London was ten and a half hours, and unlike his last flight, Archer spent most of the time asleep.

He had been lucky enough to land a spot in Business Premier again, and had quickly made himself comfortable, making the most of a movie and a bourbon to switch his mind off until after he'd eaten. As soon as dinner was finished he got his head down and slept solidly until they were an hour out from Heathrow.

They landed on time at 11:30am, but by the time he'd collected his bag and got through the queue at Customs, it was close to an hour later.

Archer made his way out into the Arrivals hall at Terminal 4, ducking into a public toilet long enough to remove the tags from his luggage, tear them into pieces and flush them. The less trace of his movements the better. As far as the Americans were concerned, he was going to London. They didn't need to know he was continuing on from there.

He stopped at an ATM to get some cash then queued again, grabbed a taxi and headed to Terminal 5. As far as he could tell there were no watchers but he expected there to be eyes on him from somewhere. He was known to the British intelligence services and they were all over Heathrow. Whether the Americans had a team on the ground to track him was anyone's guess.

Terminal 5 was busy but he put in some anti-surveillance drills anyway, just in case someone was sloppy enough to get spotted. It gave him the opportunity to grab a large coffee and a baguette to keep the engine running, and to pick up a paperback from the bookshop to help kill some time. After half an hour he checked in at the British Airways desk and was directed through to the departure lounge. Customs and Immigration paid him no mind and he was soon sitting in a corner away from any other travellers, starting his new Michael Connelly.

He glanced up as a woman approached with a smile. He smiled back and she slid into the seat beside him.

'Good afternoon, Mr Archer,' she said.

'Good afternoon, Mrs O'Loughlin.'

Sarah O'Loughlin was an MI5 officer he had met through The Division's previous resident agent in London. Moore had always spoken very highly of her and Archer had wondered whether they had something going. He knew she had been gutted when he suddenly disappeared and went off the grid last year following a particularly difficult assignment in Turkey.

She was mid-forties and attractive in a motherly type of way, with short dark hair and hazel eyes. She wore a black puffer jacket over jeans and ankle boots, and had a daypack over her shoulder.

'Berlin will be nice this time of year,' she remarked, crossing her legs and turning side-on to him. 'Not too hot, not too many tourists.'

Archer smiled. 'This isn't just a courtesy call then?'

'While you were winging your way here, your boss was on the

phone to my boss,' she said. 'My understanding is you knew your friend's private plane was in Berlin, but nothing further?'

Archer gave a short nod. 'That's right. It was a bit of a speccy recce.'

She raised her eyebrows questioningly.

'Speculative reconnaissance,' he explained.

'I know what it means, Craig,' she replied sarcastically. 'I've just never heard an adult talk like Doctor Seuss before.'

He felt his cheeks colour and she smiled cheekily at him.

'I'm just taking the piss, calm down. A bit of work has been done in the meantime.' She raised a quizzical eyebrow at him. 'Do you understand how the geeks work?'

'No,' he replied truthfully. He'd never had any interest in the workings of the UK's GCHQ or their own GCSB; he just knew they were very good at what they did. Much like they had no clue how to field-strip an MP5 in the dark, he didn't need to know how they did their job.

'Neither do I. But they've ID'd a private plane that has just landed in Germany, coming via Morocco. Looks like it originated in Jamaica.'

Archer nodded. That tied in with what Ingoe had told him. 'Whose is it?'

'We don't know. Leased by a corporation based in the Caymans. We're trying to ID who's behind the company, but you know what these places are like. The point is, it fits the picture we're building so far, so it's worth looking at.'

Sarah paused as a harassed-looking couple with a pair of sulky teenagers in tow shuffled within hearing, the woman clutching a handful of passports and boarding passes, the husband wrestling with matching trolley bags. Both kids had their ears in and scowled at the world. The boy looked at Sarah and ran his eyes over her, a sneer crossing his face. His eyes moved to Archer and the sneer quickly melted under the stare he received. He grunted something unintelligible at his mother who looked perplexed. The boy grunted again, louder this time, and the father looked frustrated. The girl snuck a glance at Archer. He looked away.

The mother said something to the father who frowned and wrestled the bags back around before dutifully following the rest of his family to another block of seats. The boy flopped down and scowled across the gap at Archer.

Archer ignored him and turned back to Sarah, who had watched the interaction with amusement.

'No kids,' she stated, and he crooked a grin at her.

'Good God, no. Could you imagine me as a father?'

She cocked the eyebrow at him again. 'You might surprise yourself, tough guy.'

'Huh,' he grunted, keen to move on. She took the hint.

'The plane is currently at a private hangar at Berlin-Tegel. It hasn't left since landing yesterday. You'll get details from your outfit. Further to that, four passengers and two pilots were on board, according to German Immigration. All on US passports, but nobody that fits the profile of being a major player.' She shrugged. 'Well, at least nobody either we or the Germans have much on.'

Archer frowned. 'Are they sure?'

Sarah gave him a look. 'They're German, Craig. Don't question their efficiency.'

He felt himself smile. 'Fair enough.'

'They have booked into a hotel in the city, but for how long, who knows. No flight plans are filed yet, but that could be done last-minute. Best idea is to get there and get into it.'

He nodded. 'Sounds about the extent of it.'

'So I've booked us into a neighbouring hotel,' Sarah finished.

Archer did a double take. 'I'm sorry, what? You've booked *us* in?'

She grinned, enjoying his surprise. 'That's what I said. Your outfit has requested assistance from mine. Our friends over the river would normally do it, but they were happy for me to come aboard for this.' She hiked her shoulders. 'It should only be a couple of days at most, anyway.'

Archer nodded again. He didn't like surprises, but what she said made sense. Security Service officers were not normally despatched overseas, so the fact that MI6 were happy to take a pass on the job showed how seriously – or otherwise – they viewed it.

'Don't worry, love,' Sarah smiled, patting his arm, 'I won't cramp your style. It's still your show.'

Archer smiled in spite of himself. 'It's not like that, Mrs O. I'd hate to slow you down.'

She gave a slight frown. 'You can leave the "Mrs" bit out now, too.' She waggled her left hand at him, and only then did he notice the absence of rings. 'We've gone our separate ways.'

'Sorry to hear that.' Archer hadn't met her husband, but it was the best he could come up with on the spot. Sympathy had never been his strong point.

She shrugged. 'Hard to be married when you're both at work all the bloody time,' she said with some feeling.

Archer was silent for a long moment. When he spoke, he chose his words carefully.

'You know I don't have a great track record with you guys, don't you?' he said, watching her face.

'You mean the girl from Six?'

'Tracy.'

'Last I heard she was still alive and kicking.'

He knew she was being generous. Tracy's involvement in the joint op a couple of years ago had ended in Samoa, after she was tortured and nearly raped by a gang of thugs. Archer had sent her a Christmas card the first year, but hadn't received one back. Fair enough, he figured. He hadn't tried again.

'Still in the Service?' he enquired, and Sarah gave a non-committal shrug.

'As far as I know.'

He accepted that and moved on. No point dwelling on the past. 'So what's our cover then?'

'Unmarried couple on a city break. Only recently together after my marriage break-up, first trip away together. We originally met a couple of years ago in London through work, stayed in touch, and began an affair last year when you were back in the UK.'

He raised his eyebrows but said nothing.

'Yes,' she said, 'we know you were. So we hooked up then, maintained a long distance online relationship, and now that you're back over for a short time we're giving it a crack to see how we like it.' She gave a wan smile. 'Chances are it'll fizzle out and end in tears because you're a cheating bastard, but I'm lonely and trying to get back in the game.' She paused a moment before trying, and failing, to give a bright smile. 'How does that sound?'

Archer blinked. 'Sounds kinda bad for you, getting stuck with a cheating bastard like me.' He crooked a grin. 'Not so bad for me, however...'

Sarah broke into a proper grin now and slapped his arm. 'Keep talking,' she said.

They got their heads together until the boarding call was made, thrashing out their cover story and testing each other on it. Sarah was clearly switched on, which gave Archer confidence; she was far more experienced in this world than he was. As they spoke he detected a sense of sadness about her. She was putting on a good front and seemed genuinely excited about the op – "a chance to get out of the office" as she put it – but he wondered about her emotional state.

Fuck it, he decided, he couldn't be concerned about that. Her issues were hers to deal with. She would just need to grip it and crack on.

For now, they were as best prepared as they could be. He couldn't get hold of Ingoe and presumed he was somewhere in the air, so he touched base briefly with the Duty Officer in Wellington to get a message passed instead.

For the next few hours there was nothing to do but wait.

# 7

Berlin was a city Archer had only briefly been through some years before, when on a training exercise with the Group. He knew his history so appreciated the significance of the place, and there were plenty of places he'd be keen to go to, perhaps on an off-duty return trip.

The guidebook he'd bought at the airport was well thumbed by the time BA986 landed at Berlin-Tegel airport, right on time at 18:25hrs. Even visitors to the country seemed to be affected by the legendary German efficiency, he reflected. Archer had always liked the Germans. Their vehicles and weapons were first rate, their food and *bier* were excellent, their country was beautiful and they were a friendly people.

According to Ingoe they were currently experiencing some low levels of civil unrest, the usual anti-immigration kind of protests that flared up now and again. It seemed to be fairly constant in this part of the world, apparently supported by some sectors of government.

He had served with a sprinkling of Brits in the army, and had quickly learned the fastest way to wind them up was to show an affinity for the Germans, the gypsies or the French. Archer had made it known he was a staunch supporter of FC Bayern, despite knowing nothing about soccer, and had used his senseless arguments to great effect with a couple of his British mates.

The hotel was the Centennial, a 4-star block of bronze-coloured stone on a side street near Zoo Berlin. It was lit up from spotlights in the ground, giving the darkened windows the impression of black eyes in a stone edifice. A liveried doorman welcomed them and helped Sarah alight from the cab, waving a young lad over to come and fetch the bags.

Archer took his time fussing over a tip for the doorman and paying off the cab, using the time for a quick recce at the neighbouring hotel. Like the Centennial, the Imperial Grand was a four-storey slab of concrete with tall windows and narrow balconies and a doorman out the front.

It was also home, at least temporarily, to a number of guests booked in under the name John Krane. He left Sarah to check in while he browsed the brochures at the desk and grabbed a handful of guides to the local sights, including a decent map of the city centre. Their room on the third floor was facing the side of the Imperial Grand, the buildings separated only by a service lane maybe five metres wide.

As soon as they got to their room Sarah pulled the drapes while Archer tipped the bellboy and locked the door behind him. He looked around the room, noting it was a basic studio with a queen-size bed and standard furnishings in polished wood and neutral colours.

'Budget constraints,' Sarah supplied with a grin, dragging her bag onto the bed. 'That and it was all we could get on this side and this floor.'

Archer nodded. The Krane party were in two rooms on the same floor next door; according to their intel, directly across from where he now stood.

'I'll take the floor,' he said, poking his head into the small bathroom. 'Fancy a bath?'

She gave him a bemused look. 'No, but you could make yourself useful and order some dinner.' She checked her watch. 'I need to get an update.'

He tossed his jacket aside and flopped onto the bed to browse the room service menu. He didn't know what Sarah would want, and she was busy on the phone now, so he went for variety based on the assumption that he would eat whatever she didn't. He dialled down, ordering a pork steak and a Viennese veal schnitzel, with a Caesar salad and a creamy tomato soup for starters.

The waiter arrived shortly after Sarah had brought him up to speed on progress. They sat and ate at the small table, and Archer was secretly pleased to see she enjoyed her food. He had dated a girl recently who had pecked at her food like a chicken in a farmyard, and it had driven him crazy.

'So we do a brush pass tonight?' he said, wiping his mouth on a white linen napkin. 'I don't suppose they're sending anyone else to help with surveillance?'

She shook her head and chewed a mouthful of steamed vegetables. He noticed she had half her schnitzel remaining. He wondered if it would remain so.

'No, just us.'

He shrugged. 'We could CTR it.'

Sarah swallowed her mouthful and contemplated that for a moment. 'Risky though.'

'Calculated.' A close target recce was always high risk; it was just a matter of mitigating the known risks as best they could, and planning for the unexpected. CTRs were a specialty of the SAS, in far more hostile environments than the Berlin city centre.

'We would need to be certain their rooms were empty.'

He nodded. 'Easy enough.'

'And not a brush pass – we'll be picking up a car.'

He nodded again. That sounded like a good plan. It paid to have transport available, whether they used it or not. He watched her slice a piece off the schnitzel. He could see she'd had enough and was just picking now.

Sarah sat back and wiped her mouth and hands on a napkin. He took that as the signal to start clearing the plates. She looked amused as he slipped the remaining meat from her plate onto his.

'God, it's like having dinner with my kids.' She smiled self-consciously.

'No point letting food go to waste,' he replied, forking it into his mouth. 'Third rule of soldiering.'

'The third? What're the first two?'

He chewed down a mouthful and swallowed. 'Sleep when you can and volunteer for nothing.'

She took a sip of water and nodded. 'So you were one of the black pyjama boys too, like Rob?'

He flicked his eyebrows. 'I was his boss at one stage, but I think he probably taught me more than I taught him.'

'He was a good man.' There was a tinge of sadness in her voice, and he wondered again about the extent of the relationship between this foreign agent and his former colleague.

'Probably still is.'

'Wherever he is.'

He nodded, saying nothing. He knew he was being probed for info; whether for personal or professional reasons didn't matter. He had nothing to pass on anyway. A confirmed sighting in Mosul several months ago. A possible sighting in Albania, another in Chechnya. A rumour in Haiti. But nothing firm, nothing more than wisps of smoke.

'I've noticed with you blokes, and Rob was just the same – you don't say much.'

He shrugged. 'No point talking just to make noise.'

'The self-contained tough guy, is that your story?' She watched him across the table. 'Actions speak louder than words and all that?'

Archer almost smiled. 'Great imagination. You make me sound like an old-time sheriff or something.' He gave a self-deprecating grin and shook his head. 'I'm probably more Elmer Fudd than Wyatt Earp.'

'Huh,' she snorted, 'somehow I doubt it.' She pushed her chair back and stood. 'Anyway, we've got things to do.'

It was time to move and Archer felt a quick buzz of adrenaline. Much and all as he enjoyed dinner and banter with a pretty lady, this was game time.

HE HAD to respect the efficiency of the Brits – they obviously had a local asset who had been given the heads-up and had got preparations in place probably even before their flight touched down.

An unremarkable black three-year-old VW Golf had been parked several blocks away, the location given to Sarah by phone. They approached on foot from different directions with Sarah staying wide to keep an external perimeter at the top of the street. It was a residential area and the car had been parked at the kerb, crammed in amongst other residents' cars. The apartment buildings that dominated the street cast long shadows, providing plenty of concealment for any watching eyes.

Archer did a walk by, taking his time as he made his way down the street, checking out the cars and general surroundings. It was almost ten o'clock but people were still moving about, giving him good cover. He turned into a walkway between buildings and stood in the shadows, checking his tail. All clear.

He stood there for several minutes, absorbing the sounds of the environment. Muffled noise from the apartments beside him. A TV, a radio. A door opening and closing. Muted chatter as a girl walked by across the road, talking on a cell phone. The odd car cruising past. A streetlight flickered.

Satisfied there was nothing out of the ordinary, he moved off again to the far end of the street. He buzzed Sarah and heard her answer immediately in his earpiece.

'Clear, go,' he said.

'That's me moving up.' She clicked off.

He found a shadow to melt into, and watched her approach from the opposite end of the footpath. She moved with purpose but not rushed, nothing to arouse suspicion, just another local on the way home. Or to her car. She paused at the rear of the black Golf, bending down for a few seconds then straightening up and moving to the driver's door. The key had been secured under the bumper in a magnetic lockbox.

The lights flashed as she bleeped the key fob.

Archer waited until she was in, the headlights had come on and she was pulling out of the parking slot, before he sifted around the corner and made some distance.

She picked him up a minute later, slowing just long enough for him to slide into the passenger's seat before moving off again.

'All good?' Her eyes were flicking between the mirrors and the windscreen as she took them away from the pick-up area. It was the hot zone and they needed to distance themselves from any potential watchers.

Archer ran his window down and adjusted the wing mirror. He was reasonably satisfied they were clear but only time would tell. The vehicle itself should be clear unless the local asset had been tagged already, so any watchers would be on to the asset themselves. They had cleared their tail on the way there so by rights it would only be dumb luck for them to have been picked up since then.

But if you were compromised, dumb luck didn't make you any less compromised than good planning.

Sarah took a circuitous route towards the city outer, ducking down side streets, pulling over and waiting, U-turning, cruising through a parking building and back out again two minutes later.

Once they were satisfied they were clear they dropped the car in a multi-storey car park a street away from the hotel. Archer kept a watch on the street just in case, while Sarah removed a black holdall from the boot. As she approached him with it over her shoulder he could tell it had some weight, and he took it from her. He put it down and was beginning to unzip it when Sarah touched his shoulder.

'What're you doing?' she said. 'We haven't got time for that right now.'

He glanced up at her as he finished opening the bag. 'Do you know the asset?'

'No, of course not.'

'Then we need to check the kit. For all we know he could be a double.'

'Jeez.' She rolled her eyes. 'And I thought I was paranoid.'

'Better to be paranoid than in jail.'

He had a quick fossick through the bag, finding a good selection of gear: a night sight, a directional microphone with a recording unit, a Canon SLR with a set of decent lenses, a Panasonic 4K camcorder and tripod, Steiner 8x44 bino's, and an array of spare batteries and chargers.

It was good kit and he was pleased with it, but he still gave the bag itself a quick search for any tracking devices attached to the lining. Sarah watched him with amusement.

'Happy now, Doubtful Dan?' she grinned.

Archer straightened up and slung the bag over his shoulder. 'Ever worked with agents in Afghanistan or Iraq?' he asked, already knowing the answer.

She gave a curt shake of the head. 'No.'

'Well I have, and you can't trust any bastard. Let's go.'

She was silent as she led the way out of the multi-storey and out to the street. He could sense her annoyance with him, but fuck it, too bad. It wouldn't be the first time a double agent had planted a tracking device, drugs, weapons or an IED on friendly forces. He had no intention of getting worked over by some shithead asset who took the money and ran.

They made it back to the hotel before eleven and set up their OP in silence. While Sarah fiddled with the directional mic – basically a long microphone with a pistol grip which could pick up conversations 100 yards away – he got busy setting up the camera gear.

The trick to not standing out like dog's balls was to avoid the pitfalls shown so proudly in the movies. Poking a camera lens out between two drawn curtains or standing backlit in a window with a pair of bino's were dead giveaways.

Instead, Archer killed the lights in the room and kept the curtains open with the nets drawn. He placed the tripod-mounted camcorder to one side and moved the coffee table under the window. The SLR was ready there with the bino's, and the charging units plugged in beneath it with the spare batteries.

Sitting at the table he had a good line of sight to the rooms across the service lane, and could see that both had light leakage around their drawn curtains. He powered up the night sight and ran it over the windows but couldn't see anything further. An infra-red scope would have been good, but beggars couldn't be choosers.

'Shove over, fatty.'

Sarah nudged him out of the chair and took his place, the earphones clamped to her head like Princess Leia's hair-do. He took the dig as a sign she'd got over her earlier huff and was pleased – it would have made for an unpleasant environment otherwise. She aimed the mic at the windows opposite and listened intently.

Archer had no idea how good this particular piece of kit was, but judging from the rest of the gear it should do the job. Sarah certainly seemed happy enough with it, nodding to herself as she listened. He waited silently for a few minutes but she showed no sign of stopping, so he moved off and got his gear together.

To save getting caught with his pants down if things unfolded quickly, he took a change of clothes out ready to jump into and packed the rest of his gear so he was good to go. He placed a couple of different tops and a hat in his daypack, added a bottle of water and a chocolate bar from the mini bar, and padded silently back over to the OP. Sarah was still listening intently, her brow furrowed, pen poised over a pad of the hotel's stationery.

He peeked over her shoulder at the notes she'd jotted already. She had the neatest writing he'd ever seen.

*3 – US? – leader – relaxed – team – rough –*

She lifted the bin from her left ear and looked up at him, whispering as if the bad guys could hear her.

'Can't hear much, they're just talking shit. They sound like squaddies.'

'Is that the "rough" bit?' he enquired with a slight smile.

Sarah smiled self-consciously. 'Of course. All squaddies are rough, didn't you know that?'

Archer grinned and stepped back. 'I'm going to take a quick shower. Give me a shout if anything kicks off.'

Sarah watched him grab his toilet bag and close the bathroom door behind him, before she turned back to the notepad before her. The chatter in the room across the way was sporadic, the sort of idle chatter that men made, laced with expletives and laughter. After a couple of minutes she heard some hooting and sexual comments, ribald enough to raise even her eyebrows, and guessed they had found a pay-per-view porno channel.

She smiled and shook her head to herself as she listened to the comments among the men. The grunting and gasping would soon begin, she guessed. Men. Just oversized children in so many ways. She wondered kind of man would sit in a hotel room and watch porn with other men. Her mind drifted to the man in the bathroom, Archer.

She barely knew him but he seemed different to most men she had known. Certainly different to her ex-husband, at least. Tim had been far more emotional. Archer seemed much more...reserved? Self-contained? Not a man to give too much away, anyway.

The men she worked with came from a variety of backgrounds – some ex-cops, some ex-military, many just normal civilians. Even if she hadn't known Archer was ex-Special Forces, she would have picked it. Far from being muscle-bound Rambo types, they tended to be quiet and confident. No need to shout from the rooftops.

And she couldn't deny there was something inherently attractive about that. At that moment the bathroom door opened and he emerged amidst a cloud of steam. A white towel was wrapped around his waist beneath a toned torso, the white almost glowing in the near-darkness.

Sarah watched as he grabbed some clothes and returned to the bathroom. He paused in the doorway and glanced at her. She could feel his eyes boring into her and a slight smirk crossed his lips. He said nothing before closing the door again, but she knew what he was thinking.

She felt her cheeks get warm and she turned back to the window, cursing him for making her feel like a silly schoolgirl. Maybe it was her own fault. It had been a long drought since the split, broken only sporadically. The first had been a drunken fumble with a self-important prick from Six at a course down on the coast, which had brought more embarrassment than pleasure. As far as icebreakers went, it had barely qualified.

The door opened again behind her and she heard him rustling about. The porno was still going in the background in the targets' room, but the conversation had stopped. Perhaps they'd gone to bed.

'Cuppa?' His voice was so close it made her jump.

'Yes.' She half-turned, lifting one of the bins so she could hear properly. He was close enough that she could smell his aftershave. It wasn't anything she recognised. Tim had worn Fahrenheit and it wasn't that – thank God. 'Yes please.'

A cup duly arrived and he told her to wake him if anything happened. She agreed that she would hit the sack as soon as the targets did, and he left her to it, bedding down on the floor with a pillow and a blanket. The room was dark and silent. Within seconds she could hear his breathing slow and settle into a steady rhythm.

Sarah turned away and stared out the window.

# 8

The airfield was a standard small operation catering to private owners and an aero club. There was a single runway and five separate hangars, with a control tower attached to the clubhouse/admin building.

At midnight the place appeared deserted and secure, the gates locked and the perimeter secured with fences topped with razor wire. Signs for a security company hung on each side of the boundary fence, but so far Archer had seen no sign of a mobile patrol.

The hangars were each lit by a single external light, with plenty of shadows to give cover to a covert infiltration.

He lay in the undergrowth and surveyed the site one last time with the naked eye. He'd circled it completely over the previous hour, using the night sight to examine every square inch and ensure he knew what he was going into.

He needed to get in there and look for any evidence to properly identify the passengers or establish the true purpose for their visit to Germany.

There was no sign of guard dogs – no kennels, food bowls, discarded bones or toys, no piles of shit. No cameras aside from at the front of the admin building, but he doubted it was infra-red.

No sign of a guard on site aside from a light in the admin building. Nothing had moved, no shadows across the window, no noise to indicate a person was in there. Maybe it was just a light left on by mistake in an office. Maybe it was a team of armed heavies waiting to ambush him.

With nothing to verify either option, he had to assume there was somebody on site who was not actively patrolling. Possibly a static guard who spent his night watching TV and sleeping instead of securing his premises.

Sarah was parked up half a klick away in the Golf, keeping open comms through the cheap walkie-talkies.

They had spent a quiet day together, talking and planning, comfortable in each other's company. They had ventured out to walk and eat, and both of them had commented later that they sensed the presence of watching eyes. Nothing seen and nothing heard, just the sensory pinging of highly-tuned antenna.

Whether it meant they had been pinged by local security forces or not, who knew? But it was the sort of instinctive response that kept operatives alive in the field. The rest of the day had been spent hunkered down in the hotel room, awaiting nightfall before sneaking out.

Archer had an earpiece taped in place and the radio itself tucked into an inside pocket of his jacket. He was clad in dark jeans, a grey and green shirt under a black windbreaker, and black trainers. He had only basic tools with him; wire cutters, a penlight torch, a multi tool, gloves and a cheap day pack.

The only non-standard tool he carried that distinguished him from an ordinary burglar was a lock-picking tool that resembled a small drill with a flat body. Even that was bought over the counter so did not necessarily identify him as anything more than a thief.

The night sight and his other kit was all wrapped in a plastic bag and stashed under a bush near the roadside where he could easily recover it.

He opened the front of his jacket and keyed the radio. 'Moving now.'

'Roger that. Moving up.'

She would move forward without lights and wait at an agreed RV point, ready for a quick getaway if he got rumbled. It would also give her some limited obs on the airfield.

He pushed up and scurried low to the fence. Fifteen seconds of cutting and there was a flap large enough to wriggle through, before lying flat and reassessing. The rattle of the chain link had seemed deafeningly loud to him but nothing else seemed to be disturbed by it.

He angled to his left, away from the admin building, crossing a stretch of green before hunkering down again and scanning. The shadows were deep and his breath steamed in the cool air. He was warm inside the jacket and was aware that he may be giving off steam from his body heat.

Another dash and he was angled across the runway towards the hangars, keeping to the shadows and moving steadily, bent over but keeping his head on a swivel.

Nothing.

He paused near the edge of the next stretch of green, taking a last couple of minutes to check his surroundings before making for the nearest hangar.

The geeks at GCHQ had come through with the info that the plane they were seeking was being housed in that particular hangar. How they knew that, Archer didn't know. He'd never understood the world of Signint (signals intelligence), never cared for it aside from what it could give him to help complete his mission.

He moved to the pedestrian door at the side, over which hung a dull sodium light. The only other way into the building was the main doors at the front, which wasn't an option. The noise of hauling one open even slightly would wake the dead.

Archer crouched at the door, his back to the wall, scanning and listening. No time to fuck about. He produced the lock-picking gun and checked the lock with his penlight. The lens was taped over with a tiny hole giving just enough light to see by.

He selected what he guessed was the right size attachment,

quickly fitted it into place and inserted it into the lock. The gun did its thing in half a minute and the lock clicked open. Archer turned the handle and moved inside, hunkering down and closing the door.

There could have been people inside but he had no way of knowing until he got in there. No point in delaying for the unknown. He listened intently, tucking the lock picking gun away again.

No noise, no movement.

A Coke machine against one wall cast a faint glow of light into the hangar, and moonlight filtered in through the large skylights.

A stairway nearby led up to a gantry with a couple of offices of some sort, overlooking the hangar floor. Another office was at ground level on the far side; he could just make out its shape beyond the plane.

'I'm in,' he breathed into the radio, getting a click in return.

He moved along the wall, checking for sensors and cameras. He expected there to be alarm sensors, but there was nothing. Strange. Maybe the light in the admin building meant there was a guard on duty, for whatever he was worth. It seemed strange to have probably millions of Euros worth of aircraft on site with no alarms.

No point wasting time second-guessing; he had to get on with it. The longer he was on site, the more likely it was he'd be discovered or something would go wrong.

He trotted over to the plane, the soles of his trainers squeaking slightly on the concrete floor.

Sure enough, it was a blue and white Cessna Denali. He checked the tail number. It was the right one. The door was open and the steps were down. Archer moved up and flicked the light around inside. Nothing obvious.

He backed out and moved around the machine, not really sure what he was looking for. It was like that sometimes. Often you didn't know what you were seeking until you fell over it. Completing a full circle, Archer paused again and looked around him. The nearest wall had a workbench along it, tools neatly arranged on the hooks above it, other gear in storage bins beneath the benchtop.

He moved to the bench and ran the penlight over it. There was unlikely to be a signed note anywhere saying, "I'm a terrorist and I was here," but there was always the chance of a scribbled note from a mechanic or member of the ground crew that may be unintentionally useful.

He found a discarded packet of cigarettes, a newspaper and a lottery ticket. A pin-up on the wall displayed a buxom blonde girl in all her glory, with a calendar courtesy of an engineering firm. A large plastic trash bin beneath the bench contained a bundle of grey fabric, maybe a tarpaulin.

The plane had been grounded long enough to have been cleaned, so anything inadvertently left on board should have disappeared by now.

He leaned against the workbench, letting his mind run on its own. There was nothing here that appeared to be of any use. The last places to check were the interior of the plane and the offices. The offices would take the longest time, so he settled on the plane first – plus, it was closest. He pushed off the bench and started to move towards the steps, when something twigged in the back of his brain.

He paused, turned, and stared at the trash bin again. Grey fabric.

He stepped back to it and pulled it out from under the bench. He grabbed a bunch of the bundled fabric and pulled it out. Not a tarp at all.

Silk. An unfolded parachute.

Archer pulled it out completely to make sure, finding the harness. He held it in his hands, adrenaline kicking in. This was it. This was the unknown clue he had been seeking, not knowing it until he saw it.

Kozlowski hadn't entered the country on a false passport at all. He hadn't been hiding on board when the Cessna landed, because he wasn't there.

He had parachuted in. The plane would have dropped him some distance away, probably over farm or woodland, and he had jumped. A guy with his background would be a competent jumper. The plane would have landed as normal, everything checked out legit, and he had been picked up by a team on the ground.

*The clever bastard.* A simple plan, but clever.

A parachute was not an unusual thing to find in an aircraft hangar, but being a private hangar – not used by a sky diving team or jump school – an unpacked one was. They were a pain to pack properly, so there was only one reason for a chute to be unpacked – it wasn't going to be needed again any time soon.

Archer stuffed the chute back into the bin and placed it back where he'd found it. He checked his watch. He'd been on site for nearly twenty minutes now. Sweat was running down his back. Having found the chute and what he believed to be Kozlowski's method of entry into Germany, he felt like he'd be pushing his luck to stick around too much longer.

He lifted the radio close to his mouth and pressed the talk button as he started up the stairs to the offices.

'Found a used parachute in the hangar. Nothing else.'

'Roger that.'

Archer was about to step into the Cessna when he heard Sarah's voice in his ear.

'Stand by, stand by. Vehicle approaching.'

He froze, listening.

'Turning in. Black SUV, at least two-up. Unlocking the gate.'

Not good. Archer backed down the steps and ran a quick check over himself to make sure he hadn't dropped anything.

'They're in, coming straight to your hangar. They're not mucking about; they've been alerted. You must've tripped something. You need to get out.'

# 9

Archer was already moving, racing to the pedestrian door he'd come through. He cracked it far enough to get a visual and could see headlights flying towards him from the direction of the gate. A quick glance towards the admin building revealed that the door was open. There had been somebody inside after all.

'Move to the ERV,' he snapped into the radio, 'I'm going off comms.'

Without waiting for a reply he ripped the earpiece out and yanked the radio from his jacket. It was a dead giveaway and he couldn't afford to be caught with it. He quickly closed the door again, the racing SUV nearly at the hangar now.

He ducked inside, shoved the radio kit into the nearest box of rags and covered it, before pausing to listen again.

Running footsteps could be heard over the rumble of an engine. He bolted across the hangar towards the main doors, but already they were opening. He cut left instead and made for the stairs up to the walkway.

If he could get up there then he could get to the roof and have a chance at escape.

Before he'd gone more than a few steps two guys burst in through the big doors, M4s in hand. Their torches fanned across the hangar, seeking a target. No time to shag around, he decided. Archer pumped his knees and arms, making a good few strides before a light swept across him. He kept going, ignoring the shouted warning.

A suppressed double-tap sounded and rounds pinged off the stairway beside him. He kept going. The third round was better placed and cracked past his ear so close he felt the wind brush the side of his head.

'Don't be a dumb-ass,' a voice shouted. 'The next one won't miss.'

Archer stopped where he was, raising his hands in the air. Someone found a switch and the hangar was flooded with light.

The pedestrian door opened and two more gunmen entered, training their carbines on him from only a few metres away. Like their colleagues they were clad in casual jeans and jackets but moved with the confident physicality of professional soldiers.

'Keep your hands up, asshole,' one of them called out. He was stocky and muscular, with a mop of blond hair. 'Come down backwards, nice and slow. Do anything stupid and we blow your ass away, unnerstand?'

Archer said nothing but did as he was told. Coming down backwards made it harder for him to try and spring a surprise attack on them; it was a smart move on their part. It also told him they knew what they were doing.

He reached ground level again and stopped. The instructions were smooth and clear; hands on the head, interlock the fingers, on your knees, look at the ground, cross the ankles. While the others covered him, one guy approached from behind and secured his hands behind his back with interlocked cable ties. A hood over the head blocked his vision and muffled his hearing.

The concrete was cold and unforgiving and his knees soon began to ache while he waited in silence. He adjusted his posture, as much as a test as to relieve the discomfort, and got a swift answer. A boot heel ground painfully into the back of his calf and he stifled a gasp.

'Stay still, asshole,' a voice told him. Like the other voices, it was an American accent. He couldn't place the regional inflection, but it didn't matter.

He stayed still, concentrating on taking in as much info as he could gather. Trouble was, there was nothing; the gunmen didn't speak and didn't even seem to move. There was no discernible sound for a good few minutes until the furthest away door opened and he heard a new set of footsteps approaching. Light and confident, quiet – rubber soles, probably. They stopped several metres away and he heard one of the gunmen move to join the unseen newcomer.

The door had let in a cool evening wind, and with it the fragrance of whatever was growing outside. Jasmine, maybe. He wasn't too good with flowers.

Archer kept his mouth half open to try and catch anything that was said, but could only hear very muffled talk. It was like listening to a conversation from underwater. In less than a minute the light, confident footsteps moved away, followed by the door closing.

'Up.'

A hand on each arm assisted him to his feet and didn't let go. He could smell aftershave on one of them.

'Okay buddy, make it easy,' the main voice said, in front of him now but a couple of metres back. Safe, and in control. 'What's your name and why are you here?'

Archer said nothing, deciding to let it play out. It played out by way of a kidney punch that blasted a bolt of pain right through his core and made him want to piss his pants. He gasped and started to buckle, but the two hands held him up. He was still gasping for breath when the question was repeated.

When no answer came, another blow came, directly on the same spot. The pain was excruciating and stars danced before his eyes. His knees gave way and he hung limply by the arms, his insides consumed with agony. He couldn't see past the pain, let alone form any kind of an answer.

'Roll 'im up.'

Archer was yanked backwards and felt himself stumble, his feet unable to keep pace with the two men dragging him by the arms.

The cable ties were biting into his wrists. He let himself go slack and heard a grunt from one of the men as they took his full weight. Better that they get tired from carrying him than him by trying to keep up.

They dragged him backwards for several metres before lifting him upright and pushing him against a steel pillar. He heard the sound of duct tape being unrolled, and a moment later he was being wrapped to the pillar. Round and round, chest and waist, knees and ankles.

'Name?' The same voice again. 'What're you doing here?'

'Stealing.' Archer muttered the word, keeping his voice low and muffled to try and disguise his accent. It was his only hope right now. A Kiwi burglar was highly unlikely in Berlin, but it seemed a better option than admitting to being a Kiwi spy.

'A thief?' The man's tone was disbelieving. 'You expect me to believe that you're just some dumb-ass burglar?'

'Lemme go.' Archer injected some desperation now, a touch of pitiful pleading. 'Need my pills.'

'Say what?'

'Nee' my pills.' Archer was giving it his best shot. If he could convince these guys he was just some vagrant out for a night's stealing, one of life's less fortunate, then he may have a chance of getting out of here alive.

'Fuck.' The man sounded pissed off now and Archer heard the movement of feet.

Maybe the guy was looking to his team for their thoughts. *Was this guy for real? Just a dumb-ass burglar?*

He heard a murmur of voices, then a decision from the team leader.

'Uh-huh. Do it.'

He knew what was coming and pushed the thought aside for now. Don't worry about what you can't control. He focussed instead on preparing himself for the inevitable as best he could. Deep breaths to oxygenate his blood and bracing himself, knowing it wouldn't be long.

They didn't disappoint. These boys were good at what they did.

No discussion, just straight into it. Gut punches first, left, right, left again.

Breathing hard, but no major damage. Yet.

Left jaw, hard enough to snap his head sideways, blinking under the hood. Gut again, nearly winding him, gasping, right jaw, head snapping back the other way, right ear now, a good solid shot that squashed the ear flat against his head. That one was going to bruise, for sure.

Up under the ribs, burying deep with rock hard knuckles. *Fuck, that one hurt*. Gasping again, trying to get some air into his lungs, but no chance. More torso shots, a constant barrage that stopped him from breathing, shot after shot landing in the same places. Didn't feel like any breaks or cracks yet, but he doubted his organs would be in great shape if they carried on like this.

And they did.

A hand grabbed his head and slammed it back against the steel pillar. He hung there, unable to move, the strips of tape holding him in place.

Bang! Left side of the head, colourful stars bursting across his vision. He let out a groan and the fist came in again, same place, his head held in place by the other hand and taking the full force, unable to ride it through. Again, a fourth, a fifth.

*Fucker. Whoever was doing that had fists like bricks.* At least they'd have some damage to their knuckles as a pay-off. Archer tried to take some satisfaction from that, but it was a weak attempt and did nothing to make him feel any better.

Gut again, and so on it went. Archer lost track, just tried to roll with it as best he could, taking each hit and absorbing it, trying not to black out. His whole torso and head ached and throbbed with pain. He searched for a happy place to go to.

His mind went back to the resistance to interrogation training he'd gone through in the Group, years ago now. It had been hell at the time, but as realistic as possible. Back then, spending hours in stress positions between bouts of interrogation by a bunch of sadistic clever bastards, he'd found a happy spot and gone to it.

A camping holiday as a kid, he was thirteen years old, and the family had camped a fortnight at a remote Coromandel beach. Bugger-all there, just other families camping, soaking in the summer sun, swimming, fishing, hiking in the hills, talking and playing board games at night before crashing out and doing it all again the next day.

The blows kept coming, solid impacts that rocked his body with each shot, but they seemed somewhat abstract now, as if he was observing it rather than taking it.

And Belinda. Oh, Belinda. A fourteen-year-old goddess from Christchurch, holidaying with her own family. Long brown hair, lean but curvy, a favourite red bikini. She could curse with the best of the boys and had her own fishing rod. And she'd let him get to second base. Thirteen-year-old Craig Archer was in love, completely infatuated with this tomboyish older girl, unable to think of anything else from the first moment he saw her on the beach, walking to the water with her younger brother.

Belinda. His happy place. For the life of him he couldn't remember her last name now. Huntly? Huntington? Something like that. Good times. He wondered had become of her. Probably married with two kids, a station wagon and a picket fence, a husband who worked too much and laughed too little.

A shot to the crotch brought him back to reality with a jolt. Pain exploded through him, right to the pit of his stomach. It had been a knee to the balls, right on the plums, and he wanted to vomit. All he could manage was a guttural growl, deep in his chest, his eyes squeezed shut tight against the excruciating agony. Bile rose in his throat, burning acid, up the back of his sinuses.

*JesusfuckingChrist, Jesusfuckthathurt. Motherfucker!*

He was sagging now, his knees buckled and his weight hanging solely on the reels of duct tape. He couldn't feel his hands anymore.

He could hear panting, heavy breathing that wasn't his own. He had no idea how long the beating had taken. Was there more to come? Who knew. Better get organised for that.

He tried to straighten up but his balls were on fire, chugging like a vintage steam engine. The slightest movement sent bolts of fire through his pelvis and made him want to spew. He struggled to breathe. Sweat was pouring off him now, soaking his hair and neck, running down his back and chest.

*Fuck me, this isn't going well.*

He heard muted conversation and tried to listen, but the blood was pounding so hard in his head he couldn't hear a thing.

Hands grabbed him and he felt movement, the bonds of tape coming loose as someone sliced through them, and suddenly he was falling forward, unable to hold himself upright.

They let him fall and he hit the concrete flat on his front, knocking the wind from his lungs and sending more bursts of pain shooting through him. Knees, left shoulder, chest, chin. Everything hurt.

'Get him up.'

Hands grabbed him and hauled him to his feet. He sensed someone stepping up close, face to hooded face.

'Count yourself lucky, pal.' The voice was soft, American, and full of menace. 'Where I come from, trespassers get shot. Don't be stupid enough to come back again. Ain't nothin' worth stealin' here, anyways. Take the hint, y'hear me?'

Archer managed a weak nod, coughing as the bile threatened to break the banks.

'Get rid of him.'

# 10

The hands dragged him sideways, he heard a door open and then felt the rush of cool evening air.

A vehicle door opened and he was hauled closer, a hard edge catching the back of his knees. He was pushed inside what felt like the back of a SUV, his legs lifted in, hand shoving him roughly onto his side.

The slam of the hatch behind him.

Doors opened, two, the vehicle rocked, the doors closed again. The engine started, a pause, then they were moving.

Archer shifted to try and get comfortable. Who knew how long the journey would be, or what would happen at the other end. For now he had to do his best to get his shit together and be as prepared as possible for the next step, whatever that might be. There was a fair chance he would be taken to a remote area and get a bullet in the head, so that was what he had to plan for.

Maybe Sarah would be in a position to intervene before that happened. She was unarmed and ill-equipped to deal with these guys. Maybe not.

There was hope though. The guy who'd spoken to him at the end, presumably the leader, was hopefully convinced he was just a thief, a chancer who got caught. If that was the case, maybe there was a chance they would just give him a good kicking and toss him aside.

Archer didn't know, and there was no point hoping for the best unless he also planned for the worst.

Could he get free and escape? As things stood right now, it seemed unlikely. These guys were good – and brutal. His hands were still bound behind him. His body had been thrashed and he ached all over. He doubted he'd be able to run with plums that felt like grapefruit.

He was unarmed and alone, and had no idea where he was – or where he would end up. There were at least two baddies with him, and presumably they would be on familiar ground. And they were armed and physically capable.

No, the chances of escape seemed slim. If you just focussed on the negatives.

On the other hand, he was Craig fuckin' Archer. Six years as a Captain in the SAS, commanding a troop fighting at the sharp end. Highly trained. More trigger time than any other officer in the Group, probably ever. A couple of years on the Circuit in Third World war zones. More trigger time. Trained more since then. Black ops missions for Division 5 of the Security Intelligence Service.

He'd been in tight scrapes before and come out in one piece. No reason today should be any different. When all else was equal, it came down to the top two inches.

The vehicle was moving at speed on tarmac, presumably city road surfaces, not speeding but not wasting any time either. It smelled newish, clean. Not a work truck then. He couldn't feel anything around him, nothing he could use.

He got his breathing under control, worked his tongue to get some moisture going in a mouth that felt like cardboard, rolled his neck and shoulders to loosen up – something popped but it felt better – and got his head together. His sweat had cooled and dried on his skin.

No point panicking. Panic wouldn't stop a 9mm round to the

skull. Fuck 'em. If he was going to go down, at least he'd go down fighting.

Finally the vehicle turned off tarmac onto a bumpy surface, slowed marginally, and rocked along for a few hundred metres. It slowed, turned a 180 and stopped.

The doors opened, the engine remained running. Footsteps, the rear hatch popped and cool air hit him. Hands grabbed his arm and waistband, dragging him out and helping him to his feet. They turned him, ran him a few steps and threw him down.

Archer tumbled and rolled, getting to a knee before he took a boot in the ribs. He went down again, gasping for breath, the bare earth damp against his exposed skin.

A boot was placed against his neck and pushed his head down into the dirt. Archer gritted his teeth and took it, waiting for the punchline. He heard a pistol being drawn, the sound of steel on leather. The metallic *snick* of a hammer being cocked.

*Where the fuck was Sarah?*

The man above him spoke. It was a different voice now, not the leader.

'You should stay off private property, asshole. It's dangerous to go snooping around. Accidents happen.'

The sound of the shot was deafeningly loud and Archer jumped involuntarily, bracing himself for the impact of a bullet. Slamming through his clothes and skin, ripping up muscle and organs, smashing bones.

Nothing but the splat of a round punching into the dirt beside his head.

The two men laughed, full belly laughs as if they were in a bar and had just heard the greatest joke in the world.

The boot shoved his head further into the dirt.

'Let's get going,' said the other guy, a few steps away.

The boot lifted off Archer's head and he lay there, collecting himself. His heart was slamming in his chest and he was panting. Footsteps moved off, doors slammed, and the vehicle revved. It eased away and the engine sound gradually receded until silence fell.

Complete silence, not even bird song. No distant vehicles.

Archer lay still for a couple of minutes, running a check over himself before he moved. Nothing seemed broken. No bullet wounds. Nothing he couldn't fix.

He got to his knees and bent forward, rubbing his head against the ground until the hood worked its way off. He shook it clear and drew in deep breaths of fresh air. It seemed like he was in a clearing of some sort, dark mounds around him, some fencing beyond that. No lights, just a quarter moon that cast a silvery sheen over the area.

He stood and paused again, shaking out his legs and letting his senses get used to his new surroundings. He had to get out of there but he had to get free first. If he came across any civilians with his hands bound behind his back, they'd call the cops and that was no good. Too much time, too much explaining to do.

He could make out his surroundings better now, and could see it was some kind of a construction site. That was good. Builders left tools and useful bits and pieces lying around. There might even be a vehicle parked up that he could hotwire.

Moving carefully through the area, his hopes were dashed. No vehicles, no tools that he could see. Nothing he could use to free himself and get the hell out of there. He sighed and reassessed. It was going to be a long walk.

He turned and started making his way along the track. It took him a moment to realise he was not alone.

Sarah stood at the top of the track, backlit by the headlights of the black VW. She silently watched him approaching. He stopped a few metres short, averting his eyes from the headlight beams.

'Gee,' he said, 'thanks for showing up. I just got my arse kicked and a pretend execution.' He scowled at her. 'Hope you've had a nice evening.'

She hiked her shoulders. 'Seemed like you had it all under control.'

## 11

An hour later they were back in the hotel room. It was close to two in the morning and nothing was moving outside.

Archer stripped to his briefs and lay on the bed while Sarah attended to his injuries. He was too sore to feel self-conscious in front of her.

She had found an all-night pharmacy on the way back and stocked up on first aid supplies. She put together ice packs using towels and ice from Room Service, and had Archer apply them to his lumps and bumps while she assessed the damage.

'Nothing broken,' was her verdict.

'Doesn't feel like it,' he grunted.

'Here, open up.'

She shoved a couple of strong anti-inflammatories into his mouth and held a cup of water for him to slurp. He drained the rest of the cup to chase them down.

'Any hits to the spine?' she asked.

He shook his head.

She ran her fingertips over his face and he grimaced. 'Might be a bit banged up tomorrow.' She grinned. 'Lucky you didn't have much to start with.'

He lifted the ice packs off his torso and shuffled back into a better sitting position against the pillows. His gut felt suitably numb. Sarah took one of the packs and applied it to his jaw while he held the other one against the side of his head.

'How's the old fella?' Sarah asked with a cheeky grin.

He frowned, not getting her meaning. She tossed her chin towards his pelvis.

'You know, the old how's-your-father? Did you get a crack in the crackers?'

He gave a grunt of understanding. 'Both sides.'

'Better sort that out too,' she said, removing the ice pack from his face and reaching for his waistband.

His hand shot out and stopped her short. She gave him a look.

'Don't be a baby. I'm a grown woman, Mr Archer; I've seen naked men before.'

'It's not...'

'Shut up. We need you fit and well otherwise you're a liability. If that means you need an ice pack on your bollocks so you can walk tomorrow, then suck it up, princess.'

He relented and released her hand. He lifted his butt while she expertly tugged his briefs down. It felt like he was carrying a package of roadkill down there.

'Oh,' Sarah said, 'is it a bit cold in here?' She looked him in the eye, completely straight-faced. 'I can turn the heating up?'

Archer pulled a face, in no position to protest too much. 'Just be gentle, doctor.'

The ice pack was like an arctic blast and it took his breath away.

'Oh no,' Sarah smirked, '*now* it's cold.'

Archer gritted his teeth and tried to block out the pain and embarrassment. But no matter which way he looked at it, he was sitting naked in a hotel room while a woman he barely knew held an ice pack to his balls.

There was nothing to do but lie back and pray for it to end.

IT SEEMED like his head had just the pillow when Sarah was shaking him awake, her tone urgent.

'Get up, we've gotta go.'

He rolled onto his back and sat up, feeling worse than when he'd gone to bed. The curtains were closed and the side lights were on, giving the room a warm orange-yellow glow. Sarah was hurriedly dismantling the OP and shoving things into the kit bag. She paused long enough to throw his clothes at him.

'They're on the move,' she said. 'Get dressed.'

Archer got dressed as fast as his aching body would allow him, tying off his boots while Sarah moved their bags to the door. She was fully dressed and he guessed she probably hadn't been to sleep. He checked his G-Shock. 03:00hrs.

'Where are they off to?' he enquired, straightening up and grabbing the painkillers from the bedside table. He threw a couple more down his neck and chased them with half a glass of water.

'Don't know yet, but they're heading to the plane.' Sarah cast a last look around the room in the half light. 'Your visit must've spooked them. Let's go.'

Archer grabbed both his bag and the kit bag and followed her out. The rest of the hotel was silent and they saw nobody on their way down to the lobby. Sarah left him to sort out the bill while she went to get the car.

Six minutes after leaving their room they were on the road, Archer at the wheel, heading towards the private airfield. Sarah was on the phone and whoever was on the other end wasn't moving fast enough to avoid a roasting.

He listened in silence as he guided the black VW through the nearly empty streets. The city was starting to come to life with early commuters rising for work and the night shift heading home.

'I'm not asking for the fucking world,' Sarah snapped into the phone, 'it would just be good to know where these fuck-holes are flying to, don't you think? ...yes, I know that, so sort it out. I need the info now, we don't have time to fuck about, so if it's okay with you... that's right...I'll be waiting.'

She rang off and scowled at him. 'For fuck's sake,' she grumbled. 'Fucking useless.'

'"Fuck-holes"?' he enquired. 'Really?'

Her cheeks coloured slightly. 'Well, for fuck's sake...'

'That's a lot of fucks this morning,' he observed.

'I wish,' she blurted before catching herself. Her cheeks burned hotter and she looked away quickly. The trill of her phone saved her. 'Yes...where? ...right, got that.' She had adopted a much friendlier tone now. 'Get us the first available flight, you've got our details... right, thanks darling. Love your work.'

She rang off again. 'They've just filed a flight plan to Croatia. Head to Tegel.'

By the time they pulled into the car park at Tegel, Sarah was back on the phone. She listened intently before pressing the handset against her chest and turning to Archer.

'The first available commercial flight is bloody twelve thirty,' she said. 'They're about to leave and they'll be there in a couple of hours; we'll be way behind them.'

Archer pulled the hand brake on but left the engine running. 'What about a private flight?'

'It'd still take too long to organise.'

He thought hard for a second before the light bulb went off. 'Any military birds currently here?'

She gave him a dubious look. 'Why?'

# 12

'I'm still not convinced this is a great idea.'

Sarah's words were almost drowned out by the thunder of the C-17's engines as they waddled down the tailgate of the big Boeing.

Archer said nothing, just shuffled forward further, secured snugly to Sarah's back. Another pair of jumpers was ahead of them, also lashed together as a tandem, the difference being that those two were fully trained and qualified. Sarah, on the other hand, had had a crash course on board from Archer. It was a big enough ask doing a jump with bugger-all training, let alone from a relatively low height and at night. All he could do was trust himself to get her through it.

The RAF crew had been in Germany to pick up some gear, and a mad dash of phone calls that went high up the chain and back down again had secured their services at short notice. The plan put forward by Archer was not perfect by any means, but in the circumstances, it was the best they had. The air force guys they were jumping with had thought it was a great lark, and even their pilot, a baby-faced Flight Lieutenant, had been up for it.

Local forces couldn't be trusted so it was a case of putting their best foot forward and seeing what happened. If it all turned to shit they would steal a boat and hightail it to international waters to await rescue.

The German authorities had agreed to delay the Cessna's take off long enough to give the intelligence officers a head start, but too much delay would cause suspicion and could abort the whole mission.

They figured they had about a forty minute lead – if the Cessna did, in fact, land at Split as planned. For all they knew it would divert off course and head for any number of countries within range. The mysterious fifth passenger might not even be on board.

Too late now.

The green light came on and the loadie gave the first pair the thumbs-up. They shuffled forward and jumped out into the dark grey of the dawn. Archer waddled forward, feeling awkward with Sarah lumbering in front of him. She was doing her best to hide her fear and he'd tried to reassure her that he'd done plenty of jumps before, but when they reached the edge of the tailgate, she pressed back against him and he could feel her tension. She didn't want to go.

'Let's go,' he shouted, edging forwards against her and flicking his NVG goggles on. 'Geronimo!'

Her scream was lost in the wind as they fell into the sky, but he was pleased that she remembered enough of her "training" to throw her arms out into a starfish. He did likewise and they plunged towards the ground, just under 5,000 feet away. A quick check showed that everything was intact so he just hung on and enjoyed the ride. The jumpsuits and helmets they wore over their civvies were warm but the exposed skin was cold. Unlike him Sarah wore standard goggles for eye protection, so was literally flying blind.

The blue ocean was somewhere in the distance but it was too dark yet to see. The grey light of dawn was just creeping over the horizon. A few lights were dotted about far below them, and he could see the odd light out where the sea should be. From the luminous compass on his wrist he could see they were on target.

Split Airport was a couple of klicks or so from the drop zone they were aiming for, and he could see the headlights of the vehicle that was waiting for them. The headlights would be pointing into the wind to help guide them down, and their contacts had also hit the hazard lights to outline the vehicle properly – there was no point finding out at the last minute that they had a tail wind and were going to get carried off-course by a sudden gust.

Ideally their contacts would also be using NVGs and the jumpers would have infra-red strobe lights, but beggars couldn't be choosers. Such was the nature of the work, Archer reflected, tucking his head to the side to avoid a loose wedge of Sarah's hair flapping in his face. Even falling through the sky he could smell her scent, and she felt warm and comfortable against the front of his torso.

The pair below them had popped their rectangular chute and were cruising in nicely. As soon as the altimeter needle hit 2,000 feet Archer did likewise, giving Sarah a warning in her ear a second before he ripped the cord. The canopy puffed open and they were pulled upright by the braking effect of the chute.

Despite the warning, Sarah let out a shriek of fright and pressed back against him.

He checked the lines above him – no snags. He tried the toggles and gave them a gentle turn each way which brought another squeal from Sarah. Everything was looking good and the breeze was carrying them nicely towards the drop zone.

As they got nearer he gave Sarah a couple of reminders about how to land – lean back, legs out in front, and relax. She nodded but he wasn't sure how much had actually gone in.

The other pair had landed in a field and moved off to the side, where the contact's dark saloon waited with two people beside it.

'Here we go.' Archer expertly guided the chute down, aiming for the cone of light from the headlights. 'Legs out front.'

Sarah did as she was told and he gripped her between his legs. He flared a few metres off the ground and they cruised in over the roof of the car for an easy landing on soft, damp grass. He took the impact on his knee pads and skidded a couple of metres before they came to a stop. He quickly dumped the chute and released Sarah from the harness, letting her roll aside as he lifted the NVGs and got to his feet.

He glanced at her as he grabbed handfuls of lines and chute and bundled it all together. Her face was white and blotchy in the yellow headlights but she had a grin from ear to ear.

'All good?' he asked.

'Uh.' She yanked off her goggles and tried to catch her breath. 'Huh.'

'Wanna go again?'

'Jesus,' was all she could manage. 'Wicked.'

Archer dumped the chute in a pile as the others gathered around. The two RAF guys were grinning too, high on adrenaline, and had already stripped out of their harnesses.

The two contacts were dressed in civilian coats and trousers. The man had a round gut and a weathered face, and was maybe fifty. The immediate impression Archer had was that he was ex-military. The woman was shorter and equally round, roughly the same age, with greying bangs protruding beneath her woollen cap. She had dark eyes and a dour expression.

The man didn't waste any time with introductions.

'Throw your shit in the boot,' he said. 'No time to fuck aboot.'

His accent was pure Glasgow, with the edgy melody of a blues guitar.

While the two RAF guys followed his direction, Archer helped Sarah to unbuckle herself and step out of her harness. He unclipped his own gear and they shoved it all into the boot of the car before Sarah slammed the lid.

'Easy there lass, don't break the fookin' thing,' the man grumbled. 'Less ye wanna pay for a new one. Didn't think so.'

The woman watched silently as he handed over a key on a ring. Archer wondered if she'd ever smiled, or if today was just a bad day. Maybe she wasn't a morning person. He accepted the key from the man, followed by a cheap plastic torch.

'Road's that way,' the man said gruffly, pointing off behind them. 'Car's waiting. Maps in it, and a phone. The rest ye'll have to sort yesel', right? Know where ye're goin'?'

'Basically,' Archer shrugged.

'Didn't think so,' the man snorted, then peered closer at him. 'Ye an Aussie?'

'Good ears, mate,' Archer grinned. 'You a Paddy?'

The man scowled for a long second before grinning. His teeth were gappy and yellowed. 'Cheeky fooker. Must be Kiwi then.' He stuck out his mitt and shook hard. 'Welcome to Croatia, pal. Gi' us a few minutes then get yesel's movin', right? Don't fook aboot here, someone may've seen ye comin' in and yer cover story won't stand for shite.'

He was probably right. The cover was that there had been two solo jumpers – the RAF guys – and Archer and Sarah were never there. It didn't explain the multiple sets of gear, but the nameless contacts were supposed to ditch that immediately to minimise the risk.

Archer didn't know who these contacts were, but he was guessing the man was probably an ex-squaddie and the woman looked to be a Croatian. Probably met when the bloke was serving in the Balkans back in the early nineties, and would now be on a nominal retainer for jobs like this on an as-required basis.

He gave the RAF guys a wave and watched as they piled into the car with the two contacts. Like its owners, it had seen better days. Perfect camouflage.

The bloke threw a U-turn and the car headed off towards the vague outline of a farm gate. Archer and Sarah slowly followed, taking their time to give the others a good lead. Their eyes gradually adjusted to the dark and by the time they reached the gate everything was quiet and still again.

They emerged onto a deserted side road and found a tired-looking red VW Passat parked on the shoulder a hundred metres away.

'Can't get enough of the Vee Dubs,' Archer observed as he unlocked the driver's door. Red wasn't ideal for an inconspicuous vehicle, but beggars couldn't be choosers. Obviously the other car was the contacts' favourite.

The car smelt musty and needed a wash, but it fired first time and there was a local map on the seat as promised. There was also a plastic shopping bag containing a burn phone with a charger and a small wad of kuna, the local currency. The needle on the fuel gauge showed a full tank.

Sarah busied herself with the map while Archer got them moving, heading in the same direction he'd seen the other vehicle go. There hadn't been time for a proper briefing of any sort due to the fast exit from Germany, so he had to assume that they were heading towards the city. He had a rough image of the area in his mind and decided to follow his nose until Sarah could place them properly.

He ran his tongue around his mouth, feeling the fur on his teeth and tasting stale sleep breath. A freshen-up would probably have to wait, but hopefully they may be able to at least get a feed on the run. He saw the airport off to the right and Sarah traced a route with her finger on the map.

'Next right,' she said, 'should be sign posted to the airport.'

They made their way into the airport car park and Sarah jumped out while Archer went to find a park. Their phones were on international roaming, so there was no issue with comms, and he needed to remain as out of sight as possible after his run in with the goons in Berlin.

He backed the red Passat into a slot not too far from the terminal and sat back to wait, using the time to study the map and get his bearings. The plan was to find where the private planes landed, pick up the passengers when they disembarked and surveil them. They knew who the guys were, thanks to the efficiency of the German Customs team, but so far they had nothing from either of their agencies on background checks. Names on passports, legit or not, meant little. Archer needed to know the men were behind the names. Knowing the enemy was the first step towards beating them.

Quite how it would all work was yet to be seen. Right now they were illegally in a foreign country with little in the way of resources – not even luggage – and a support infrastructure that was pretty basic.

Archer mentally shrugged. Fuck it – at least it wasn't a war zone any more. He'd heard some horror stories from Ingoe and some of the other old sweats about the atrocities they'd seen in the Balkans back in the nineties, and it hadn't been a pretty picture.

He saw Sarah heading back towards him, wheeling a pair of trolley bags behind her and clutching a copy of a newspaper under one arm.

She tossed the bags into the back seat and fossicked around for a moment before dropping into the passenger's seat beside him. She handed him a pre-packed sandwich and a chocolate bar of some make he didn't recognise, along with a bottle of water and the newspaper.

'Thanks,' he said, unscrewing the bottle cap. The newspaper was in Croatian. 'What's this for?'

'You look like a sexo sitting in a car,' she replied, ripping open her own sandwich. 'At least with that you'll look like a sexo who's up with current events.'

'Fair enough.' He took a long swallow of the cold water and wiped his mouth. 'Any luggage in the bags?'

'I grabbed a few clothes for a quick change, and some more food. The private flights still have to come through the main hall. They've landed, according to the lady at the info desk.' She cracked her bottle to take a drink, but paused as a black Hummer cruised up towards the terminal. The windows were blacked out and it screamed gangster. 'What d'you think; that their ride?'

'Chances are.' Archer capped his bottle and slipped it down beside Sarah's feet. 'Good for us if it is.'

Sarah nodded silently. Using a vehicle like that told them a lot about their target, if it was indeed his. He was happy to be overt and easy to surveil, so probably had no fear of that, indicating high confidence if not arrogance. He likely had local authorities on the payroll. He liked the image that went with such a bling vehicle. It was all good stuff for the watchers to know, and being just the two of them, the more they knew the better armed they were.

The Hummer stopped at the front of the terminal and waited, the massive engine running. A heavy alighted from the driver's seat, all decked out in a black leather coat with a shaved head and shades. Archer labelled him as Kojak.

'Shall I do a walk past?' Sarah suggested.

Archer was about to agree, when the glass doors of the terminal slid open and a small group emerged. They headed straight for the Hummer.

'That's them,' Archer said, spotting a familiar face in the group. It was the guy who had stopped him in the hangar. Stocky and muscular with a mop of blond hair. He moved around to the rear and loaded a couple of kit bags into the back. Archer mentally tagged him as Blondie.

While the luggage was loaded, a couple of the group stood off to one side, smoking. One was a thickset heavy in a bomber jacket. The other was tall and thin, with dark hair swept back and longish curls at the neck. He wore a plain black leather coat and black jeans. He smoked what looked like a cigar and moved like a wraith, barely seeming to move at all.

Instinctively, Archer knew he was the boss. Even at this distance he could tell the guy had an aura about him. The other seemed to be his lieutenant, so Archer tagged him Number Two.

Archer fired up the Passat and waited for the off. Sarah kept eyeball, smoothly taking the role from him, knowing it was less obvious for a passenger to be watching than the driver.

'Moving.' Sarah's experience showed in her calm tone.

Archer slipped it into gear and eased forward, not rushing it. The Hummer would stand out like a bulldog's bollocks; there was no need to get right up on it. The black Hummer turned and headed back towards the road, the tinted windows giving nothing away.

He let it get to the exit before he turned from their aisle and followed suit.

# 13

The Hummer was a good hundred and fifty metres ahead by the time the Passat emerged onto the main road and aimed for Split, twenty-odd k's away.

A white van was between them and Archer knew Sarah would be sussing it for any indication it was linked to the Hummer. He concentrated on maintaining a steady speed and not losing sight of the target vehicle.

If they'd had time to organise a second car it would have been handy, but having a spotter with him took the pressure off. At least right now it wasn't unusual to have a couple in a car heading from the airport towards the city.

He made a mental note to grab a rental as soon as they could as a back-up. He ran through a mental list of kit they should try and get their hands on as he drove. Sarah sat in comfortable silence. The radio played soft European pop. The fuel tank was still nearly full and the temperature gauge showed normal.

They were soon at the edge of the city and the Hummer showed no signs of evasive action. The white van turned off and Archer let another car get in front of him, wary of standing out now they had reached the obvious destination.

The city of Split opened up ahead, all terracotta tiles and stone buildings, with the blue Adriatic Sea spreading beyond it.

The Hummer followed main roads for a few minutes before turning right without indicating. Archer moved on past, wondering whether they'd been spotted or if the driver was throwing in some anti-surveillance drills as SOP. Or maybe he didn't indicate because he was driving a Hummer and therefore was the king of the road.

He kept his eyes straight ahead, hearing Sarah murmur, 'They're heading towards the hills. No one behind them.'

Archer threw a U-turn and went back to the mouth of the road, waiting for another car to turn ahead of him. Sarah had produced a small pair of bino's from the glovebox and focussed them as he drove. Aside from the car in front of them he couldn't see another vehicle. The road wound up into the hills above the city and he could see houses tucked back from the road. Small family homes, nothing flashy. The foothills climbed steeply and were thick with trees.

The ancient Fiat in front of them slowed and took an age to turn into a driveway. Archer cursed and cut around it, gunning the Passat to make ground.

'Easy,' Sarah warned, her eyes glued to the bino's. 'They're still there, about four hundred ahead. Chill.'

He took a breath and checked himself. No point coming this far to blow it by getting impatient. He saw a glimpse of the black wagon well ahead as the road took a turn to the left. They weren't wasting any time but didn't appear to be trying to outrun anyone either. He felt more confident that they hadn't been pinged.

The higher they went the more infrequent the houses became. The quality seemed to increase as well, and the vehicles he spotted were later model European jobs.

'Turning in,' Sarah said, getting a last glimpse before the road took them behind an outcropping.

Archer gave it some gas and the tyres hung grimly to the tarmac as he belted the old Passat around the tight bends. It wasn't built for racing and he could feel the grip slipping, forcing him to ease back.

'Easy, tiger,' Sarah cooed beside him, a smile playing at her lips.

'You'll get there. It's about technique, not speed.'

He smiled despite himself and wondered if she flirted with everyone, or if he was getting special treatment.

'Round the next bend,' she said, 'just up on the right. Looked like a driveway.'

They rounded the last bend and spotted a driveway cutting uphill on the right, high black steel gates blocking the entrance, set back far enough to allow a vehicle to clear the road before stopping. They drove past and negotiated another few bends before Archer could pull into an observation area.

A small car park with a huge set of binoculars bolted to a stand allowed tourists to drop a coin and check out the sights. A green and white Kombi van was there, the young couple taking selfies with the Adriatic in the background.

He had to admit, it was a hell of a view, but they weren't here to play tourist.

'What'd you see?' he said, turning the car around to face downhill.

'Big house up in the trees,' Sarah said, 'couldn't see much else.'

'Vehicles?'

'Couldn't see.'

'Security?'

'Couldn't see, but yeah, you'd think so. It's obviously money up here, and looking at that Hummer, probably not all legit.'

He nodded, thinking hard. 'I think we need to swap vehicles,' he said. 'This thing stands out being red, and they may have clocked it already.'

'You want me to call the contact and get a car brought up?'

'No.' He glanced at her. 'You ever used that guy before?'

'No, don't know him.'

'I don't want to get him too involved. We don't know him well enough. Drop me off here and you shoot down to the city, find a Hertz or whatever and grab a better car. You know what to look for.'

She nodded her agreement. 'What if they bugger off while you're on your todd?'

He frowned. 'What the hell is that?'

She chuckled. 'While you're on your own. You'll be high and dry without a motor.'

'If they bug out I'll ring you straight away. At least you'll be in a position to intercept them at the bottom of the hill as they come down.'

She pointed in the other direction, further into the hills. 'And if they go that way?'

He shrugged. 'Then we're fucked.'

She nodded. 'Fair enough.'

'My guess is they're staying here, so hopefully they'll be here for the day. I'll get into an OP and get some eyeball. You get a vehicle sorted, and a hotel I guess. I'll give you a buzz when there's something to report, and in the meantime try and find somewhere handy that you can stash the car up here.'

They trimmed down the details until they were both happy with the plan. They agreed timings for comms and an ERV (emergency rendezvous) point. The young couple at the Kombi had finished taking their selfies and now sat on the low wooden barrier, sharing a joint. The sickly sweet smell wafted over the air and the guy gave Archer a lazy grin as he swapped seats with Sarah. The girl dragged on the joint, her eyes half closed. Archer hoped they were staying off the road for a while.

He took a few minutes to sort himself out, grabbing the binos before going through the things Sarah had bought. He took some water and chocolate bars, a grey hoody and a black cap with a picture of a palm tree and *I Love Croatia* on it, and shoved them into the small dark blue day sack. He added the flashlight and a dirty grey-brown groundsheet from the boot and secured the bag shut.

'Let's go.'

Sarah started back down hill, pulling up a hundred metres or so from the driveway where the Hummer had disappeared. Archer rolled out quickly while the car was still moving, diving into the undergrowth at the side of the road while she moved off smoothly. He clambered through overhanging branches and low bushes until he was out of sight of the road and crouched down, taking stock of his surroundings.

No traffic on the road and no noise from the direction of the properties. Any birds in the immediate vicinity had gone quiet. There were no warning shouts and no whirring of CCTV cameras zeroing in on him. He took a few minutes to listen, watch and wait. If he got sprung by anyone this close to the road it would easier to sell the story of ducking into the bush for an emergency dump than if he was crossing their back yard.

Satisfied he was okay for now, he got the day pack settled on his back and began working his way uphill, using the scrubby weeds and small bushes for handholds. It was impossible not to leave any sign in the dirt so he just did the best he could. The ground soon levelled out and he stayed low under the olive trees that covered the place, moving to his right parallel to the road. He couldn't see if he was on a separate property or the same one the Hummer had gone to.

Pausing in the undergrowth, Archer caught his breath and listened again. A car on the road, working hard to get up the hill. A back-up team? Cops? He waited, poised to move. The car moved on past, the driver chopping down a gear and giving it more guts. The car sounded ready to drop its load.

Archer knew how it felt. He took a few moments to dig his hand under some leaf litter and get into the dirt. He rubbed it on his face, neck and hands and also onto the day pack. It would help to camouflage him in a natural environment and reduce the glare of his white skin in the light. Should any dogs turn up it might also help reduce his scent if they were at a distance.

He plotted out his next few movements and carried on, moving from cover to cover and stopping every few metres to re-evaluate. He'd seen no sign of a security system yet; no cameras in trees, no infrared beams at ground level, no trip wires, no pressure pads, no dog shit. Maybe they were closer to the actual house, or maybe the householder felt safe enough up here without them.

He could see a house through the trees now. He estimated it was a good couple of hundred metres back from the road and slightly lower than his current position. He moved towards it, keeping low and moving tactically – being careful where he placed his feet, not breaking any branches, trying not to disturb the undergrowth at all.

It was slow going and tiring, but he had always been a believer in investing at the front end. Doing things right at the start saved him from fixing fuck ups later.

Eventually he got to a spot where the olive trees thinned out and dropped away to an orchard of what looked like young citrus covering a decent sized field.

He slid down on his belly with everything zipped up and secure to prevent losing anything and the day pack at his side to minimise his profile. He crawled forward on his toes and elbows, inching up until he was two metres or so back from the edge of the undergrowth.

He lay flat and observed again, only moving his eyes. His mouth was half open to maximise his hearing. His breathing slowed and he quickly felt at one with his surroundings.

Beyond the citrus orchard was a manicured lawn with well-tended flower gardens and water features. The driveway was stone chip from the road until it reached a turning circle, where it turned into slabs of paving stone.

The centre of the turning circle was a water feature of a naked guy in a toga with a pair of damsels hanging off his legs.

Archer chuckled to himself. The front of the model's toga was open and the sculptor obviously had a fascination with the phallus. Maybe the place was some kind of freaky European sex club where wealthy fat men came to pork slaves.

With any luck he'd soon find out.

The black Hummer was parked at the top of the turning circle, right at the front door. Kojak from the airport with the shaved head and shades was standing beside it, smoking. Another guy was with him, also bulky and also smoking. Bling rings glinted in the sunlight.

Knuckles.

Both wore black suits. They looked like a pair of 'roiders, and he pegged them as local muscle.

The house itself was a large stone affair, three storeys high, the top of which must have given great views. It looked well cared for and very Mediterranean. No sign of anyone else. The other side of the driveway dropped away on a slope, and looked to be another mini orchard leading to more olives. He could see the edge of another stone building on that side of the house, maybe a garage or secondary dwelling.

Shifting his gaze, Archer could see the tended lawn ran around towards the back of the house. He could see a hint of blue and wondered if it was a pool. He wouldn't be able to see more without moving.

He stayed put for now, slowly working the burn phone out of his pocket and checking it. No messages and it was still muted. He thumbed a quick text to Sarah to let her know he was in position and the Hummer was on site. He kept the phone in his hand until he received an acknowledgement a minute later, then put it away again.

The guys at the front of the house were still standing around like drivers and BGs always did. Their body language was relaxed and there were no weapons visible.

Archer lay there, running through an appreciation of the scene. No visible CCTV cameras, security lights on each side of the house, about a hundred metres from where he lay to the front door, another forty to the back of the house. No obvious path to follow through the citrus orchard.

He checked his watch. Nearly 09:00. He edged slowly back into the undergrowth, taking his time, moving on toes and elbows again. Satisfied he was properly out of sight, he moved behind a tree, slung the day pack on and began a full circuit of the house.

It wasn't ideal to recce the place in daylight, but having no idea how long these guys would be there, Archer figured it was worth the risk. He took his time and moved tactically through the greenery, keeping it low and slow until he had circumnavigated round the back of the property to the far side of the house. None of the curtains were closed.

The pool at the rear was an inviting blue and immaculately tidy. Two of the guys they'd tracked were sprawled on loungers beside it, seemingly asleep. Blondie and a Latino-looking guy that Archer automatically tagged as Chachi.

He could hear faint music from within the house. A third guy was visible just inside the rear door, standing in the shadows with an Uzi over his shoulder, but Archer couldn't make him out.

The odd snatch of conversation could be heard and he paused to listen. A woman's voice, light and bouncy. Must've already been at the house when they arrived.

He spotted movement inside, through the open rear doors. A woman emerged onto the patio with a towel in one hand and a bottle of sunscreen in the other. She moved like a dancer – long and balanced. Her long dark hair was tied loosely at the back. Her bikini was white with red love-hearts, barely keeping her ample assets in place, the thong at the back cutting between two perfectly sculpted cheeks. Her skin was tanned and unblemished.

Archer watched as she sauntered across the pavers to a free lounger, where she dropped her towel and bottle. She slowly removed her sun gigs and placed them down on the towel. Chachi stirred and Archer could tell he was watching the girl. He could also tell that the girl knew. She stretched, accentuating her full breasts, and loosened the hair tie.

The blue water rippled as she took a neat dive and quickly resurfaced, blowing spray and wiping at her face as she giggled.

Her sporting talents probably weren't aquatic then, Archer thought wryly.

He looked beyond her splashing around and spotted the Boss standing in the shadows by the back door, watching her. He had bare feet and three-quarter-length black pants with a loose white shirt. His hands were in his pockets and he wore black shades. He reminded Archer of Nick Cave, the Aussie singer.

Archer held still, feeling as if the man was staring directly at him. There was something about the guy he didn't like, something more than the whole gangster image.

After a couple of minutes the girl emerged from the water, wringing out her wet hair and Archer got a better look at her. She looked to be in her early twenties, had a Cyrillic tattoo running up her spine from some kind of winged tramp stamp at the base, and definite implants. A hooker, he mused, or a dancer – not that there was much difference, in his experience. Presumably the boss' bit of fluff.

Sure enough, just as she was about to start applying sunscreen, he said something. She looked up, hesitating for a second. He didn't speak again, just looked, and she took the hint. She put the bottle down, quickly dried her legs with the towel and followed him inside.

The guy with the Uzi stepped outside and said something to the two guys on the loungers. They all chuckled. Obviously some insider joke about the boss having the horn on.

Archer was about to start backing away when he saw the girl appear in an upstairs window. Her bikini top was gone and her silicone bags were on full display as she pulled the curtains closed. He waited a few more minutes until normality had resumed before easing back into the undergrowth and continuing his recce.

CCTV cameras were visible at the top of the house, with another at the rear of the secondary building. As far as Archer could tell, it was some sort of garage. He paused to take photos as he went and sent them to Sarah.

He took the time to examine all sides of the house, paying particular attention to the windows and doors. If they were to try and enter the place, it was good to know which doors opened inwards and which went outwards, the types of locks, the location of any catches. They were all things that caused problems for a CTR and slowed you down, potentially compromising an operation.

By the time he hunkered down in a shallow dip beneath the scrubby juvenile trees on the far side of the house, an agonising two hours had passed and he was drenched in sweat.

He took a few moments to drain a bottle of water and regather himself, before tucking the empty bottle back into his bag and getting the phone out. He read a text from Sarah, reporting an hour ago that she had a rental car and was standing by.

He relayed his new position and his intention to wait the day out.

# 14

It was getting on towards midday and the sun was fully up.

The trees gave him shade but he could see heat waves coming off the steel of the black Hummer. The two guys at the front had rotated with another guy Archer hadn't seen. He looked like he would have been one of the team from the airport, and Archer labelled him Biff based on nothing more than it sounding American and the guy had the clean-cut look of an all-American boy.

Biff had a pistol holstered at his hip and a folding stock AK47 in his hands. He looked more alert than the two heavies and patrolled the front area at irregular intervals, not moving far but remaining constantly alert.

Archer noted the difference and the weaponry. It confirmed his suspicions that the other two were local muscle.

His new position was a few metres back from the edge of the scrub, with a good line of sight to both the house and the driveway. The shade of the trees shielded him from the sun and also – hopefully – from the house. He considered digging in, using the old tarp from the boot and the ground litter to make a proper OP, but leaned more towards mobility in case he needed to bug out in a hurry. Being unarmed, the last thing he wanted to be doing with a bunch of heavies coming at him was scrambling out of a hide before he could leg it.

Decision made, he scraped up more dirt and re-applied it to his skin. He rubbed some over his clothes as well – anything to break up the texture and lines of clothing was worth the effort. That done, he got a chocolate bar down his neck and followed it with more water. One of the dangers of being in an OP was dehydration. He secured his rubbish in the bag and scanned around to make sure he'd dropped no litter.

The sun shifted and the guards rotated. Blondie ended up at the front. Archer noted that he brought his own weapons; another hip-holstered pistol and a folding stock AK. These boys were certainly well prepared.

At the turn of the hour he texted an update to Sarah and got one back quickly. She was obviously bored. He deleted the messages and put the phone away again. It was 1400 and nothing was stirring.

He took some time to reassess himself. His body still ached from last night and the slow recce hadn't done him any favours, but at least he could rest for now. The trick was not to seize up. To counter that he made tiny movements, stretching out a limb at a time, squeezing and releasing the muscles to keep some blood flow going. He took on more fluids, but being halfway through the second-to-last bottle now, he took it easy. Who knew how long he had until he could resupply.

In the meantime, the previous bottle and a half were knocking to get out. Digging out the empty, he rolled onto his side and unzipped, got himself into position, and carefully let loose. The bottle filled before he was done.

Typical.

He carefully screwed the cap onto the now-warm bottle and put it back into the day pack. He downed the second bottle and refilled it from the other end, managing to complete his task with minimum spillage, which he considered an accomplishment in itself. Any OP where you left without smelling like piss or crap was a good OP.

Job done, Archer stashed the second bottle in the bag and lay back on his front. He could smell his own sweat.

The temperature dropped as the afternoon wore on and it was nearly four when he heard motors approaching up the hill. Vehicles had been up and down all day but nothing had entered or left the property since the Hummer had arrived. This was different. At least two cars, and they sounded like performance machines.

The hum of electric gates opening followed by the crunch of tyres on gravel confirmed it.

The Boss emerged from the house, standing with Number Two and Chachi, as the new arrivals pulled up. Chachi openly carried an Uzi over his shoulder.

Archer gave a silent nod of appreciation. Performance machine was a very apt description alright.

The lead vehicle was a Ferrari LaFerrari in traditional Italian red. According to a blog Archer had read recently, it was a 789 horse V12 hybrid. He had no idea what year it was but that had no bearing on the fact it was the fastest production car in the world. 0-60mph in 2.5 seconds.

The one behind it, staying back a respectable distance to avoid any stone chips, was a sleek silver Porsche 918 Spyder. Its 608hp 4.6 litre V8 had similar performance stats to the Ferrari but was slightly quicker over the quarter mile, if his memory served him correctly. Like the lead vehicle, the Porsche was a lean, mean, growling beast.

The two cars turned slowly and came to a stop near the Hummer. Archer got his phone out and switched the camera on, zooming as best he could given the distance.

The two men that alighted from the cars looked like brothers. Both wore sharp dark suits without ties, had shoulder-length dark hair, and goatees. The women with them were cut from the same cloth as the girl in the pool – fake tits, fake nails, hair thrashed to within an inch of its life, and stripper bodies.

Everything about the little group reeked of gangster. Archer guessed the connection between these clowns and the group he'd followed was probably the age-old solution – money. The new arrivals clearly had it in spades. He snapped away on the phone, getting the vehicle plates and the best shots he could of all the players.

Number Two and Chachi stepped forward, gesturing for the new arrivals to lift their arms. Both men were given an expert pat-down, and each was relieved of a pistol. The two bimbos were then searched – not that there were many places to hide anything. They giggled and flirted with the men as they were patted down, and one of the newcomers made some kind of crude remark that got his mate laughing and the bimbos giggling more.

None of the others cracked a smile, and to Archer, it accentuated the difference between the two groups.

They stood around chatting for a few minutes, and Archer noticed the Boss gesture towards the second building as he did so. He wondered again what was inside. Maybe the guy was also into sports cars and was showing off to the newcomers.

After some more bullshitting the group retired inside, leaving just Blondie out the front. Archer watched as Blondie took a closer look at each of the two cars, letting himself be distracted for a few minutes while he drank in the beauty of the two machines. It would be hard not to, but it also indicated a lack of discipline, which he found interesting.

The late afternoon rolled into the evening and Archer stayed put, watching and listening. He'd once spent the better part of a month in an OP on an Afghani mountain in winter, so a day in Croatia was no hardship. The biggest risk he could see so far was boredom. The guards were armed and relatively alert, probably well trained too, but they weren't active. Unless things changed for some reason, he could probably lie there all week and remain undetected.

Boredom, on the other hand, led to carelessness. Carelessness led to disaster. He double-checked his belongings, ensured the phone was still on silent and he'd cleared all the messages. Everything was in order.

That was when all hell broke loose.

Shouts broke out from the rear of the property, a woman

screamed, another joined in. There was a crash as something broke, and more shouting.

Archer watched and waited. Chachi was on guard at the front of the house, and he was listening intently to his earpiece. Obviously something had turned to shit inside, and he was sussing whether he needed to get involved or not.

More crashing, a shriek and a shout. A terrified wail.

Chachi nodded to himself and stayed put, scanning his surroundings, the Uzi in his fist. Whatever was happening didn't need his intervention, but Archer still wanted to determine what was going on.

He slowly moved further back into the undergrowth, keeping his eyes on Chachi, and made his way towards the rear of the house. The pool area was all lit up and chaos had certainly descended.

Kojak and Knuckles were both on their knees on the patio area, completely naked. Kojak had both hands on his head and was cringing away from the barrel of Blondie's AK, which was aimed at his skull. Knuckles was using his left hand to cradle his right arm, which appeared to be injured. Even from where he crouched, Archer could see he was out of the game.

The two gangsters sat at an outdoors table nearby, their bimbos standing behind them. Both girls looked shocked and had their arms crossed, watching silently. The two men didn't appear to be too disturbed by the scene in front of them.

Another table was turned over nearby and broken glass glittered in the light. A guy Archer hadn't seen before was rifling through a pile of clothes, and it was horribly apparent what was going on.

The Boss and Number Two stood together, each with a pistol in their hand. The Boss was talking but Archer couldn't hear what he was saying. Kojak shook his head, his voice pleading. The Boss said something else, very cool and calm. Kojak shook his head again, pleading some more. Knuckles stayed silent, seemingly deep in a world of hurt.

The Boss glanced towards Blondie and gave an order.

The blonde guy stepped forward, rear-slinging the AK as he pushed Knuckles flat on the paving stones. The guy squealed with pain and tried to protect his injured arm, but in a second he was flat on his face with Blondie over him.

Kojak tried to say something and earned himself a cuff across the head from Number Two's pistol.

Blondie knelt on Knuckles' back, seized hold of his injured arm and wrenched it up and back. The guy screamed in agony and even Archer heard a distinct crack as a joint or bone popped.

One of the bimbos took an unsteady step before collapsing on her friend, out for the count. Probably not quite how she'd thought the night would pan out. The other bimbo lowered her to the ground and stood again, unable to tear herself away from the show. It was like watching a car wreck.

Kojak was shouting now, his tone pleading and desperate. He may as well have saved his breath, because the guy with the clothes found something and handed it to the Boss.

The Boss examined it before waving it at Kojak and asking something. Kojak went silent. He may as well have admitted guilt.

Blondie went to work on Knuckles again, standing up while holding the injured arm. Archer could see the wounded man was still conscious, but just barely. Right about now he'd be praying for the waves of pain to pound him into unconsciousness.

Holding the arm near the elbow joint, Blondie braced his knee against it.

The Boss spoke again and Kojak shook his head in silence. The Boss nodded, and Blondie popped the elbow against his knee, one smooth move folding it completely the wrong way.

Knuckles shrieked, bucked once and collapsed like a deflated parachute. Kojak bellowed something unintelligible and tried to get to his feet. Number Two pistol whipped him again. The second bimbo put a hand to her mouth, retched, tried to straighten up, and lost it. She vomited on the pavers, staggering away from the two seated men. The two men glanced at each other and a comment passed between them.

The Boss and Number Two had their heads together now as they conferred. Blondie had stepped back and was covering the two prisoners with his AK. The other guy had finished with the clothes and was standing back, an Uzi in his hands.

It seemed obvious to Archer that one or other of the two locals had been burned either as an informant or traitor. Neither were good options, and it was only ever going to end one way. He got the phone out and snapped a few photos, for what they were worth.

He quickly messaged them to Sarah and was deleting the message when he spied movement from his left. It was Chachi, moving fast towards him, one hand at his earpiece as he spoke into the radio mic clipped to his front.

The guys round the pool began to move too.

# 15

Archer cursed himself for not shielding the screen of the phone better as he rammed it back into his pocket and began to edge backwards. Chachi didn't have NVGs on, and maybe he hadn't pinpointed Archer's exact spot.

Any hope of that was blown when the Uzi came out and hammered a short burst into the undergrowth just a metre from Archer's position. He moved faster, rolling sideways as the Latino heavy reached the edge of the lawn and brought the Uzi up again. Another burst ripped through the branches and leaves and buzzed past Archer as he kept moving.

Any hesitation right now and he'd be dead. With Chachi so close, there was no chance of getting away without neutralising the threat of the Uzi first.

'Come out, homes,' Chachi called out, scanning the undergrowth. 'Come out or I'll blow your ass away.'

A scrubby bush to his right moved and he swung that way, finger tightening on the trigger.

Archer's daypack hurtled through the air, crashing into Chachi's side and knocking him off-balance. Archer was on him in a flash, body slamming him in a ball-and-all tackle, getting a hand to the Uzi as he drove the man sideways and rode him down to the ground. Chachi was no rookie though, and was twisting and bucking the whole time, trying to throw his attacker off.

They hit the deck with Archer on top, scrabbling at the submachine gun with his left hand, getting his right forearm across the side of Chachi's neck and forcing his head into the ground. He leaned his full weight on the forearm, feeling Chachi's legs thrashing beneath his, the guy's left hand coming round to grab at his face.

Archer tucked his head down as best he could, the fingers still tearing at his hair, his ears, scratching and searching for his eyes. He could smell coffee and cologne, with a waft of spearmint gum. The guy was strong and wiry and had a tattoo of a flaming half-moon behind his ear.

Control of the Uzi was locked in a stalemate and he knew it was going to be a war of attrition – he had to grind Chachi into submission before his mates arrived.

The searching hand found its way to the side of his face and a finger hooked into the corner of his mouth, ripping at it, forcing his lips apart. Archer bit down, chomping hard on the finger and locking onto it, crushing it between his teeth. Chachi let out a yowl of pain and tried to pull his hand free. Archer kept hold of it, tasting blood and sweat and gun oil, maintaining the pressure across the man's neck at the same time.

He felt the resistance going, the thrashing of the legs slowing, the arm going slack. Footsteps were approaching, running from the pool area, and a torch was sweeping the grass.

Archer pulled himself up higher on Chachi's body, grabbing at the Uzi and plucking it from Chachi's weak grasp. The torch beam cut their way as he rolled off the other man, bringing the Uzi up, seeing one guy behind the beam as the light found them, a shout sounding.

He squinted against the light and triggered a 3-round burst then another, hearing a scream and seeing the torch go flying. He crabbed to the side, checking for more enemy, seeing another stepping onto the lawn from the pool area. Archer sent another burst his way and the guy ducked back, returning fire wildly with an AK.

Archer turned back towards Chachi, realising the guy was not dead. He was weakly trying to draw his sidearm when Archer pumped a burst into his torso, making his body jump like he'd touched a power main.

More fire came from the direction of the pool area. There was shouting and screaming and the lights went out. He crabbed back over to Chachi, searching him quickly and coming up with a spare 32-round magazine for the Uzi. He shoved it in his waistband and took the guy's pistol too. He was still gurgling and moving slightly. *Too fucking bad* – Archer left him where he was and found his daypack, before scampering back towards the front of the house.

Glass exploded behind him and AK rounds ripped up the grass around him as someone opened up from inside. Archer fired a one-handed burst in the general direction and ran for it, sprinting down the side of the house several metres before spinning and dropping to a knee.

The gunman was framed in a shattered window, AK in the shoulder, and Archer cut loose, rattling off half a dozen rounds into the window before the magazine ran dry and he was moving again. He dropped the empty magazine as he ran and rammed the spare up the butt of the pistol grip, working the bolt to chamber a new round.

He reached the side of the house, hearing car doors bleeping and panicked shouting. Risking a peek, he saw the two hoods and their bimbos trying to get into their cars.

There were no gunmen in sight.

Archer popped out, the Uzi up in the aim, and challenged them.

'Get on the fucking ground! Now!'

The closest guy, about to drop into the driver's seat of the Ferrari, completely froze, his face going white. The other guy, several metres back at the door to the Porsche, was bolder.

'Fuck you, asshole,' he growled in a heavy accent.

'Gimme the keys!'

Archer moved towards the Ferrari driver, his hand out for the key. A glance over his shoulder told him that trouble was about to arrive. He dropped and spun, ripping off several rounds at the two shadows charging down the side of the house. They took cover and returned fire, one with an AK, the other a pistol. Archer gave them another burst and darted for the Ferrari.

The driver stood frozen still, the key in his hand. Archer snatched it from him with one hand, yanked him aside and threw him to the ground.

He sensed the other guy coming at him, the guy roaring now like a wounded bull. There was no time for niceties. Archer half turned and pumped a double tap into his gut, dropping him. The two bimbos were shrieking now and rounds started coming from the guys in the darkness. He sent another couple of bursts their way, threw his daypack inside the car and followed it fast.

Two seconds later the V12 let out a ferocious growl and the red beast leaped forward like a fuck-starved jackrabbit. Rounds slammed into the left hand side as Archer flung the car around the drive and aimed for the gates, spraying stones out behind him. It took him a second to realise one of the bimbos had jumped in with him.

'What the fuck?!'

'Look out!'

He looked up in time to see the steel gates blocking the way, gave it a kick in the guts and covered his face with one arm as the other wrestled the wheel.

The nose of the Ferrari impacted the gates with a hell of a thump, there was a tearing screech of metal giving way, and they burst through, fishtailing right onto the road.

'Fuck! Wrong way!'

Archer hit the picks, slammed it into reverse and threw a fast J-turn, throwing it back into second and gunning it down the hill towards the city. He couldn't see any flashing lights coming but surely it wouldn't be long before the place was swarming with cops, and he needed to be far away from there when it was.

'Who the fuck are you?' the bimbo shrieked at him. 'You fucking kill those guys and steal their car? You fucking know who they fucking are? You fucking crazy bastard!'

Archer ignored her and concentrated on staying on the road. The

Ferrari had more power than he'd ever experienced, and the adrenaline surge of the battle was making his gross movements clumsy and his foot heavy on the gas.

He eased off and took a slow breath, checking the rear view mirror. They were a good few hundred metres from the house but already a set of headlights was flying after them. He could feel the phone vibrating in his pocket and guessed Sarah was wanting to know what exactly was going on.

He ignored the phone for now and concentrated on losing the pursuers.

The Ferrari clung to the tarmac as he threw it round the bends, the machine seeming to revel in the challenge that would have flung any other car off the side of the road. The engine was a highly-tuned growl, and the controls responded like an eager virgin in his hands as he belted down the mountainous road. The city lights burned and twinkled to the right but he didn't dare take his eyes off the road to check for flashing red and blues.

Rounding a tight left-hander he saw another car approaching at speed, some kind of dark sedan with its high beams on. He cut hard left back onto his own side of the road, missing the front of the sedan by scarce millimetres, and threw a quick look at the other driver as he flew past.

Sarah's eyes were like saucers as she stared back at him, her mouth open with fright.

He saw her brake lights flare at the same time as he hit the picks, skidding to a halt. He slapped the car into neutral and yanked the emergency brake on, leaping out as the sedan came careening round the corner in reverse, shooting past him and braking again.

'Get out of the car!' he barked at the bimbo in the passenger seat. She sat and stared at him before unleashing another volley of abuse.

Ignoring her, he waved at Sarah to turn the car around. She was already starting a thousand point turn on the narrow road as he raced back towards the corner, hearing the sound of approaching engines. They were coming fast and were only seconds away.

He looked back, seeing Sarah finally getting round to face downhill again. Beyond her he could see the first flashing blue light down in the city, and knew it wouldn't be long before the cops were there.

He sprinted back to the Ferrari, the Uzi in his hands, shouting at the girl again to get out of the vehicle. She opened the door and was starting to get out when headlights swept round the bend and the Porsche was on them.

It was going too fast to stop and slammed straight into the rear of the Ferrari, shunting it hard forward with a deafening crunch of shattered plastic and metal. The girl was flung aside and Archer kept moving, trying to get past the wreck before anything blew.

He glanced into the cab of the Porsche as it skidded past him and saw the face of the guy he'd taken the Ferrari from. There was someone else in the passenger's seat but he couldn't make them out.

Archer brought the Uzi round and put a burst through the driver's window, shattering it and blowing pieces off the dashboard as the car slid by.

Headlights washed over him as the black Hummer blew round the corner, bearing down on him as he raced back towards the waiting sedan. He dived to the left, hitting the tarmac hard on his shoulder and rolling out of the path of the big truck. It was already skidding to a halt and he didn't have time to waste.

He got to his feet, Uzi up in the aim, and paced towards the Hummer as the front passenger's door opened. A guy was half out of the vehicle when Archer raked him with a short burst through the back, spraying blood across the inside of the windscreen. The driver panicked and stalled the truck as Archer got closer, letting the body fall to the ground so he had a clear view into the Hummer.

The driver was scrabbling for a folded AK on the front seat but was too flustered. Archer recognised the guy who had been searching the clothes by the poolside. He brought the Uzi on line and pumped a short burst into his chest, slamming him back against the driver's door. He glanced down at the body by his feet, not recognising the man. He guessed there must have been more guys inside the house, thugs he had never seen, and realised how lucky he'd actually been to get away like he did.

He ran past the stalled Hummer, checking the Porsche when he got to it.

The gangster driver was trying to pull himself out of the wreck, blood running down his face from a cut, and Archer saw the other bimbo in the passenger's seat, slumped forward and apparently out cold. He grabbed the driver and yanked him free, dropping him to the ground and standing over him.

'Who are you doing business with?' he shouted, the Uzi's stubby barrel pointing at the guy's face.

The guy groaned and put a hand to his head. Sirens sounded, approaching fast. A small fire had broken out under the front of the Porsche and flames were licking up the panels where the Porsche was mashed into the back of the Ferrari.

'Who were you meeting with?' Archer demanded, giving him a kick for emphasis.

'Fuck you...'

'Hurry up!' Sarah was outside the car now, shouting to him. 'The cops're coming!'

'Who is he?' Archer stood on the guy's knee and ground it into the tarmac, making him squeal with pain. 'Give me a name!'

'You will never find him, Mr Policeman.' The gangster had a sick grin on his face. 'He is ghost.'

'We need to go!' Sarah hollered. The sirens were deadly close now and he could hear the police cars being pushed hard up the hill.

'There's no such thing,' Archer growled, jabbing the Uzi at the guy's face. 'Name!'

The guy was remarkably calm, maybe figuring he was safe now the cops were coming. He gave a nonchalant shrug. 'I don't know it. You want my advice?'

'Not really. I want a fuckin' name.'

'Just walk away and forget you ever saw him.'

'Move your arse!' Sarah bellowed.

'It's more than you'll be doing, shit head.' Archer stepped back, lowered the submachine gun's muzzle, and put a single round through the guy's kneecap.

The guy was screaming blue murder as Archer sprinted towards Sarah. He recognised her car now as a dark grey Skoda. He heard a low crump behind him, followed by the shatter of glass as the Porsche went up properly. He knew the Ferrari wouldn't be far behind it.

Sarah was already rolling as he fell in the passenger's door. They had just got to the first corner when a police car flew round it, bells and whistles going, the two cops inside apparently not even seeing them as they went past.

'Keep going,' Archer urged her as she checked the rear view mirror.

'Well I'm not bloody stopping!'

There was a loud bang somewhere behind them, followed by another a second later.

'There goes about a million bucks worth of cars,' Archer observed.

# 16

They continued down the hill, and were only a hundred metres from the main road when another police car approached. This one slowed and the two guys in it were eyeballing them, the passenger saying something into the radio.

The driver started to crank the wheel around to cut them off.

Before Archer had a chance to speak, Sarah gunned it, bolting forward as if to try and get past the police car. The cop accelerated to cut her off and she swerved to the right at the last second, cutting around behind him and shearing off the wing mirror on Archer's side as she did so. There was a screech of metal and the car shuddered then they were past it and Sarah was slamming on the brakes.

She whacked it into reverse and smashed backwards into the driver's door of the cop car, threw it into first again and laid rubber as she floored it.

Archer threw a surprised look at her as she changed up, wringing the engine out. She looked back at him with the hint of a smile.

'We're not here to fuck ducks, darlin'.'

They hit the main road and cut right, heading in towards the city. They could hear sirens approaching and Sarah threw the car into a tyre-squealing turn down a side street. Flashing lights crossed behind them, and up to the right they could see the flicker of flames from two very expensive burning wrecks.

Archer finally got his seatbelt on and she shot him an amused look. Despite the chaos all around them, or maybe because of it, she seemed to be enjoying herself.

'Worried about my driving, love?'

'Did you have to pick a Skoda? I don't want my life to end in a friggin' Skoda.'

'Terribly sorry.' She down changed violently and took a left at speed, the tyres protesting loudly. 'There wasn't too much choice today.'

'I was just driving a Ferrari,' he griped. 'A goddamn Ferrari.'

'And look what you did to that.'

He grinned. 'Fair point.'

She slowed as they entered the city proper, and took an audible breath. He saw her eyes flick up to the rear view mirror at the same time as he saw blue flashing lights bouncing off the buildings around them.

'Shit!'

Sarah gunned it, throwing a hard right and flooring it, the first left, then left again. The streets were narrow and lined tightly with buildings, the howl of the engine echoing in the narrow avenues. Archer could hear the roar of the cop car behind them, siren screaming and blue lights flashing. He didn't know how big the *Policija* force was in Split, but he had no doubt they would be swamped with angry cops before too long. They were an armed force and had a tough reputation.

'Ram them and get us the fuck out of here,' he told Sarah, as she hurtled right into a side street.

She responded without question, slamming on the brakes and whacking it into reverse. The blue and white police car screeched round the corner and she smashed into the front of it, gassing it and riding up on onto the bonnet of the other car.

A second later, with the tearing of metal, the Skoda bounced back down and rocketed forward again. The police car was spewing steam from its caved-in front end as they disappeared down the side street.

'In there!'

Sarah skidded into a car park behind a shop and they leaped out, running like hell down an alleyway that led to the next street over. He remembered to grab his day pack and deliberately left the Uzi behind, knowing that running round with a gun was an open invitation to get mowed by the cops.

They could hear sirens all around now, but with the sounds bouncing off all the buildings it was impossible to tell where they were coming from.

'Up there!' Archer sprinted across the road and threw himself at a concrete wall, getting a foothold half way up and grabbing the top with both hands. He hauled himself up, reaching down to grab Sarah's hand and help her up. She was lighter than he'd expected but obviously not used to climbing walls, and no sooner was she up than she overbalanced and tumbled over the other side.

A string of expletives he'd usually associate with sailors spewed forth as she disentangled herself from the bicycle she'd landed on. He dropped down beside her, scanning the courtyard they found themselves in. It appeared to be the back of a business premises, with rubbish bins and boxes of crap strewn about.

Archer led her down a narrow access way along the side of the building and found himself at a cobbled pedestrian area. A bunch of eateries attracted foot traffic, and a pub a few doors down had punters milling around outside.

He ducked back into the shadows and dug the last water bottle out of his bag, using it and his sweat to wash as much of the dirt and crap off his face and hands as he could. He dried himself on his sleeve and re-slung the day pack.

'Let's go.'

He took her hand and led the way out to the cobbles, turning right and acting as if he knew what he was doing.

'Where are we going?' Sarah asked, gripping his hand. 'You do have a plan, don't you?'

Archer grinned as if she had just cracked a funny. 'Hell no. I thought we'd just suck it and see.'

She cocked an eyebrow at him. 'Could you not think of a less vulgar term for getting us out of the shit?'

He grinned again. 'You know, I've always thought that when you're running close to the edge, the normal rules go out the window. It's a dog-eat-dog world and instinct takes over.'

'So we're all just animals then, is that what you're saying?'

'Basically, yeah.' They reached a cobbled plaza with little cafés dotted around each side and people sitting out at tables, dining and laughing. 'We put on our finery and act like we're civilised, but when the pretence of civility is stripped away, we're just cave men and women, gnawing on bones and beating each other with clubs.'

Sarah looked like she didn't know whether he was serious or not. Her hand felt warm in his and he noticed she hadn't made any attempt to let go. He didn't mind.

A police car blasted past somewhere nearby, the blue lights flickering across the plaza as it went by, and he felt Sarah's grip tighten.

'Just keep walking,' he said calmly. 'Nobody knows it's us and we're just another tourist couple out for a walk and a bite to eat, okay?'

'Of course. Just don't beat me with a club and we'll all be happy.'

They reached the other side of the plaza and took a walkway through to another street. This was a narrow side street lined with parked cars. The tall buildings on either side had plenty of windows and little balconies, presumably apartments or hotels. They paused at the footpath and Archer was about to speak when he heard a call from behind them.

He turned and saw a pair of policemen approaching down the walkway, their eyes locked on the two civilians. One had his radio out but wasn't using it just yet. The other was gesturing at them and saying something in what Archer presumed was Croatian.

'Stay cool,' Sarah murmured.

The cops were nearly with them now and Archer gave them a smile. The older guy was heavyset, maybe in his forties. The younger guy was more athletic looking and probably mid-twenties. Both looked confident.

'*Bonjour*,' he said. They had to blag their way out of this somehow, and it was always good to blame the French.

The leader of the two hesitated before waving his hand at them and saying something else that Archer didn't understand.

'*Passport*,' Sarah said in her best French accent.

'Ahh...' Archer touched his pockets, giving it the proper Aussie haka before "remembering". '*Le 'otel.*' He gestured vaguely down the street and shrugged apologetically.

The two cops glanced at each other and he could sense they didn't believe him. The leader stepped forward as the second stepped away, starting to lift his radio. This was no good. If they got arrested they were fucked.

As the leader opened his mouth to speak again, Archer exploded into action. He hit the leader with a brutal short jab to the nose. Blood sprayed out and the guy grabbed at his face. As he stumbled back the younger guy reacted, going for his holstered sidearm.

Archer was on him before he cleared it, seizing the gun hand with his left and delivering a throat punch with his right. The young cop gasped and tried to grab his throat to relieve the sudden, crippling pain. Archer drove a knee into his crotch, yanked the sidearm away and swept the guy's legs to dump him on the ground. He turned back to the leader, who was struggling to see through his tears, his face running red.

Sarah followed Archer's lead, sweeping the guy's right leg and dropping him to a knee. He tried to grab at her but missed, and she smashed her foot into his crotch. He gasped in agony and fell flat on his back, one hand at his shattered nose, the other cupping his squashed fruit.

Archer stripped him of his radio and tossed it aside, did the same to the younger guy and skittered both cops' side arms across the cobbles. He glanced around, seeing a few people gathered at the plaza end of the walkway, watching. Somebody already had their phone out and was shouting into it.

'Come on.' He grabbed Sarah's hand again and they bolted out to the street, going right. He yanked off his jacket as he ran and shoved it into the bag. Sarah did the same, cramming hers in on top and zipping it again. They crossed over, hearing sirens echoing about the city centre, and headed down another side street.

They kept running for a couple of minutes, not speaking, just focussed on getting the hell out of there while they could. Eventually Archer pulled up into an alleyway, dragging Sarah into the shadows and checking their tail. They were clear for now, but they could hear engines and sirens still going, seemingly a few blocks away. At least the cops hadn't got a chopper up. That would've been problematic, to say the least.

Both of them were sweating and heaving with the exertion, and Archer guessed it was probably the hardest running Sarah had done for a while, maybe ever. He stayed up straight and sucked down air, feeling the lactic acid burn in his legs. Sarah was bent over and breathless. He took a minute to get himself under control before putting a hand on her shoulder and guiding her upright. Bent over like that she was never going to fill her lungs.

'Stay here,' he said. 'I'll be back within five minutes. If I'm not, you're on your own. Right?'

She nodded, her chest heaving. Sweat was running freely down her face and neck and she felt like she'd been dragged through a bush. She watched him disappear back up the side street, hands in his pockets and walking with relaxed purpose.

She sucked in deep breaths, gradually getting herself under control, glad for the regular gym sessions since the split. At the time it had given her something to focus on other than her misery, and not only had she lost weight and toned up, but she'd also fallen into a short-term fling with one of the gym instructors. Six-two and buff as buff could be, with the stamina of a professional athlete. A few tats and far too much hair product, but nobody was perfect.

Not that it had done much for her aside from the initial self-esteem boost of shagging a bloke fifteen years younger than her –

turned out the bastard was notorious for nailing "older" birds at the gym. *Older*. The little fucker.

He'd got his comeuppance shortly afterwards, however, when a fast-acting liquid laxative had somehow found its way into his water bottle. He'd shit his pants on the gym floor in front of a bunch of members, who had found it hilarious. Sarah had changed gyms by that time and never looked back, except to chuckle.

At least now she could say that the hours of training had literally saved her life – well, so far, at least. She wondered what Archer was up to. Here she was, almost ready to lose her lunch, and he seemed to have barely broken a sweat. The man was a friggin' machine.

A new sound reached her ears and she edged to the mouth of the alleyway to check.

A motorbike was purring down the road, nice and easy. The rider was helmeted but she recognised him anyway. He eased to a stop at the kerb and gave her a thumbs up. The bike was a red and white Suzuki road machine of some sort. She hurried over, slinging the day pack onto her back. He handed her a spare helmet and she climbed aboard, snuggling up behind him and encircling her arms round his waist.

He gave the bike a rev and they moved off.

## 17

Zadar was another coastal city, 160k north of Split.

The Suzuki ate up the miles on the E65 and they made it there in an hour and a half. As soon as they arrived they ditched the bike in a side street and made their way on foot into the central city area, moving fast and rubbing their exposed skin to get some feeling back after the cold ride. Sarah had been shielded behind Archer, but he was freezing.

A quick stop at a convenience store gave them large coffees, fresh bottles of water and snacks, a pair of spectacles and a new sweater for Archer, and a plain hoody and cap for Sarah.

They paused long enough to rehydrate and neck some food. The hot coffee in his belly instantly made Archer feel better, and the movement and calories got him focussed again.

Sensing he needed a break, Sarah took point and soon found a late night internet café. She left Archer outside on a park bench to watch her back while she went inside and booked a terminal for half an hour.

In less than ten minutes she was back and they quickly put distance between themselves and the café. Archer had researched a travel book he'd grabbed from the convenience store, and navigated their way towards a hostel. Turning up at a hotel without luggage would be too suss right now, but hostels catered to a different clientele.

'I got through to the duty desk,' Sarah said in low tones as they hustled along, 'got some bell-end I've never heard of. Took a couple of goes to get the message through to him that we needed help.'

She was referring to the emergency contact she'd had to make. Archer hadn't asked, but he guessed it was through an internet chat room or one of the untraceable chat services. There was always somebody at the other end, back in a nice warm office in HQ with the telly on and their feet up, praying for the end of their shift, hoping they wouldn't get such a call from an officer in the field.

'ETA?'

'Gotta wait for a call.' They turned into a side street and could see the sign for the hostel further down. There was still a light on above the door. 'Has to be within twenty-four hours, but I'm picking it'll be sooner, given the circumstances.'

Archer nodded, hoping it would be soon enough. He didn't fancy a stint in a Croatian jail.

Sarah took the lead again at the hostel, paying cash to a long-haired desk clerk who was either stoned or mentally retarded. Either way, he barely gave them a glance as he passed over a key, a set of linen and a pair of towels. They paid extra for some basic toiletries and let him return to the Twilight Zone.

The room was on the second floor overlooking a neighbouring rooftop. It was small and had a threadbare curtain and worn carpet tiles, but it seemed clean enough and the door locked behind them.

The bathroom was equally tiny and had a cracked basin.

'Home, sweet home,' Sarah murmured. She tossed her head towards the bathroom. 'Get yourself cleaned up if you like. I'll get the bed sorted.' She saw him pause and grinned. 'Don't worry, tiger, I'll trust you to be a gentleman.'

'Mighty generous of you, cheers.'

The shower was old and tired but the water was hot enough to get a good lather going and he scrubbed hard, getting the dirt and sweat and unidentifiable crap off his skin. He washed his hair as well and felt a million times better by the time he stepped out.

As he scraped his skin on the rough towel, his tired mind drifted to his companion. She had impressed him with her cool head under stress, and he knew she had his back, which was always comforting to know.

He wondered again about her relationship with his former colleague, Moore. There was no doubt they'd been tight. She didn't seem to be the type to stray from her marriage, but who really knew? It was obviously a different ball game now that she was separated, but he sensed a feeling of loss about her, the sort of deep sadness within that only time could heal.

He dried his hair vigorously. He was no counsellor and he was certainly no expert on marriage – it was something he had done well to avoid so far. All he cared about right now was getting the job done. Anything else could wait; he had neither the time nor the inclination for any kind of romantic entanglement. Mind you, she was out there in that double bed, and she had hardly been shy about flirting with him so far...

Archer pulled his briefs and pants back on and hung the towel over the door handle as he left the bathroom. Sarah was flicking through the tourist guide when he emerged, and she gave him a smile before disappearing into the bathroom.

He took a minute to check their security, making sure the door was locked and wedging a folded wad of newspaper under it as a doorstop. He shifted the only chair in the room over against the door before stripping off his pants and arranging his gear by the side of the bed. None of the precautions would slow a determined intruder very much at all, but something was better than nothing.

The last precaution was checking the pistol he'd taken. It was a standard CZ75, a Czech-made 9mm semi auto with a fifteen round magazine. He had no spare ammo for it but at least the mag was full. He emptied it, checked each round and the weapon for damage, refilled the magazine and set it aside.

He stripped the weapon down, checked the inner working parts and reassembled it. He slid the mag into place, racked a round into the chamber, and set the safety. The CZ75 was one of numerous weapons he'd become intimately familiar with during his SAS service, and the whole process took less than two minutes.

Satisfied now, he tucked the pistol under his pillow and slipped into bed. His body ached and was begging him for sleep, and in seconds he was out for the count.

The next thing he became aware of was a hand sliding across his chest and a warm naked body tucking in behind him. He tried to ignore it for a long moment, undecided whether this was a good idea or not, but the hand slid down to his belly and nature took over.

Sarah smelled fresh and clean and felt warm as he rolled onto his back and she slid into his arms, pulling his mouth down onto hers, her tongue inquisitively seeking a playmate.

*Fuck it*, he decided, *I could die tomorrow.*

THE BUZZ of the phone cut the silence in the room and Archer was awake immediately, one hand sliding the CZ out from under the pillow while the other threw the covers back.

It took a moment to realise they weren't being raided and he sat back down, rubbing a hand over his face and stifling a yawn. Sarah was sitting up beside him, holding the covers up over her breasts while she listened intently to whoever was calling.

'Got it,' she said, and disconnected. Her face was illuminated by the glow from the screen as she turned to him. 'We've got a pick-up at the docks in one hour. They'll call five minutes beforehand and we need to be there or they'll go without us.'

'Fair enough.' He nodded in the darkness. 'What's the time now?'

'Just on six.'

He groaned and lay back down, tucking the pistol under the pillow again. It felt like he'd barely slept at all, although he couldn't deny it had been a great way to get to sleep. Sarah put the phone down and leaned in for a kiss.

'Anyway,' she said brightly, 'good morning.'

When the phone rang again exactly fifty-five minutes later, they were ready and waiting. They had washed, dressed, eaten, found the location and done a walk-by well before the pick-up was due.

If the stolen Suzuki had been found, it hadn't resulted in a huge descent of angry cops on the town. As far as they could tell, nobody even knew they were there. The port was alive even at this time of the morning, being a ferry terminal and commercial dock. People were out walking, some fishing, others snapping photos as the sun spread across the Adriatic Sea.

It was their first chance for a decent look at the town on the short walk from the hostel, and Archer was taken by the beauty of the place. Whitewashed walls, orange and red roofs, old churches and regal-looking buildings everywhere. It was the sort of place you'd come for a weekend with a girlfriend, taking in the sights and dining out, walking for hours down the marble streets of the old town, drinking coffee at the little cafés that were on every corner.

He glanced at Sarah beside him. Neither of them had mentioned the night before and had slipped instead into a functional groove of doing what they needed to do to get the hell out of there.

Their instructions had been to be ready near an old man sitting on a red bucket, fishing from the seawall. He was easy to find and they stood off, admiring their surroundings, watching the old boy as he sat patiently with one hand on his rod and the other holding a hand-rolled cigarette to his mouth. He wore a long tatty coat and a bright yellow knitted hat, and had a grizzly grey beard.

'He the contact or just a landmark?' Archer wondered aloud.

The phone buzzed and Sarah put it to her ear. She listened for a moment before disconnecting. She looked at Archer as she put the phone away.

'Just a landmark,' she replied. 'Let's go.'

She led the way, walking purposefully past the old fisherman towards the private docks a hundred yards away. The piers there were lined with sporty, expensive-looking cabin cruisers. They went through a wire mesh gate and descended a ramp to the docks.

A man appeared at the end of the next pier over and gave them a toss of the head before turning away again. They followed him along the pier to a sharp-looking white and blue cruiser that had to be forty foot long. The pilot seat or whatever it was called – Archer had never spent much time on boats – was upstairs and the cabin windows were tinted.

The man waited on the pier beside it, and gestured for them to go aboard. They stepped through the pedestrian gate onto the rear deck and found themselves face to face with another man, standing in the open sliding doors of the cabin.

Like the first man he was somewhere in his early thirties, stockily built and fit looking.

'Come in.' Like the contact from yesterday, his accent was pure Glaswegian. Archer wondered idly if they were related. 'Hands on the table.'

They did as they were told and he gave them each a thorough pat down, relieving Archer of the CZ75.

'Ye'll not be needin' that, pal.' He handed it off to his companion, who stood guard at the door.

Once he was satisfied they were clean they were allowed to stand and turn around. He took Sarah's phone and handed that to his mate too.

'Right,' he said, 'I'm Ricky, he's Steve. We're here to take ye to safety, which means a boat ride over t' Italy. There you'll be picked up by ano'er team, Miss.' He turned his gaze to Archer. 'An' ye'll be helped on yer way, right?'

'Whatever you say, skipper.' Archer had a pretty fair idea these guys were members of the Increment, a special-ops team attached to MI6. It was a similar unit to The Division, tasked with deniable and highly dangerous operations that required specialist skills. Extracting operatives from foreign states was bread and butter for them. 'You're in charge of the shaky boat.'

"Shaky Boats" was a term used by the SAS for their Special Boat Service colleagues. The rivalry between the two units was fierce, with each vying for bragging rights as the best UKSF outfit. Archer had worked with both and knew the strengths of each unit. The respect he had for the SBS didn't prevent him having a dig, however – it would've been rude not to.

Ricky glanced at Steve, a wry smile crossing his lips. 'Looks like we've got one o' them tossers aboard, pal,' he said. 'An' a fookin' Kiwi one at that.'

'Fookin' great,' Steve agreed. He was also Scots but his accent was much softer than Ricky's. 'Better than havin' a fookin' Aussie, I guess.'

'Aye, just.' Ricky looked Archer up and down appraisingly. 'Even if he is a fookin' Rupert.'

Archer grinned, the ice well and truly broken. The Brit military was full of Scotsmen and they had always had a healthy disrespect for officers.

'Get yersel's below decks,' Ricky told them, 'there's food and drink down below, a bed if ye wanna wee lie doon. Stay there 'til we call yer, right?'

They did as they were told and a few minutes later they were easing away from the docks, the rumble of the engine a comfortable throb in the background as they looked across the harbour towards Ugljan Island.

Ricky reappeared once they were underway, letting them know they wouldn't dock in Italy until after dark and pointing out where the emergency equipment was.

'And if there's any trouble,' he added, 'keep yer fookin' heads doon and let us deal wi' it, right?'

With that he closed the cabin door and they heard his feet ascend the stairs to the main saloon.

Sarah perched herself on the side of the bed and crossed her legs. 'So,' she smiled impishly, 'how should we pass the time then?'

Archer gave her a questioning look. 'Really? Have you unleashed the beast?'

'Huh.' She stood and pulled her top over her head. She wore a plain black bra underneath, supportive enough to give a tantalising swell at her cleavage. 'The beast has been dormant for some time.'

She undid her jeans and started to skin them off her legs. 'Now it's time to get crazy.'

Fair enough, he decided. She was a big girl, and there were no misunderstandings about what this was.

Some time later he lay on his back, Sarah nestled in beside him and sleeping heavily. He was as relaxed as he could be, with the rolling of the waves, the comfortable double bed and the afterglow of energetic love-making, but still his mind would not let him drift off.

It frustrated him that, even after all that had happened in the last few days, he still felt like he was chasing a ghost. The Boss, the main guy, the mastermind, whatever you chose to call him, he had no name. The bastard was out there somewhere, weaving his evil webs, laughing at the hopeless fools who tried to catch him. Laughing at him personally, Archer himself, mocking him.

*Think you can catch me, fool? Think again.*

It felt like he was chasing ghosts in the dark with his ankles shackled, working hard and knowing he was close, but just unable to seal the deal.

He tried to push the thought from his mind and focus on what was right in front of him. He dropped his hand to Sarah's back and gently stroked it. She slowly stirred, pressing into him, and he felt her lips on his neck. His other hand moved to her breast, cupping it, his fingers finding the nipple and gently squeezing. She moaned into his neck, shifting, her own hand sliding down from his chest, lower, finding him.

Their mouths met, tenderly at first then with more passion, hungrily feeding off each other as Archer rolled her onto her back and their bodies began to move together.

Archer lost himself in the moment, casting aside all thoughts of his mystery target as he concentrated all his energy on the woman in his arms.

## 18

It was dusk when they got the stand-by.

Archer stared out the windows of the saloon, watching the dark, rocky coastline getting closer. It was a rugged section of coast with a small bay where waves broke and spilled up a narrow beach. A rickety-looking wharf extended into the water and he could see two men walking along it towards them.

The engines eased back to a gentle throb and Ricky expertly guided the craft alongside the wharf. He held it there, bobbing on the swell, while Archer climbed up to the wharf. He reached back and helped Sarah up.

Ricky and Steve stayed on deck, silent in the darkness. Archer wondered idly if they were aware of how their passengers had spent the afternoon. Not that it mattered.

Before they had a chance to say thanks, the cruiser was moving off again, heading back towards open water.

He turned as the two men reached them, shivering slightly in the cool evening sea breeze. The two blokes were dressed in standard jeans, dark bomber jackets and desert boots. Both were in their thirties and wiry. They had Special Forces written all over them, and Archer assumed they were more guys from the Increment.

'Welcome to Italy,' one of them said. 'Ma'am, you're coming with us.' He had a south London accent and a day's stubble. 'If you'd like to follow us.'

The two men took the point and tail and led them from the wharf across a short section of sand, up a rough inland path through some undergrowth until they reached an unlit parking area beside a road. Two sedans were parked at opposite sides of the parking area; a blue Audi and a green Citroen.

'Right mate,' the spokesman said, handing a set of keys to Archer and tossing his head towards the Audi. 'That's yours. It's a clean and legal rental, so try not to bang it up, yeah?'

Archer nodded, seeing the other guy bleep the locks on the Citroen and open the rear door for Sarah. She hesitated, looking at him.

'Cheers mate,' he said. 'Ah...where exactly are we?'

The guy grinned in the darkness. 'Just south of Ancona. You've got a sat nav and all the shit in your car. I'm sure you'll be able to navigate your way from here to wherever you're going. Just stay the fuck away from us and give us a head start, and we'll all be happy campers, yeah?'

'Fair enough.' Archer nodded. He started to move towards the Citroen to say goodbye to Sarah, but the guy blocked his way.

'Your car's over there,' he said firmly. 'Time to get going, yeah?'

Archer took the hint and nodded. Sarah had the rear door open but the interior light was off. Even though he couldn't see her face, he knew she was staring at him.

'Travel safe,' he called out, before turning abruptly and walking away. It wasn't quite the farewell he had imagined and he knew it would leave a sour taste with her, but it would have to do. She was a big girl, and he had shit to do.

The Citroen disappeared and he fired up the Audi. It was an A3, a couple of years or so old. It didn't have all the bollocks of the top range but it did have a large bubble wrap envelope on the front passenger's seat.

Inside was a standard "legend" pack. A three-year-old NZ passport in the name of Craig Ascot, with his date of birth and photo. With it were a Visa and driver license in the same name, and a wad of folded euros held together with a rubber band.

A new iPhone, fully charged with an accompanying charger, was the last item out. The documents all went into his pockets and the phone was plugged in to keep it juiced.

That done, he checked the sat nav system and got moving.

The A3 was comfortable and had enough grunt, and the gas tank showed full. The iPhone got through to the duty officer and after a short wait he had Ingoe on the line. The Ops Officer was straight to the point.

'All good?'

'Yep, on the road now.' There was no need for details; Ingoe knew where he was, or close enough to it.

'Alone?'

'Yep.'

'Head back to where you last flew from,' Ingoe instructed him. 'Call me back when you get to that area and I'll give you further.'

'Got that.'

'Drive safe.' There was a pause and he could almost hear Ingoe smiling. 'Don't blow any more shit up.'

Ingoe cut the line and Archer tucked the phone back into his pocket. He thumbed Berlin into the sat nav. A few seconds later it brought up the route. 1382 kilometres from his current location. Slightly over fourteen hours driving.

Archer turned the radio on and started scanning for a decent station.

IT WAS A CLASSIC MILITARY HURRY-UP-AND-WAIT.

After the better part of fifteen hours on the road, stopping only briefly to refuel, eat and stretch his legs, Archer reached Berlin. Italy, Lichtenstein, and Bavaria had all passed in a blur as he pushed himself to get to the German capital as fast as possible.

The call to Ingoe from the outskirts of the city had given him the address of a hotel and the instruction to get there and wait for further.

The hotel turned out to be a Holiday Inn on the west side of the city. The young lady at the Reception desk greeted him with a smile and tapped away at her computer when he checked in.

'Thank you, Mr Ascot,' she said, 'I am pleased to say you have received a complimentary upgrade to one of our suites.'

'Well that's lovely, thank you very much.' He gave her his best winning smile. 'I don't suppose that comes with a bottle of bubbles, by any chance?'

She smiled graciously. 'Unfortunately no, Mr Ascot. But you are welcome to dine with us and perhaps have your bubbles later in the evening if you wish. I see your luggage has arrived ahead of you, and we have a parking space reserved in the garage for your car.'

Archer nodded and smiled. Ingoe had outdone himself. He swapped her the car keys for the room key and made his way upstairs to the suite. It was a standard Holiday Inn with standard Holiday Inn décor and furnishings. It could have been a Holiday Inn in any city round the world, but Archer couldn't have cared less.

After checking his room and luggage he flopped onto the bed and closed his eyes. Right now, sleep was calling and he gladly answered it.

# 19

Woken by his rumbling stomach, Archer had hit the weights in the hotel gym for half an hour, rinsed off, and moved on to the pool. He cranked out lengths for twenty minutes, maintaining a steady, even pace. That done, he took a long shower, got dressed in a casual shirt and jeans, and headed downstairs.

Rather than using the hotel facilities he found a little eatery round the corner and parked himself in the corner near the fire exit. A stein of Pilsner and the biggest schnitzel he'd ever seen satisfied his gut, and in the absence of any tasks, he decided to settle in for the evening. A giant wedge of calorie-laden Bavarian chocolate cake topped with rum cream was washed down with a frothy coffee strong enough to strip paint.

He took his time, savouring the last vestiges of the meal and watching his fellow diners – mostly couples or small groups, the odd person on their own.

One of these he noticed at a table in the far corner from him, enjoying a large bowl of soup and a glass of white. She had a phone on the table beside her and a newspaper folded neatly which she was reading between spoonfuls. The light of a street lamp outside cast a yellow glow in the window and her long blonde hair seemed almost luminescent, giving her an ethereal quality. Despite the back-lighting he could tell instinctively that she was very attractive. She wore a dark top of some sort and jeans, and had a jacket slung over the back of her chair.

As he watched her over the rim of his cup, he saw her slip a surreptitious look his way, as if she had felt his eyes on her.

He lowered the cup and smiled. She ignored him and turned back to her dinner.

*Bugger it*, he decided. He had nothing better to do.

He got up, tucked some notes under his empty plate and carried his coffee over to her table. He half pulled the chair out and she looked up. She looked mildly irritated but not surprised.

'Do you mind if I sit?' he asked, giving her his best attempt at charming.

She shrugged noncommittally. He took it as a yes and sat. She made a point of taking another spoonful of soup. It looked like ham and pea, thick and hearty and accompanied by a chunk of crusty bread.

He took a moment to assess her while she ate.

She was average height with an athletic build. Her blonde hair was shoulder length and styled by someone who probably charged more than Archer earned in a week. She had that timeless European style that you never found anywhere else. She could have been anywhere in her thirties, maybe older if she had good genes.

She swallowed and sat back, looking at him as she wiped her mouth carefully on a napkin. Her eyes were a very clear ice blue and there was an intelligence behind them. He knew she was assessing him as much as he was her.

'Can I help you?' she asked. Her English was perfect, with a strong German accent.

'I was just wondering if you'd like some company, that's all,' he replied easily, lifting his coffee cup. It was cold and nearly gone, but it didn't matter. She was more confident than he'd predicted and he found himself suddenly wondering whether it had been such a good idea. Perhaps now was not the best time to be hitting on a strange woman in a café.

'I am fine, thank you.' She lifted her spoon pointedly. 'I have my dinner to eat and my newspaper to read.'

'Fair enough.' He nodded and forced a smile, feeling his resolve slipping away. This had definitely been a bad idea. He was striking out like a fourteen-year-old at his first school dance. He peered at her soup. 'Looks good.'

'It would be,' she said, her tone cool, 'if I was able to eat it while it is still hot.'

'Point taken.' He drained his cup and pushed the chair back. 'I'm sorry for disturbing you.'

She waited until he was half standing before she spoke again. 'You have an interesting accent. Are you from New Zealand?'

Archer paused, unsure now whether she was opening the door or not. 'Good spotting,' he said, feeling his cheeks burn immediately. *Good spotting – what an idiot*. 'Have you been there?'

'No.' The tiniest hint of a smile played at her lips. Her blue eyes seemed to be laughing at him. 'I don't really like hobbits.'

Archer opened his mouth to speak, felt his cheeks getting hotter still, and closed it again. Best to cut and run, he figured. He was going to need a beer to put these flames out.

'Have a good evening,' he managed, before turning and heading for the door. His humiliation was overwhelming and he couldn't wait any longer to get the hell out of there.

The night air was cool and refreshing when he emerged onto the street.

He took a slow breath and tried to regather himself.

'Fuck you, Peter Jackson,' he muttered. It was time to call it a night.

# 20

Archer could see the screen of his phone flashing as he padded across the concrete floor towards it, fresh from the pool and dripping water with every movement. He snatched it up off the towel.

'Yes?'

'Where the hell've you been?' Ingoe sounded grumpy. 'I've been trying to get you for the last half hour.'

'Sitting round with my finger up my date,' Archer snapped back. 'There's fuck all else to do at sparrow fart.'

That wasn't entirely true, but he was bored and irritable and not in the mood for a serve. He'd risen at dawn, hit the floor for some stretching and exercises, and had been doing lengths for the better part of 45 minutes. His arms and shoulders were humming and he needed to rehydrate.

'Well untangle your panties, you've got somewhere to be.'

Archer wiped his face on the towel as he listened intently.

'Get moving to Prague, it's about four hours driving from Berlin. There's a cobbler there you need to see. We believe our friend is likely to be in contact.'

Archer knew that a cobbler in their parlance had nothing to do with shoemaking, but rather was a forger, usually for identification and travel documents.

'How likely is likely?'

'That crew you met, or what's left of them, haven't surfaced anywhere yet, but this particular cobbler has supplied shoes to the likes of them before.'

'But we don't even know who these clowns are; how can we be so sure?' He could almost hear Ingoe's teeth grind down the line. 'What I mean is, if I'm going to rock in there and brace some joker, I need to be on fairly solid ground.'

There was a tense silence for a moment.

'It is my arse in the sling, after all,' he added, feeling somewhat defensive now. A Czech prison held no more appeal to him than a Croatian one.

'Just chill the fuck out, Arch,' Ingoe said tersely. 'Some of us are actually quite competent as well, okay? There is plenty of intel about this coozer in Prague supplying documents to terrorists and criminals. We know that an outfit like this will use forged documents. Making sense so far?'

'Yep.' Archer's tone was just as terse.

'After the bunfight in Croatia, there was an incident just outside Bratislava, where some traffic cops tried to stop a stolen vehicle and ended up getting shot – one dead, one critical. The car had been stolen just hours beforehand in Zagreb. The bad guys got away, and a few hours after that a different car was hired in Vienna. It's been sighted heading through the Czech border.'

Archer mentally traced the route. Croatia through Hungary to Slovakia, over to Austria and north to the Czech Republic.

'The car was hired using documents we have confirmed as forged. The stolen car was found dumped in a public car park about a klick or so from the rental agency.'

'Were the docs done by this guy in Prague?'

'Unconfirmed on that, but definitely bogus. And the hirer was an American male, so things are falling into place pretty well.'

Archer nodded to himself, feeling his earlier irritation sliding away, replaced by the buzz of anticipation. This was what it was all about.

It was a concern how things were developing – torturing and killing business associates was never a good thing, and killing a cop was an open invitation for the authorities to unleash hell. It indicated either desperation or recklessness, and nothing he had learned so far gave him any reason to believe these guys were reckless.

Or it could be something far more dangerous. If the bad guys were unravelling then it created a whole different beast to deal with.

He could scent the quarry and it was time to get on the trail.

'So where am I going, and what am I doing there?'

'I'll flick you the address. I think, considering the current situation, a direct approach may be needed.'

'Got that. Who's the target there?'

'A Russian named Vladimir Semenov. Previously worked at the Kremlin in some kind of capacity, not sure exactly what, and is now freelance. Aged about 55.'

'Ex-KGB?'

'I'd say.'

'Security?'

'Probably.'

'High risk then.'

Ingoe chuckled. 'Abso-fucking-lutely.'

Archer nodded to himself again, keeping the iPhone clamped to his ear as he dried his torso with the hotel towel. 'If he's so well known, how come he's still in business?'

'Who knows mate? You gotta remember, this is still Eastern Europe; they don't play by the same rules as us.'

'Speaking of playing, are our friends playing with us now?'

'Your recent ones are, the other ones not so much – only as much as they want to, like normal.'

'So we still don't have an ID on the main man yet?'

'Nope.' Ingoe's tone took on an edge. 'All the chatter we're getting though indicates some kind of spectacular is coming.'

'Where?'

'Don't know. We had thought it was the LA incident, but the chatter has continued since then, so it must still be coming. The same groups are still talking, the same terminology and all that, so nothing seems to have changed in the last few days. All indications are that it's imminent though; we just don't know exactly when.'

'GCSB must be working overtime,' Archer murmured, referring to the Wellington-based sig-int agency.

'They are. We're getting this from the Yanks though.' Ingoe gave a snort. 'They seem to have a line into a vein we can't tap ourselves. It's about all they're sharing at the moment.'

'And we think this main player's probably American as well?'

'That's the indication.'

'Surely we must be able to drill down a bit further than that?' Archer pressed. 'How many American bad guys are there in this scene? Can't be that many.'

'You wouldn't think so,' Ingoe agreed. 'Believe me mate, we're working on it. Our friends are getting a lot of pressure, particularly after the LA incident. It's been highlighted to them that they owe us big for that.'

'Well, good luck with that.' Archer had a lot of respect for the US agencies, but he also knew how stubborn and self-contained they could be. 'I'll be in touch.'

He disconnected and headed for his room, anticipation tingling in his veins.

PRAGUE WAS ABOUT 350 k's from Berlin, and after Archer had showered and dressed, he fuelled the car and himself and headed south. After stopping near the border to purchase the required highway tolls vignette, he arrived in the Czech capital nearly five hours later.

It was midday and the cities and towns of south-east Germany and north-west Czechia were a blur behind him. He stopped at a service centre on the outskirts of the city and topped up the blue Audi again. He took a few minutes more for a toilet stop, grabbed some refreshments for himself, added a Lonely Planet guide and a folding road map, and hit the road again.

The address Ingoe had sent him was right in the heart of Kyje, one of the higher crime areas in the north-eastern part of the city. Archer followed his sat nav for a drive by, and was directed to a street named Koberkova. It was a residential area with a mixture of houses and apartment blocks.

His target appeared to be the worst of the blocks – a plain concrete structure, five storeys high with satellite dishes and aerials dotting it like zits on a teenager.

The car park out the front was partially full, and he noticed a small group of youths sidling around aimlessly. He ignored them as they watched him cruise past. He hooked a left and made his way back towards the central city.

He'd called ahead and made a reservation, and now navigated his way to the Hilton Prague. They had another hotel in the Old Town but he had taken the more modern one simply because the advertised price was cheaper. Ingoe seemed grumpy enough at the moment without Archer blowing the budget.

The young guy at the desk was happy to book him in early, and within ten minutes of arriving Archer had dumped his bag in his room, left the car with the concierge and made his way on foot to Palladium shopping mall.

After all the time in the car it was good to stretch his legs, and it also gave him the opportunity to check his tail with a couple of basic but reliable anti-surveillance moves. Satisfied he hadn't picked up any obvious watchers, he entered the mall and wandered from store to store, ducking in and out and doubling back on himself to be sure he was clear.

He picked up a coffee to go and grabbed a cab outside, asking the driver to take him to the Saint Bartholomew church in Kyje. It was an obvious tourist destination for those foreigners doing the standard ABC – Another Bloody Church/Castle-tour, and Archer had the Lonely Planet book in his hand tagged at the appropriate page.

The cabbie dropped him right outside and accepted the cash

Archer passed over, before disappearing to find another punter. Archer took the time to enter and admire the 13th century church before ditching his empty coffee cup and striding out for his true destination.

It was a walk of several minutes and Archer used the time to familiarise himself with the area. His plan was simple, but it always paid to be prepared. Murphy was a cantankerous bastard but his laws always seemed to be accurate, and if something could go wrong, it would. Archer identified a couple of places on this side of the target address that could serve as somewhere to hide if things went pear-shaped and he ended up needing to leg it.

He walked down the street backing onto the target address, getting eyes on it from a different angle and noting the lack of a rear entrance. This was going to be a frontal approach out of necessity, which brought with it its own challenges. One way out meant only one way in. One way meant that if the entry was blocked, whoever was inside was trapped like a rat. But one way in was also always easier to defend, and created a death funnel for the attacker.

Archer hooked right and came into the rear of the apartment block, via a rubbish-strewn walkway with graffiti on both walls. He counted the apartments as he walked, noting that there were eight on each floor. Apartment 31, the target address, would be on the fourth floor.

The building was a bland brown and grey block of concrete, standard fare for the old Communist bloc. Street appeal hadn't been high on the agenda back then, and it looked like the developers had overlooked this little gem so far.

As he reached the mouth of the walkway he spotted the group of youths he'd seen earlier, still loitering in the car park. They were visible in the sunlight on the other side of the basement garage, the garage itself dark and shadowy between their location and his. He continued on, hands in his pockets and head down, just another guy on his way to nowhere in particular.

Entering the darkened garage, which was ground level and open on both sides, he saw it was home to a few cars, a row of dumpsters against one wall, and another small group of youngsters. These ones were scattered about in ones and twos, but the way they all watched him told him they were together. At least a couple of joints were on the go between them and the sickly-sweet smoke hung in the air.

One of the youths, a skinny girl who was maybe 15, pushed herself off a concrete pillar and approached him, saying something in Czech.

Archer shook his head and kept on going, only glancing at her when she repeated her question. She had a denim skirt up around her arse and the shimmery top under a stained khaki jacket plunged so low at the front that her barely-there tits were practically falling out.

He picked her for a crack whore, and felt a kick inside at the sight of her, peddling her body to some stranger in a shitty car park under a shitty apartment block.

He shook his head again and walked on.

She called out something at his back, no doubt questioning his sexuality, and he heard a couple of others titter in the background. The scrape of a foot on dirty concrete brought his head round sharply to the right.

An older youth was standing in the shadows, watching him carefully as he went by. He was maybe 20, give or take, solidly built with long greasy brown hair. He wore a black jacket that could have been leather but was probably vinyl, and even in the shadows Archer spotted the bulge of a weapon in his waistband.

The pimp maybe, but a heavy regardless. He made a mental note to keep an eye out for the guy.

The guy watched him pass by, saying nothing, and a few moments later Archer emerged into the sunlight. He took a hard right to another path along the front of the building, staying away from the other group of youths.

He reached an enclosed concrete stairwell and started up. As expected, the stairwell stank of piss and cigarette smoke. Discarded butts, wrappers and pieces of tinfoil dotted the ground. Archer continued climbing, stepping aside at the second floor to let a world-weary mother battle her way down with two snot-nosed young kids in tow.

Reaching the fourth floor, he paused to take a breath and regather himself before the final approach. There was no going back once he knocked on that door, and he would just have to deal with things as they unfolded. He had no gun, no back up and a good chance of coming off second best if things went pear-shaped.

On the plus side though, he had speed, aggression and surprise.

# 21

He took the walkway to his left, checking off the door numbers as he went. Not every door was numbered but there were enough to keep track. He reached 31, stopped, and rapped on the door. It was a solid unit, definitely lined internally with something better than plywood. Probably a steel sheet through the core. The windows to the left of the door were closed, barred and had the curtains pulled.

A fish-eye camera clung to the wall above the door and he stepped back, giving it a full facial. Whoever was monitoring it would want to see who he was, and there was no chance of getting inside without playing the game.

A long moment later the door opened fractionally and he could just detect a person in the darkened interior.

'Yes?' The voice was deep and guttural, with some kind of European accent. Archer's Russian was a bit rusty, but it sounded close enough.

'I need some help,' Archer said calmly. 'A friend sent me.'

'I don't know you.'

'And I don't know you, but this is business.' He glanced in both directions. 'I'd rather not stand round here with my balls dangling in the wind, if it's all the same to you.'

'Fuck your balls and fuck you, I don't know you. Go do your business somewhere else, Mr Balls.'

The door started to close. Archer opened his jacket and heard the snick of a pistol hammer being drawn back.

'Relax,' he said, showing the wad of cash protruding from his shirt pocket. 'It's only money. Like I said, I need help and I've got the cash to pay for it. I've been referred here to get the best product. Yeah?'

There was a long pause and he wondered if he'd played this all wrong, but in the end the lure of cash sealed the deal. The door opened and he could see a man half behind it, standing in the shadows. The pistol in his hand was pointing at Archer's gut. The man was tall and solid and dressed in a black Gore-Tex jacket. His hair and beard were both grey and clipped short.

'Hurry up,' he growled. 'Come inside, Mr Balls.'

Archer stepped over the threshold and took another step forward into a dark entranceway. The door shut behind him, reducing the room to almost complete darkness, and he was shoved hard face first against a wall. A hand braced him between the shoulder blades and the barrel of the gun ground into the back of his neck.

'Now, Mr Balls, who the fuck are you? You come here say you need help, you got cash; I say bullshit. Who the fuck you think you are?' The gun ground harder and he could feel the guy's hot breath in his ear. 'You a cop? Secret agent?'

'I'm just a guy who needs help,' Archer replied, trying to sound calm. It wasn't easy with a gorilla breathing down his neck. 'I'm not a fuckin' cop.'

'You tell me now or I blow your fuckin' head off, Mr Balls.'

'I got referred to you,' Archer told him. He wondered if the guy was just going to rob him and leave him for dead. Probably happened all the time in this estate. 'I need to get out of Europe and I need some papers to do it.'

The guy's voice was so close now that Archer could feel the brush of his lips against his ear.

'I don't know what you talk about. You turn up here spouting all this shit and I think you a cop. Maybe I can just blow you away for the funs, huh?'

Archer could see this was going nowhere fast. It was time to change tack.

He turned his head as far as he could, managing to see the guy out the corner of his eye now.

'If I was a cop,' he said, 'would I do this?'

Before he was finished speaking he dropped sharply, twisting hard at the same time, getting under the gun and freeing himself from the hand on his back. He raked the side of his boot down the guy's closest shin, caught the gun hand in his own left and shoved it skyward, and slammed a hard right to the guy's exposed ribs.

He wrenched the gun hand down now, twisting, got a knee into the guy's thigh, twisting more, stamping against the inside of his other ankle, bending the guy double now. The gun came free, the guy was pushing up and back, kicking out at Archer's legs and grunting with effort, and Archer rammed the gun against his ear, swiping for the safety with his thumb and finding it already off.

The gun felt like a locally-made CZ82, probably pilfered from military supplies.

'I don't think a cop would be allowed to do that, do you?'

The guy growled something that Archer didn't understand, and he realised he wasn't Russian after all. It sounded maybe Polish.

'Stop whining like a bitch,' Archer said. 'You can get up, but stop being an arsehole. I don't have time to fuck around.'

With that he stepped back, dropped the magazine from the pistol and racked the slide to pop the round out. He couldn't see it in the darkness, but heard it bounce off the wall.

The guy was getting up when an internal door opened and the entranceway was flooded with light. Another man stood there, an older man with a pot gut, wearing a floral Hawaiian shirt over beige slacks and fluffy slippers.

'Come in,' he said in almost flawless English. 'Would you like a cup of tea?'

THE RADIATORS in the apartment were cranked up and Archer could feel sweat dribbling down his neck and back as he sat on Semenov's lumpy, floral sofa. The lack of furniture and belongings indicated that this was a business place rather than a home.

The tea was black and scalding hot, which wasn't helping matters. Semenov himself was quietly spoken and studious; he reminded Archer of his high school geography teacher. The heavy hung around the door, constantly looking away from the CCTV monitor to glower at Archer. He hadn't said a word since Archer had been invited in.

'So,' Semenov said, pausing to take a sip from his tea cup. The cup was delicate bone china. He set it down carefully on the matching saucer on his coffee table, and settled back into his armchair. 'You are here because you need help. You say you are referred to me by a friend. You need to get out of Europe and you need papers to do this. Yes?'

'Yes.' Archer put his own tea cup aside. He was gagging for a glass of cold water, but didn't want to offend his host.

'You are in a spot of bother then.' Semenov watched him carefully, not a trace of humour in his eyes.

'Yes.' Archer nodded.

'Such things are costly, Mr...?'

'Smith.' Archer didn't smile. 'Let's go with that for now.' At least it was better than Balls.

'Very good, Mr Smith.' Semenov nodded sagely. 'So you will need a passport, at the least.'

Archer nodded again. 'That should be enough.'

'A driver license?'

Archer shook his head. It was a fair attempt at an upsell, he had to give him that. 'No, I just need to get through Immigration.'

Semenov nodded again.

'I see. When do you need it by? Tomorrow, I expect?'

'As soon as I can get it.' He spread his hands deferentially to the older man. 'I'm in your hands.'

Semenov nodded again. His eyes had barely left Archer's face through the whole discussion. He had a very controlled, unhurried air about him.

'Nationality?'

Archer wasn't sure whether the man was asking for his own, or what type of passport he wanted. He went with the latter.

'Canadian or Australian,' he said. He knew that, along with NZ papers, these two were among the most sought after by Western intelligence agencies due to their wide acceptability. They were also among the easiest for him to handle with his accent.

'Canadian,' Semenov confirmed. 'Eight thousand US. Cash.'

It was above market price, but urgency brought with it a premium tag.

'No problem.'

'You will pay in full in advance.' It wasn't open for discussion.

Archer nodded and opened his jacket. He held the wad of cash out to Semenov. The heavy moved off the wall and took it instead, snatching it from his fingers with a glare. He thumbed through it.

'Short,' he scowled, glancing at his boss for direction. 'Six thousand.'

Semenov raised an eyebrow, his eyes on Archer.

'I may be in a bind,' Archer said evenly, 'but I'm no fool. I give you everything now and what happens? I turn up with a bullet in my head.'

'Who's to say it won't happen anyway?' the heavy growled.

Archer ignored him. 'I'll pay the rest when I get the passport. Fair enough?'

Semenov frowned but gave the smallest of nods.

'Tomorrow,' he said. 'You will meet my friend and make the exchange. Yes?'

'No problem.'

Semenov gave him the name and address of a café in the city centre. 'You will do a brush pass with a copy of tomorrow's newspaper,' he said. 'You know what I mean?'

Archer nodded. It made sense, and was another indication of

Semenov's background. They refined the details and Archer stood, ready to go.

'Of course, Mr Smith,' Semenov said, picking up his cup. He took a slow sip before replacing it on the table. 'This arrangement is confidential. If you should discuss it, or me, with anyone, I will of course find out.' His gaze was steady and cold. 'I would not advise this.'

Archer nodded his acceptance. He noted that Semenov had been careful not to make any explicit threat. 'The same applies to me, I have to say. I don't have any interest in a holiday at the Czech government's expense, you know what I mean?'

Semenov nodded his acceptance. They took another few minutes to get a decent digital head shot and confirm the personal details, then shook hands. Semenov's grip was moist and strong. He pumped Archer's hand once and looked him in the eye.

'Remember, Mr Smith,' he said quietly. 'Discretion is protection.'

Archer nodded and smiled. Maybe that was his business slogan. He released the grip and turned to go, finding his way blocked by the heavy, up so close that their chests bumped.

'We will meet again,' the heavy rasped, giving a shit-eating grin, 'Mr Balls.'

Archer sniffed and gave a frown. 'Can't wait,' he said. 'Before we do, perhaps you could invest in a tooth brush.' He moved around the heavy towards the door. 'There's a good lad.'

Clicking the door shut behind him, he took a breath and moved quickly away. The heat in the apartment had been stifling and his shirt and jeans felt damp. He needed hydration and he needed to get away from the heavy at the door. Gun-toting idiots with the mentality of a twelve-year-old gave him the shits.

He had the feeling that tomorrow would be very interesting indeed.

# 22

Archer knew he was playing a dangerous game.

He felt the pressure of the assignment weighing on him; the need to catch this mysterious player and prevent a major tragedy was immense. Even though he knew there were other people working hard in the background, each contributing their own small piece to the bigger picture, he was alone.

Nobody else was out at the coalface, striving to get their hands on the bad guy. Nobody else was putting their neck on the block and waiting for the axe to fall. It was a cold and lonely place to be, but Archer was comfortable with it. There was nobody else he had to rely on, nobody else to consult. Nobody else to fuck it up. His decisions were his and his alone, and likewise, if he fucked it up it was on him.

From his position at a table inside the café, he had good eyeball on the entrance. His long black was half gone and he had a ball of anxiety in his gut. It was time for the exchange and he had a nagging doubt that it was going to happen. He'd been back over his interactions with Semenov a million times, turning over and analysing every little step.

Had he given the man any reason to doubt him? Had he somehow smelt a rat? Had he been tipped off? They had his six grand already –

maybe they'd just fuck him off and take the chance that he wouldn't come back.

Cold-calling a bad man like Semenov carried inherent risk, but it also wasn't unusual. It wasn't like these guys advertised on Facebook or Craig's List. A pop-up window for *Get your forged passports here* probably wasn't a great business strategy.

He took a small mouthful of coffee, letting it slide down slowly. He knew his coffee intake had been excessive lately, but the caffeine hit was welcome nonetheless. His eyes felt tired and scratchy and his body ached. What he needed, he thought to himself with an internal smile, was a little Thai to walk up and down his back. That'd soon sort things out.

He glanced to the door again as he put the cup down on the scarred table top. No sign of Semenov or his sidekick. They were now officially late and he forced himself to take a breath and calm his anxiety. They were criminals after all; hardly the most reliable section of society.

Normally he wouldn't have worried too much about time-keeping with such people, but Semenov had worked for the Kremlin, and presumably was actually ex-KGB. They weren't an organisation known for their tolerance of failure or sloppy practices, so Archer had put some stock in his likely reliability.

A middle-aged couple entered the café, huffing and talking loudly as they surveyed the blackboard menu above the counter. Even before they opened their mouths he pegged them as American. The comfortable beige slacks and sneakers on the man, ruddy cheeks and a Dodgers cap. The woman had bright red lipstick badly applied, a peach-coloured cashmere sweater and Levis struggling to contain a substantial diff above glaringly white Reeboks.

Chad and Minnie from Iowa, he guessed, on the Prague leg of their European coach tour.

He looked past them to the door, using them as cover from anyone who wondered why he was still there, lingering alone over an average coffee in an average café.

The door opened, the bell above it tinkling again, and a man in a bulky puffer jacket entered. It was Semenov's side kick.

He queued behind Chad and Minnie, waiting patiently while they faffed about with their order. Minnie wanted cream and an extra shot. Chad took his straight black, same as he liked his women. He looked to Minnie for approval as he guffawed. She ignored him and gave the girl behind the counter an apologetic look. The girl looked blankly at both of them and pushed the EFTPOS terminal across the counter.

By the time they'd finished their order and shuffled off to find a table, Semenov's side kick had called out his order to the girl and slapped a note down on the counter, jabbering something in Czech and pointing towards a table outside. She nodded and he went back out the door, the bell tinkling again.

Chad was getting a real earful in hushed tones from Minnie over at the window. Archer almost felt sorry for him. Prague was probably a far more exciting place than Bumfuck, Iowa, and he was just getting carried away. Or maybe he was just a dickhead.

Either way, Archer had things to do. He picked up his copy of the Prague Post from the table, folded it in half, and threw down the last of his coffee. It was lukewarm and bitter enough to make him blink. He put the cup down, stood, and made his way towards the door.

The next few seconds would be the making or breaking of this phase. Semenov's side kick was to stand up as Archer came out, drop his copy of the Post, and Archer would pick it up for him. He would give the man his own copy, retain the other and they would go their separate ways.

Archer's copy had two grand in cash in an envelope taped inside, and the other copy would have instructions on where to pick up his passport. He would follow the direction to a dead drop somewhere nearby, pick it up and that would be the end of the transaction. If there wasn't two thousand bucks in the envelope, the side kick would soon know and Archer could expect to be ambushed before he got his hands on the passport.

Fair enough, but a bloke in his assumed position was unlikely to try and rip off the supplier. Or, at least, extremely foolish.

The bell tinkled, Archer felt the warm afternoon sun on his face as he stepped outside, and he saw the heavy start to move. He stood, turned, and dropped his paper as he bumped into Archer.

There was a brief exchange of muttered apologies and Archer bent, scooping up the fallen newspaper in his left hand and straightening up. He passed the paper from his right hand to the heavy, nodded and smiled and stepped past him, moving onto the pavement and turning left.

He tucked the folded paper under his arm, strolling purposefully as if he had somewhere to be, until he got to a side street and waited for the traffic, glancing left and right. As he did so, he opened up the first fold of the newspaper, as if checking the headlines.

Instead of a discreet note with directions to the DLB, there was a square of white A4 with a hand-drawn sketch in pencil and a single line of text beneath it.

The sketch showed a man – presumably Archer – about to devour a penis that was almost as big as his head. It was the sort of drawing boys had put in each other's schoolbooks when Archer was a kid. The text beneath it read, in child-like lettering, *Fuk U*.

It was crude, but effective.

Archer folded the paper and turned back towards the café. The heavy was standing on the footpath, watching him with a huge grin. The man gave him the universal wanker gesture, turned, and walked off in the opposite direction.

Sighing, Archer started after him. The guy's intentions were obvious, but right now he couldn't see a way around it. He still wanted the passport and needed the in with Semenov, and if that meant he first had to deal with this idiot, then so be it.

The heavy was wearing the standard uniform of a European gangster – black leather jacket, jeans, boots and mirrored shades. He wasn't hard to track. He walked half a block before stopping and looking back directly at Archer. He gave that shit-eating grin again, flipped him the bird, and crossed the street.

Archer knew he was being drawn in, but the available options were pretty limited right now. Ignore this clown and go back to

Semenov's pad? Could do, but if this interaction with the heavy was authorised by the boss man himself, then chances were the fucker had bugged out. If not, if this was just the heavy having his own little play at Archer, then Semenov would be none the wiser and he could be reached later.

And he had to admit to himself, a part of him wanted to settle things with this guy. He didn't even know anything about him, let alone his name, but he couldn't afford to have a loose cannon running around behind him when he was trying to get the job done.

*Fuck it. Just get on with it.*

He crossed the road, dodging round a pair of students on bikes, and reached the opposite pavement in time to see the heavy enter an alleyway a few doors down. Archer went after him, moving with purpose but not rushing. Rushing led to mistakes; mistakes were fatal. He paused at the top of the alley, seeing the heavy reach another alleyway half way down. He watched the heavy turn and look at him before disappearing from sight.

Archer sighed again, knowing he was walking into a trap. They were still in the central city, so he was reasonably confident that gunplay was unlikely.

He headed into the first alleyway, keeping wide against the wall just in case. It seemed to be a service lane for the neighbouring businesses and a thoroughfare for pedestrians, but aside from a few rubbish bins and a stack of broken plastic pallets, it was deserted.

Archer paused a moment by the pallets, seeking a weapon. The pallets were all cracked and broken and he spotted one that looked like it had been run over by a delivery truck. Shards of broken plastic jutted out at all angles. He twisted a narrow piece off and tucked it up his sleeve. It was rough and jagged and would do as a makeshift shiv.

He moved on to the next alley, realising it was actually a cobbled backyard between a couple of businesses. Large steel gates were open right now, presumably shut later to deter thieves. Multiple doors led off the yard and he saw no sign of Semenov's heavy. Glancing down at the twin gates, folded back to the sides like bat wings, he saw a pair of boots behind each one.

*Not so clever.*

Archer could see the left gate was up against the rear concrete wall of the building fronting the street, while the right gate was a good couple of metres away from the brick wall that formed the side of the service lane.

He took a short run and threw his weight against the left gate, slamming it against whoever was behind it, and that person against the concrete wall. There was a grunt and he grabbed the edge of the gate, yanked it back and slammed it again against the unseen ambusher.

He spun back, hearing the squeak of tired hinges and the scuff of boots on cobbles as the guy from the behind the right hand gate made himself known. The gate was swinging at him, fast, and he just managed to dodge it as the guy came at him.

He was short and stocky, a bulldog in a black leather jacket, and he had an extended ASP baton in his grip.

Archer stepped round a big swing, stepped again, and landed a front kick to the guy's thigh that knocked him back. A scuff behind him and he half turned, ducking, the left gate swinging past him, the guy he'd squashed behind it now emerging. Blood ran from a previously-broken nose and the guy was pissed. Tall, broad and stubbly, with a matching black leather jacket. Maybe they all shopped together. The thugs that shop together, stay together.

This guy didn't bother with the ASP in his hand, keeping it closed while he charged in, swinging fists the size of pumpkins.

Archer backed up rapidly, ducking and weaving, knowing that one of those hits would sit him on his arse and then he'd really be in trouble. The shorter guy flanked him, grinning now he had some back-up, the ASP cocked over his shoulder ready to go. Archer spotted movement out of the corner of his eye, seeing Semenov's heavy step out of a doorway, his game face on. A flick knife clicked open in his paw.

The big guy wasn't too mobile but Archer had to keep his distance. He stumbled over a discarded box, hopping to his left to get his balance, which brought him closer to the shorter guy.

'Mr Balls,' Semenov's heavy growled, 'I told you we'd meet again.'

Archer kept his gaze on the other two who were closer to him, with his hands up in a defensive position. He circled further left, the shorter guy backing off slightly as he tried to line up a shot with the ASP.

The other two chuckled, enjoying their leader's jibe. He was clearly quite the card, and probably the brains of the outfit.

'You didn't actually,' Archer countered, 'but here we are anyway.'

'Huh?'

The shorter guy went for a head strike with the ASP while the heavy tried to compute what Archer had just said. Archer weaved back, slapped it aside and got him with a solid left jab to the ribs before the guy got out of range.

'You didn't say that,' Archer told him, watching the big guy shuffling in, his big mitts up, blood still trickling down his chin. 'You're just pretending you did so these two jerk-offs will think you're cool. Trying to appear superior doesn't actually *make* you superior.' He risked a look at the guy and gave him a cheeky smirk. 'See, if you were smarter, you'd know that. And you'd know that this whole scene here is a really, *really* bad idea.'

The heavy scowled, hearing him but not quite getting it. 'Three on one, Mr Balls,' he rasped. 'I think you fucked.'

'Well clearly you do,' Archer said, his tone that of an exasperated teacher with a particularly slow child, 'but that's because you're not thinking.'

The three thugs all looked at each other. The tall guy smirked first, then the shorter guy. The heavy didn't like it that they were amused.

'Fuck you,' he growled. 'You some kinda tough guy, Mr Balls?'

Archer gave a modest shrug, still shuffling round in the circle with the other two, nobody quite ready to make a real move yet. 'I'm nothing special,' he said. 'But I was in the Army for a bit. You ever hear of the SAS?'

The heavy sneered at him and made the wanker gesture again. 'SAS,' he sneered. 'Saturdays and Sundays?'

'Close,' Archer said, edging slightly forward, keeping the conversation going. If these clowns were listening, they probably weren't watching. 'It's not what you think, you see. People think it's the Special Air Service, but it's not.'

'Sausage and Salami?' the heavy tried. 'Slip and Slide?'

The other two chuckled again. He was on a roll now. That was good. The shuffling circle continued moving, Archer tightening it up a little now, getting to about seven o'clock to the heavy's twelve.

'That's good,' Archer said, smirking at him again, 'there are some big words there. Well done.'

The heavy scowled.

'No, see, what it really means is speed, aggression and SURPRISE!'

The last word he bellowed as he leaped forward, loud enough to startle the big guy who was directly in front of him. Archer landed a front kick straight to the family jewels, danced back, ducked the shorter guy's swinging ASP and grabbed the arm that came with it, twisted, wrenched the wrist to drop the baton, got a hand to the guy's tricep and locked the elbow back straight.

He levered hard, hyper-extending the elbow and swinging, propelling the shorter guy into the taller guy, who must've had balls of steel because he was barely fazed by the kick.

As they crashed into each other, Archer scooped up the dropped baton and lashed out at the closest target, landing a solid strike across the shorter guy's lower back. He howled and clutched at himself even as his mate was throwing him aside to get to Archer.

Archer dodged left, ducking behind the shorter guy who was staggering as he tried to keep his feet, using him as a shield from the big guy. The big guy knocked his mate aside now with a sweeping arm and Archer ducked his next strike, lashing out with the ASP, low and brutal. The steel baton cracked the guy across the knee, the guy's huge left mitt clubbed Archer across the shoulder and knocked him sideways, and the shorter guy fell against the wall.

The big guy growled, snorted, and lined up Archer for his next go. He took a step forward, the knee folded under him with a sickening crunch of smashed cartilage, and he fell awkwardly on his side, grabbing at his shattered knee.

Archer stepped in again, slammed him across the side of the neck with the tip of the ASP with his full weight, and stooped to grab the big guy's fallen ASP. From the corner of his eye he saw both the heavy and the shorter guy moving in, side by side.

He snatched hold of the unopened ASP and hurled it backhand at the heavy. Despite the foam grip, the unopened baton was solid and heavy, and it smashed straight into the heavy's chest with a dull thud. He gasped and stopped still, winded, gaping like a fish. Archer spun, dropped to his hands as if to do a press up, and launched both feet up and back in a surprise kick to the shorter guy's gut. He was propelled back into the brick wall, and Archer leaped to his feet, snatching up the extended ASP again.

The shorter guy was reaching inside his jacket, trying to get his hands on a weapon, and the heavy was sucking in air as he readied himself again.

Time to stop fucking around.

Archer flicked the baton into his left hand, and belted the shorter guy across his left elbow with a vicious backhand strike. He heard a bone crack and the guy's face went white. It wasn't enough – he could still use his right hand.

The heavy didn't even see the strike coming, but he certainly felt it. The shaft of the ASP took him flat across the left side of his neck, swept through and came back. The return strike cracked him across his right arm, causing him to drop the flick knife.

The shorter guy was in the dreaded No Man's Land of wanting to fight, knowing he had to, but being in so much pain his body was ignoring his brain's signals. He was still weakly trying to grab at his concealed weapon. Archer stepped back, lined him up, and slammed the butt of the baton into his right temple. It was lights out and the guy slid down the wall, collapsing in a heap.

The heavy was almost at Archer now, pistol in his hand, his face sweaty with pain but looking determined. Archer saw the big guy behind him and to the left, drawing a weapon from under his jacket, the pistol almost clear now. He flicked the baton like a throwing knife, spinning through the air end over end before it smacked into the big guy's forehead and knocked him back flat.

The heavy was right there now, just a metre away, the pistol coming round, and Archer had no time. He hit him in the face, bent knuckles under the fulcrum, driving the nose up and back, getting some space. The plastic shiv dropped into his palm and he rammed it forward into the soft flesh of the man's throat. The heavy gasped, gurgled and jerked. He dropped the pistol, grabbing for his throat.

Archer twisted the shiv and yanked it out, warm blood flooding over his hand. He gave the heavy a hard push in the chest, knocking him backwards. The man stumbled, fell on his arse and flopped down. His eyes were wide and blood was pissing out the ragged hole in his throat.

Leaving him, Archer checked the other two. The shorter guy was starting to stir and the big guy was moaning, half conscious. Archer went back to the heavy, ignoring the other two for now, and quickly frisked him. He found his cash and recovered it, along with a plain brown envelope that contained the passport. He took the guy's phone and wallet too, for good measure.

Turning to the other two, Archer saw the shorter guy as the main threat right now, being conscious and still armed with a pistol. He took a step forward, booted the guy under the chin and knocked him out cold again. The bigger guy was conscious enough to still have fighting instincts, but was too out of it to follow through. Archer kicked his gun away and left him there. He doubted the big guy would ever walk properly again. There was no need to kill him.

Archer grabbed up the big guy's pistol, a worn Browning High Power, and tucked it into the back of his waistband.

He scanned the yard once more. No immediate threats left behind, nothing belonging to him, and hopefully nobody had seen it. No guarantees of that, though.

He stepped through the gates, keeping his head down, and walked away.

# 23

By the time Archer got to the apartment block it was early evening and the scene had changed again. Workers were heading home from the city, the joggers and walkers had emerged and the streets were busy.

The junkies and whores were still hanging around the basement garage, more or less the same faces as before. As Archer cut through the garage he could see a bloke back-on, standing with both hands braced against a wall in the shadows. One of the girls was on her knees dealing to him.

Another young guy was furtively making an exchange with a guy and a girl, equally as young but slightly better dressed. They glanced at Archer but continued anyway, cash changing hands for a tiny snaplock bag.

Modesty and discretion were obviously foreign concepts around here. Archer continued walking, ignoring the activities in the jungle. He didn't see the leader but could feel his eyes. The guy would be like a shark, always moving and watching, sniffing out bait and ready to attack. He was the one to watch.

The crew that hung round the front of the block were still there, kicking a football around with about as much enthusiasm as a nun at a Black Sabbath gig.

Archer took the stairs to the fourth floor, passing a couple of residents and stepping over a dero who was slumped against the wall with his legs sprawled out, blazing on a skinny joint that smelt more chemical than herbal.

He rapped on the door of apartment 31 and stood back, letting his face be seen. He was desperately hoping that Semenov was still there, but he somehow doubted it. It seemed unlikely for him to be at his place of business without his muscle around.

He rapped again. Nothing moved. He tried the door handle and leaned into it. The door was as solid as a vault.

Fuck it. He'd missed the window of opportunity. Semenov was gone.

Archer felt his heart start to race, panic surging up inside him, threatening to overflow. *Fuck fuck fuck! The one lead they had to get to the mystery man and he'd blown it!*

His hands started to tremble and he took an involuntary step backwards. It was all crumbling down around his ears and there wasn't a goddamn thing he could do about it. Without getting his hands on Semenov, there was sure to be another major terrorist attack, only this time it would succeed. The local intelligence services could find him, no doubt, but by then it would be too late.

Scores of innocents would be dead and maimed, and all because Archer had let his ego rule his head. Rather than tangling with the three heavies, he should have scarpered straight back here and dealt with Semenov face to face. Instead, he'd wasted over an hour and now faced a crippling failure.

He could hear his blood rushing in his ears and his chest felt tight, threatening to crush his lungs.

*Sonofabitch!*

He turned on his heel abruptly and stalked away, his jaw so tight he could feel his teeth grinding hard against each other. He bounded down the steps, his mind racing, searching desperately for an answer, a way out of this fucking mess. It felt like trying to plug the holes in the Titanic with a napkin. The fucker was going down fast, and he was going with it.

The dero he'd passed earlier had finished his joint and was trying to get to his feet. He saw Archer descending towards him and stretched out a hand, palm up, pleading for something in words Archer didn't understand and didn't want to hear.

'No,' was the best he could muster right now.

The dero tried to grab at him as Archer came level, and Archer slapped his hand away angrily, moving past. The dero swore and spat at him, a gob of saliva splatting on Archer's sleeve. In a split second Archer had whirled, lunged forward and grabbed the dero by the front of his stained coat, his right fist hurtling towards the dero's unshaven, sunken face.

At the last moment something snapped in Archer's brain and he stopped, his fist a centimetre from the dero's nose, balled and tight and trembling with rage. He sucked in a short breath through pinched lips, eyeball to eyeball with the dero. The guy stank of BO and weed and fear. They hung there for a long moment, one man struggling not to wet himself, the other struggling to contain the rage that wanted to erupt from inside him. Nothing would have given him more satisfaction right then than to unload on that poor, sad, broken man.

He pushed away, the dero putting his hands up defensively and cowering back against the cold brick wall as if it were shelter from the unhinged man before him.

Archer straightened, uncurled his fists, and turned away. He sucked in a breath, fighting to get a grip of himself and move on. Panicking solved nothing.

He continued down the stairs, slower now, getting his head together. The more he thought about it, all was not lost. Yet.

The basement garage was almost completely dark now, the light bulbs long gone – either smashed or redeployed as drug utensils. The hangabouts were still hanging about, although it seemed a couple of them had drifted off, presumably servicing clients.

Archer walked into the shadows and stopped. He stood still, listening. Waiting.

It took several long moments, but eventually he heard movement. Grit crunching under a shoe, the rustle of clothing. The shark was circling, assessing the bait. Archer couldn't see him yet, but sensed his presence, a few metres away to the right. He could hear him breathing.

The young guy said something in Czech, his tone soft.

'English,' Archer said.

The guy got the message. 'You want something?'

'Yeah.'

'What d'you want?' The shark moved forward, materialising out of the shadows. He wore a scruffy old blue denim jacket today, dotted with various badges. His greasy hair hung limply to his shoulders.

'What've you got?' Archer countered. He needed the guy closer. He didn't fancy a foot chase through this place, not knowing where the fuck he was going or who was waiting there.

The guy shrugged. 'Some smoke. Girls.' He looked Archer up and down. 'Boys.'

Archer flicked his eyebrows. 'A girl.'

'You like young?' The guy had no facial expression at all. It was like his soul had eroded and all that was left was a talking shell. 'Tweeny?'

'Whatever.' Archer shrugged. 'How much?'

The shark rattled off a shopping list of services and matching prices that made Archer's gut churn. He struggled to keep the feeling of revulsion from showing in his face, and was grateful for the dark.

He reached into his pocket, took out a fold of notes, and began to thumb through them. The shark automatically stepped forward, ready to close the deal. Archer's right hand shot out, knuckles folded, and slammed him straight in the Adam's apple.

The shark let out a strangled gasp and both hands went straight to his throat, his eyes bulging with terror. Archer rammed the cash back into his pocket, swept the guy's legs from under him, and dropped him to the ground.

Despite the blitz attack, the guy had enough willpower to scrabble under his jacket for his weapon.

Archer seized the gun hand, ripped it towards himself to straighten the arm and locked the hand forward like the neck of a crane. The shark squealed in pain and tried to push up off the ground. A second later Archer had drawn the pilfered Browning and jammed the muzzle against the guy's left eye. He thumbed the hammer back with a loud click and the guy froze.

Archer relieved him of a pistol of some sort, slipped it into his waistband and let the guy fall back to the ground. He followed him down, keeping the pressure of the gun barrel against his eyeball, and dropped a knee onto his gun arm to pin him there.

'Fuck you, cop,' the shark hissed through the pain, 'you fuck. You can't do this.'

'Oh, I'm no cop,' Archer replied softly, digging the Browning in a bit harder. 'I'm much worse.' He let that sink in, letting the guy's mind churn it over and turn him inside out.

'What...what you want?' The guy was in serious pain, and was trying to wriggle his arm out from beneath Archer's knee. Archer leaned in harder, grinding the bones into the concrete. The guy squealed again and Archer caught the distinct whiff of urine.

Clearly this guy was a force to be reckoned with in his own crew, but he wasn't used to playing with the big boys.

'I want information,' Archer told him. 'You give it to me, and you'll live. You don't...' He let the threat hang there and do its thing.

'What...ahhh... what...you know?'

'The Russian guy upstairs,' Archer said, 'where is he?'

'Up...stairs...ahhh, fuck...thirty-one.'

'That's it. Where is he?'

'Upstairs.'

'No.' Archer gave the pistol some body weight, digging it into the guy's eyeball. It must have hurt like fuck, because he smelt a fresh waft of urine as the guy let loose. 'I've been to his apartment; he's not there. Where do I find him?'

'Upstairs!' The guy was pleading now, his voice getting higher and more desperate every time he spoke. 'I tell you!'

Archer leaned down, almost nose to nose with him now. 'I said I've been there. I don't have time for your bullshit. Lie to me again and I'll blow your fuckin' brains out, understand you little cunt?'

The guy tried to nod, but it was hard with a pistol shoving his head back against the ground. 'Not thirty-one... he live in different... one...ahhh, fuck, Jesus...he...live in...twenty-four...the end one.'

His face was screwed up with pain, probably waiting for the hammer to fall. Archer was tempted.

'Any security there?'

'No...just him.'

'Guns?'

'I...probably.'

'Who else lives there?' It didn't really matter; Archer was going in anyway.

'I think...nobody...just the Russian.'

Archer nodded. He was pretty sure the shark was telling him the truth. It would take bigger balls than he had to lie in these circumstances. He pushed up, releasing the pressure on the guy. The shark immediately pulled his injured arm onto his chest and cradled it. His left eye remained screwed tight shut.

Archer frisked him, relieving him of two phones and a folding knife, plus a wad of cash. He tucked them into his pockets and straightened up, looking down at the guy. He raised the Browning, aiming it at the shark's face. He slowly lowered the hammer and snicked the safety back on.

The shark unscrewed his eyes and looked up at him, his face a pale blur in the darkness. He seemed to realise he was going to live. With the relief came a misplaced sense of bravado.

'You fuck,' he panted, 'I see you again and I'll...'

'You'll what? Piss your pants again like a little girl?'

The shark opened his mouth to speak again, and Archer cut him off with a vicious stomp to the crotch. A shriek of pain cut the air and

Archer pushed down, grinding the guy's balls under his heel. He felt not a shred of sympathy for the guy. As far as he was concerned, someone who could peddle human misery like he did deserved far worse.

Without a word, Archer turned and headed back towards the stairs.

Apartment 24 was at the far end of the third floor. The door was closed and the curtains drawn.

Archer slowed as he passed the neighbouring unit, and could hear a TV coming from inside. He carried on to Semenov's door and paused to listen again. Nothing.

He rapped on the door and stepped back. It gave Semenov a good view through the peep hole plus it gave him room to put a boot to the door if he needed to – although, going on the door downstairs, he'd likely break a foot if he tried to smash it in.

It took half a minute before he heard movement behind the door. Presumably Semenov had checked the peep hole and knew who he was talking to.

'Yes, what do you want?'

'We need to talk.' Archer made a point of looking around him. 'In private.'

'We have talked. The deal is done. No refunds.'

'I don't want a refund.'

'Then you go away. I have no need to talk to you.'

Archer sighed, looking exasperated. 'We have a problem. Your man ripped me off.'

There was a pause.

He guessed Semenov was assessing his options. He could try and fuck Mr Smith off but there was the chance it would just attract attention. He couldn't call the cops, and calling in some heavy support would bring more attention and also took time – besides, he wouldn't be able to get hold of his sidekick just yet. The only other option was to deal with the problem right now, which would mean he'd be armed.

Archer held his hands up for the peephole, palms open. 'Look man, I haven't got time to fuck around. I need what I paid for, then I can fuck off and leave you alone.'

'What you mean, he ripped you off?' Semenov was naturally suspicious and still not opening the door, and Archer couldn't blame him.

'He took my money and fucked off. I don't have my papers, man. I need to get outta here.'

'Who sent you here?'

'The young guy down in the garage, the pimp. Long hair.' He threw the guy under the bus without hesitation. If it meant he suffered some street justice later then so be it.

'I meet you downstairs. Ten minutes.'

Archer shook his head, looking properly pissed off now. 'No, how do I know you'll turn up? I need that passport, man, or I'm fucked. You come and sort it out now.'

There was another pause, before he heard the rattle of a security chain followed by a lock opening. The door cracked open and Semenov peered out at him. A pistol was in his hand, pointing at Archer's gut.

'Step back, walk in front,' he said.

Archer did as he was told, keeping his hands out to his sides, clearly visible. He led the way to the stairs and started up. Reaching the top, he stopped and waited. Semenov was slow on the stairs and watched him carefully. The Kremlin's former master forger wore a brown cardigan that was badly pilled, beige polyester slacks and fluffy slippers. In another world he'd be a doddery grandad. Maybe he was in his private life.

Semenov had the pistol tucked under his cardy now, and gestured for Archer to move on. They got to the door of apartment 31 and Semenov unlocked it before ushering Archer inside. He shut the door and hit the lights, pointing Archer to a seat in the lounge. The pistol was back in view now, and Semenov took out a cell phone with the other hand.

'You speak to my friend?' he said.

'Yes. He told me to fuck off and laughed at me. He had a gun.'

Semenov frowned and thumbed the keypad on his phone. 'This is not right.'

'I think he has a discipline problem,' Archer said, 'you need to watch him.'

Semenov said nothing, but glanced down at the phone to hit Send.

Archer was out of the seat and on him before the older man even registered what was going on. He ripped the pistol away, elbowed Semenov hard in the side of the head and hip threw him to the floor.

Semenov's glasses went flying and his lungs emptied with a gasping whoosh. Archer pinned him down with a knee on his chest and jammed the barrel of the Browning under his chin.

'Catch your breath,' he said softly, 'because you're going to start talking.'

Semenov gave a weak nod, his chest heaving. Archer eased off the weight to let him recover a bit.

'I'm looking for a man,' Archer told him. 'He came to you recently for papers.'

'This...is...my job.' Semenov licked his lips nervously. 'I do papers...for people. What man?'

'I don't know his name. He's a big player, a terrorist. Arms dealer.'

He saw a flicker in Semenov's eye; he knew who Archer was talking about.

'What...nationality?'

'You tell me. When did he come?'

'I think of...a man. He come...yesterday. He got papers.'

'Name?'

Semenov managed a small smile despite his predicament. 'Mr Smith,' he said. 'I have many Mr Smiths, you understand.'

'I get that,' Archer acknowledged, 'but you know this man, so stop fucking about. I don't have a lot of time, Mr Semenov.'

Semenov's eyes narrowed ever so slightly. 'So you know who I am. Why your interest in me, Mr Smith?'

'I don't give a shit about you, I just want this guy. Who is he?'

'I have no name. He is an American; that is all I know.'

'You made him a passport?'

'Of course.' Archer applied more pressure to the Browning under his chin and Semenov grimaced. 'Please, enough. I am an old man, I am no threat to you.' He looked Archer in the eye. 'I knew this day would come. Time will always run out. Please, let us sit like gentlemen. I will tell you what you seek to know.'

Archer got up and watched the other man make his way painfully to the couch. Archer remained standing, the Browning in his hand. He knew he should have cleared the apartment but time was against him. His senses were pinging flat out but he was satisfied they were alone.

'Are you going to kill me?' Semenov's tone was calm and controlled, like he was discussing plans for the evening with an old friend.

Archer gave a thin smile. The barrel of the Browning didn't waver. 'That's up to you. Start talking.'

Semenov sighed. 'I do not like to talk about my clients, it is not a good business option.'

'It's a better option than a nine mil in the head,' Archer reminded him. 'Stop fucking about.'

Semenov nodded his agreeance. 'I gave him a new passport, Australian. The name was Vincent Granger.' He spelled the surname. 'The date of birth was July 5$^{th}$, 1957.'

'What else did he tell you?'

'Nothing.' Semenov looked mildly amused. 'I simply supply documents, Mr Smith. I have no interest in their travel plans.'

'You have a photo?'

Semenov shook his head. 'No.' His eyes flickered as he said the words. 'It is part of the deal.'

'Bullshit. You took a digital photo, like you did with me.'

'I gave him the memory card,' Semenov said quickly. 'He was very insistent.'

'You've dealt with him before,' Archer said, following his gut now. He knew Semenov was lying, but instinct told him it wouldn't take much to make him talk. 'You've kept a photo. I bet you keep photos of all your customers.'

'Why would I do that?' Semenov said, looking curiously at him. 'Privacy is essential in my line of work.'

'Insurance policy.' Archer smiled thinly again, knowing he was on the right track. 'So if you ever got caught you'd have something to trade with.'

'Mr Smith,' Semenov protested, 'I am a man of honour. How dare you...'

'You'd sell your clients to save your own hide,' Archer retorted. 'I want that photo.'

'Mr Smith...'

Archer took three fast steps forward, raising the Browning, and Semenov cowered away. 'Okay, okay. I have a photo of the man. You may have it.'

'Very kind of you.' Archer stepped back. 'Get it.'

'It is in the cloud.'

Archer frowned, taking a moment to click that the man was talking about a cloud-based server.

He watched Semenov carefully as the older man took out his smart phone and got the connection. He had Semenov hold the phone out and use just one hand, hoping to ensure the man didn't delete whatever data he had. He didn't have time to shag about with obtaining passwords and codes.

The Russian brought up a photo on his phone and turned the screen for Archer to see. It was a standard head and shoulders passport shot, but Archer knew immediately that it was the man he'd seen in Croatia, the man he'd nicknamed the Boss. Dark hair swept back, dark eyes, high forehead. Intense-looking. Maybe in his mid-fifties.

He snapped a photo of the screenshot and tucked his phone away, before relieving Semenov of his own device.

The Russian looked up at him as he stepped back again, his eyes shrewd. 'So now you are going to kill me, Mr Smith?' he said. 'It is hardly sporting behaviour, is it?'

'We're not playing games, Semenov. People's lives are at stake.'

'Who do you work for?' Semenov had a distinct aura of calm about him, still in his conversational mode.

'It doesn't matter who I work for.'

'Do they know what you are truly like, Mr Smith? A loose cannon, I think they say?'

Archer knew the Russian was playing with him now, but couldn't resist giving a snort. 'I'm no loose cannon, Semenov. What I do, I do for a purpose.'

'Oh, the greater good,' Semenov mocked him. 'Does this greater good help you sleep at night, Mr Smith?' His eyes were dark and glittering. 'Does it stop the nightmares for the people you kill?'

'I sleep just fine,' Archer replied coldly, his grip tightening on the butt of the Browning. 'The only nightmares I have are for the people I couldn't save.'

'Oh, how heroic you must feel. You wrap yourself in your security blanket of ignorance, thinking you are doing good, saving the world. It must be wonderful to be so...altruistic.'

'Not altruistic,' Archer started to say, catching the tiniest flicker of movement in Semenov's left arm. Even as he raised the Browning the other man's hand was coming up, pulling a compact pistol from between the cushions on the sofa.

Archer fired, one shot that was loud enough to echo in the small apartment.

The bullet took Semenov high in the chest and his mouth gaped open. His lips moved soundlessly, his eyes bulging, his body stiffening as if held in an electrical current. The entry wound leaked red onto his shirt front. His left foot twitched briefly before rolling to the side and resting.

The body slumped backwards, the head lolling towards the ceiling, before it began to slip slowly sideways. It came to rest halfway down the back of the couch, slouching awkwardly.

Cordite hung in the air and Archer's ears rang. He slipped the Browning into his waistband and looked at the body. Semenov was staring at the door as if seeking help that would never come.

'Maybe not altruistic,' he finally said, in answer to the dead man's jibes, 'but at least I'm not a fuckin' terrorist.'

He headed for the door.

# 24

The drive from Vienna had been circuitous but steady, avoiding main roads and anywhere likely to be subject to cameras or checkpoints. There was little traffic on the road and he stuck to the speed limit.

It was unlikely that the killing would attract too much attention, if it had even been reported to the authorities yet, but there was no point in being careless.

He diverted towards the Elbe River and found a lookout spot overhanging the dark water. He stripped the Browning down, wiped it clean and threw the pieces one by one into the river, hearing a decent plop with every throw. The river was long and winding and in theory he could have stopped anywhere along its banks to ditch his gear. Only if he was seen here would this particular place become an area of interest for the authorities, otherwise the gun was now effectively gone for good.

He made his way back into a small town he missed the name of and found a public toilet to clean up in, washing his exposed surfaces and ditching his clothes in a storm water drain, securing them all in a bundle and dropping them into the darkness.

Freshly changed and rehydrated, he drove further on before pulling off the road long enough to place a call to Ingoe.

It was a succinct conversation. The Ops Officer was neither surprised nor saddened to hear of Semenov's demise, although he noted that it was now even more vital that Archer was not detected in Austria.

It took only a few seconds to send the target photo through, then Archer was on the move again, eager to put some distance between himself and Prague.

He jumped back onto Highway 8 and crossed the border with no issue, making his way past Dresden and north on Bundesautobahn 13 towards Berlin. Trucks blasted past on their way to and from the industrial hub, hauling heavy loads into the darkness beyond the cones of his headlights. He turned off short of the capital, following his nose to a town called Zeuthen.

He avoided the town centre and parked up in a lay-by area off a secondary road that seemed to be popular with budget travellers. There was a camper van off to one side, all in darkness.

Archer killed the engine and lights, locked the doors, and set his watch alarm for 05:00. He reclined his seat and curled up as best he could, getting a few hours' much-needed kip before continuing on his way.

A service centre stop gave him the opportunity to freshen up and stretch his achy body. He washed down one of yesterday's bratwurst in a stale bun with a large coffee before driving on, and made the capital by eight.

Berlin was already alive when he arrived.

He dropped the car on the second-to-top level of a multi-storey car park, sitting for a few minutes to watch for any followers. Not seeing anyone didn't mean they weren't there, so he took the stairs down to street level and beat the feet, taking a walk down random streets for twenty minutes. He called the Ops desk while he did so to report his safe return to Berlin.

'Wait one,' the desk officer told him, 'the boss wants a chat.'

Ingoe came on the line. 'No dramas?'

'No. Just clearing my tail.'

'No matches on that photo, we've flicked it over to a couple of other outfits to check their records. I've got no doubt he'll be known to someone. We'll let you know. In the meantime, thin out and do some sight-seeing.'

'All good.'

Archer rang off and tucked the phone away. It was half past eight now and workers were busy getting themselves off to their faceless offices for another beige day at the coalface. It was important now that Archer laid a trail of activity for the day. He needed something to show his whereabouts for the day on the off-chance he was somehow linked to the killing in Prague.

He retrieved the car and returned to the Holiday Inn, taking the time to grab a late breakfast from room service and a decent shower. It felt good to be washed and dressed in clean clothes, and with a full stomach and a spring in his step, he was ready to play tourist.

It wasn't often that he got downtime on a job like this – usually his time was spent surveilling a target or taking direct action. For now at least, his time was free.

He made his way to Checkpoint Charlie, the scene of so much dissent and skulduggery during the Cold War, had a look at the remains of the Berlin Wall and, quite by chance, stumbled across a walking tour of the city. He handed over his cash, took a guidebook, and tagged along with a bunch of multi-national tourists, all festooned with cameras and trendy walking kit.

The tour guide was a well-spoken German girl in her late twenties with a bright yellow floppy hat and little round John Lennon glasses. Archer joined in the group, listening avidly to her tales of the Gestapo, the bombing during the war, the Stasi and the desperate attempts to escape East Berlin.

David Hasselhoff was mentioned more than once and Archer couldn't help but think of the talking black Trans Am, a perm that no man could ever reasonably excuse and spiffy Devon in the big truck.

As they walked the streets Archer noticed people handing out flyers to passers-by in at least three different locations. He took one out of idle curiosity and scanned the brightly coloured writing. It was short and concise; *Stop immigration! Save the Deutschland from foreign criminals!*

There was more scrawl after that but Archer quickly lost interest. It was the same old dribble that had been around for years. The only thing that stood out to him was the fact that, far from being skinheads in denim and chains, the people passing out the flyers were middle class, normal-looking people. One even reminded him of his mother.

He screwed the flyer into a ball and tossed it in the nearest bin. He had bigger things to worry about than this crap. Besides, the girl in the yellow hat had an engaging smile and a toned set of legs that were holding his interest.

Eventually he felt the hit of fatigue so slipped away from the group, picked up a large frothy coffee from a café and a bratwurst from a street vendor – fresher and hotter than the earlier effort – and fed himself while he walked to find a cab. He felt himself nodding off on the way back to the hotel, and it seemed like the driver had taken him on the tourist route for a few extra notes, but he was beyond caring.

He made his way into the Holiday Inn, took the lift to his floor, and buzzed open the door. He had plans for an afternoon nap before he hit the gym, but as soon as he crossed the threshold of his room, he realised he was not alone.

The woman standing by the window was facing him, her hands in front of her, fingers laced together, seemingly loose and relaxed. Her face gave the game away. It was watchful, sharp, her eyes running over him in an instant and watching every move. Archer had no doubt he was being assessed by a professional.

She was dressed in a smart dark blue pantsuit. The whole scene was a lot more formal than when he'd spoken to her in the café over a bowl of ham and pea soup.

The man to Archer's left was bigger, strong in the shoulders, his jaw square and solid. His body language was quietly intimidating, as if he was waiting for something to kick off so he could explode into action.

Looking at him, Archer had no interest in provoking such a reaction. It took a blade to know a blade, and this guy was clearly an operator. Probably GSG9, he figured. His bald dome gleamed and his dark beard was flecked with salt, his eyes hard and inquisitive. His nose had been broken at least once, and his black suit was functional and off-the-rack.

'Please,' Archer said, turning back to the woman, 'let yourselves in. Make yourselves at home.'

She didn't smile, but produced an ID wallet which she held out for him to see. He couldn't read it from where he stood, but it looked official and they clearly weren't there to play games.

'Come in, sit down,' she said in flawless English, her tone neutral.

'How kind,' he said, 'considering it is my room...'

The guy gave a harrumph and Archer looked at him.

'What the hell is this about?' he demanded, giving his best impression of an indignant tourist. 'Who are you people and why are you breaking into my room? I've a good mind to call the police. I'm a bloody tourist...'

'No.' The woman cut him off sharply. 'You're not a bloody tourist, Mr Archer. You're a bloody foreign asset operating on German soil without German authority.' She eyed him coolly. 'So stop the bullshit and please, take a seat. It is best if we talk civilly about why you are here and when you will be leaving.'

Archer cocked an eyebrow and tossed his chin towards the man.

'Or what?' he said. 'Smiley here breaks out his best moves?'

The man grunted, unamused. He glanced at the woman as if seeking her direction. She gave a tiny shake of the head and gestured again for Archer to sit. Clearly she was in charge.

'Please, sit,' she said. 'I am getting tired of asking, Mr Craig Archer from New Zealand.'

Archer hiked his shoulders and moved to the bed. The comfortable studio room was suddenly crowded with three people in it. He sat on the edge of the bed and the woman took the armchair, angling it around to face him. Her companion moved positions, staying behind Archer, close enough to hear him breathe. Archer ignored him and focussed for now on the woman before him.

Whatever was going to happen would be initiated by her. He knew he'd been rumbled, but how badly remained to be seen. Perhaps he could still bluff his way out of the hotel room.

The woman's next words blew that hope to hell.

'Mr Archer, we know you work for the Security Intelligence Service,' she said, 'and we know why you are in Germany. You have no diplomatic status here and as soon as we are finished talking you will be escorted to the airport where you will board a plane and return home.'

Archer said nothing. His only real hope now was that they didn't know about his overnight trip to Prague. That wouldn't be good.

Her cool blue eyes watched him. She could have passed for Scandinavian, he thought idly. High cheekbones, perfect skin. The blue of her eyes was darker than he would have expected from such an Aryan-looking specimen. She was studying him closely and he felt exposed.

There were procedures for dealing with exactly this sort of situation, which were drummed home to all officers throughout their training and beyond. The primary goal was always to avoid arrest and prevent political embarrassment. Archer had the feeling they'd moved beyond that already.

'ID,' he said, holding his hand out expectantly. She arched an eyebrow at him like a school teacher with a petulant child. 'Please,' he added.

She removed the black leather wallet from her pocket again and handed it over, and he took his time checking her credentials

*Bundesamt für Verfassungsschutz* – Federal Office for the Protection of the Constitution – as he'd thought. The BfV was the federal government's domestic security service, and despite the odd scandal, they were very good. If his memory was right, they were an unarmed agency, and he wondered whether he would be able to use that to his advantage somehow.

Her name was Eva Graf, or so the identification card said.

He took his time as he tossed up his options. Getting kicked out of Germany was hardly ideal, not when he was hot on the trail right now. The political fallout, however, would be significant and unexplainable if he pushed the envelope with an agency such as the BfV. These were not Third World thugs who could be bribed or bullied. He decided to go for some solidarity instead.

'Department 5 or 6?' he inquired, passing the ID wallet back to her. Department 5 dealt with foreign extremists, whereas 6 focussed exclusively on Islamic terrorists. It could prove handy to know what her assignment was.

She arched an eyebrow again and looked mildly amused. 'Does it matter?' she replied.

He shrugged nonchalantly as if he didn't really care. 'Not really.'

'However, if I were to be from Department 5, that would make us almost the same, would it not?' Her gaze was coolly calculating.

Archer felt a kick in his chest at the reference to Division 5. Jesus, these people were very well informed. He did his best to look unconcerned. 'I'm not sure what you're talking about,' he said blandly.

Still no mention of a dead ex-KGB forger in Prague. So far, so good.

The woman smiled. Her lips were full and a deep maroon. 'I'm sure you don't,' she said. 'Now unless there is something you would like to tell us, Mr Archer, it is time for us to go.'

She rose to her feet, gesturing for him to get up. She stepped aside and pointed to the chair she had just vacated. Archer gave her a questioning look.

'Sit,' she said, 'while we pack your things. It would not be nice to have any surprises, would it?'

He sat reluctantly, grateful that he didn't have any weapons with him. Such a find would have made things very difficult indeed. He watched while the woman – Eva – dragged his suitcase onto the bed and searched it. She was quick and thorough. That done, she recovered his toiletries from the bathroom and checked them carefully before adding them to his case.

'No exploding toothpaste,' he tried, 'it's okay.'

The man eyed him like he was an idiot.

'KSK?' Archer inquired. 'GSG9? KSM?'

The guy's eyes flickered at the mention of KSM, the naval Special Forces unit, and Archer nodded. The guy was, or had been, a maritime operator. He'd have plenty to talk about with the Shaky Boats guys. He'd never worked with the KSM, but knew of their reputation. It validated his reluctance to want to tangle with the guy.

'Alright,' Eva said briskly, securing the lock on his suitcase. 'Let's go.'

Archer stood and moved towards the door, only for the man to block his way. He was a couple of inches taller than Archer and his dark eyes bored holes in Archer's skull.

'No funny business,' he growled in a heavy accent, 'no playing games, Mr Archer. It would be mistake for you, yes?'

Archer gave a short nod and a reassuring smile. 'No worries mate,' he said, 'message received and understood.' He glanced back to where Eva watched the interaction between the two men. 'Don't worry, I'll behave myself.'

The man opened the door and Eva handed the suitcase to Archer, being careful not to touch him as she did so. She held his passport up for him to see. 'I will hold this until we check in.'

'We?' Archer was surprised. 'Are we all going?'

'No, not all,' she said. 'Just you. But we must check you in. Understand?'

Despite the situation and his impending deportation, he had to admit she had an X factor about her. Sexy in a very composed, Germanic way. He wondered what she was like in bed. Probably very efficient, he decided.

'What is so funny?' she said sharply and he quickly wiped the smile from his face.

'Nothing,' he said apologetically, giving himself a mental reminder to keep his fantasies to himself. He paused in the doorway, giving her his best winning smile. 'It's a shame we won't have the opportunity to work more closely, don't you think Miss Graf?'

Eva gave him a cool look. 'No, I don't think, Mr Archer. Now please get moving. You have a plane to catch.'

He began to turn away but caught her smiling to herself as he did so. She saw him clock her and immediately applied her game face again, but it was too late.

He'd made a connection, and they both knew it.

# 25

The ride to Berlin's Schoenefeld airport was smooth in a plain black Mercedes V-Class MPV.

Archer sat in the rear with the heavy behind him and Eva in front of him, twisting in her seat so she was side-on to him. Another muscle-man drove, using a heavy foot on both the accelerator and brake.

The airport was just outside the city and Archer knew he had a limited time to do anything, if the opportunity rose at all. He didn't trust the German officers not to be armed, and he didn't fancy his chances with the two heavies. Running would be his only option, but he would have to be fast and effective, and his face would soon be taped to the front dash of every cop car in the country.

Deciding that discretion might be the better part of valour right now, he queried Eva on the travel arrangements.

'Sixteen twenty five, EasyJet to Gatwick,' she replied shortly. 'ETA seventeen thirty.'

He nodded his thanks but stayed sitting with his elbows on the back of her seat. 'Am I able to make a call to get picked up at the other end?'

She considered that for about a nano-second, and gave the

answer he had expected. 'No.' Then she gave a slight smile. 'Gatwick is not a dangerous place, Mr Archer. You will be safe while you wait for a pick-up, I am sure.'

'Oh, you never know.' He gave her a straight face. 'There could be Moonies, overweight Americans with their cameras and loud voices and Hawaiian shirts...there might even be some English football fans. They can get pretty unruly, y'know. I wouldn't fancy my chances most days of the week.' He gave her smiley eyes and could see she was amused, despite herself. 'But I appreciate your faith in me, Eva. It's doing wonders for international relations.'

She cocked her eyebrow again. He was getting used to that, in the short time they'd known each other. 'Are all New Zealand men so full of shit?' she asked.

Archer pretended to mull that for a moment, before nodding. 'Some, yeah. It's a gift we have Down Under.' He followed her lead and cocked an eyebrow at her. 'Have you ever been Down Under with a Kiwi, Eva?'

She did her best not to laugh aloud at his blatant come-on, but couldn't hide a bemused smile. 'No, Mr Archer, I have not been... Down Under, as you say.'

The heavy behind him made a growling noise in his throat to let them know he was listening and disapproved.

Archer ignored him and kept his focus on Eva. Aside from being sexy as hell, she was also the leader of this little contingent, and he knew that any concessions he could get would come from her.

'Look,' he said, lowering his voice conspiratorially, 'I'd really appreciate it if I could touch base with my head office. It could be pretty embarrassing for both our governments, you know...perhaps a courtesy call...'

She was about to answer when her own cell phone rang. She answered it with a simple 'Ja' then listened for nearly a minute, nodding occasionally to herself. She rang off and turned back to him.

'Do not worry, Mr Archer,' she said, 'a courtesy call has been made from my superiors to yours. They will be expecting you at

Gatwick and then I understand you will be flying straight back to Wellington.'

Archer felt his heart sink. He could imagine the Director's reaction to this debacle. It was going to be an unwelcome reception, and if he was going back to Wellington rather than Auckland, then it meant he was being sent to front up to the Director himself. A cloud of doom started to settle on him.

Eva was silent for a moment. The tyres were rhythmic on the tar seal. The heavy in the back breathed loudly.

'I am sorry,' she said softly. 'But you know how it is.'

Archer nodded and was about to speak when the driver cut him off sharply. His eyes were fixed on the rear view mirror and his shoulders were tense. He barked something in German and both Eva and the heavy in the rear craned to look out the back window. Archer followed suit, just in time to see a grey BMW 5-series racing up the right hand side of the MPV. The windows were tinted but he could make out two shapes in the front and maybe a third in the back.

The BMW was moving fast, and so was the vehicle behind it, this one a white VW sedan.

The driver shouted something else and there was a rapid exchange between the three Germans, too fast for him to catch. Archer had no idea what was happening but figured whatever it was, it wasn't good. He was suddenly slammed into the back of Eva's seat as the driver hit the brakes. There was a heavy impact from behind and the crunch of crumpling panel work. The BMW went past and the driver floored the gas again.

'What the fuck's going on?' Archer shouted.

He heard pinging sounds from the front of the MPV and lifted himself to see the windshield spider webbing under the impact of multiple shots. There was a spray of red and the driver slumped to the side, letting go of the wheel and pinning the accelerator to the floor.

Archer was turning to look behind them when he felt another big shunt from the VW, shoving them forward. The driverless MPV swerved to the left and they were all thrown like rag dolls.

Pushing himself up off the floor, Archer stepped over Eva and dived for the front seat, reaching over the bloodied driver to grab the steering wheel. He could see now that they were on a stretch of highway with farmland ahead of them on what should have been their right.

They were heading straight for a hard shoulder that dropped quickly into a ditch with a raised berm beyond that. Cars were dodging the out-of-control Mercedes MPV, one spinning out as it went by, horns blaring all around. The grey BMW was tracking them across the autobahn like a sheep dog. A guy was leaning out of the rear passenger's window with a submachine gun of some sort in his hands.

Archer grabbed for the driver's leg, trying desperately to free it from the accelerator, knowing they had barely seconds to avoid catastrophe. It was no use, he had a handful of the guy's pants leg but couldn't budge it. If he yanked on the emergency brake at this speed they would roll, and be in a worse position than before.

A fresh burst of gunfire raked the driver's window, showering Archer with glass, hornets cracking close by his head as he desperately tried to swerve back onto the road and avoid the inevitable collision. The ditch and berm were screaming towards them like a looming mountainside.

'Hold on!' he bellowed, throwing himself back into the rear of the vehicle. He crashed into Eva as she was getting up and they hit the deck with her beneath him. A split second later there was a sickening lurch, a deafening crash and thump, the vehicle dropped and shuddered, metal screeched and glass shattered, and the side windows blew out as the SMG cut loose again.

The MPV stopped moving with its nose jammed down into the ditch. The engine still roared, and he could feel the wheels churning into the earth or whatever was beneath them.

'Move! Move!' Archer pushed up and crabbed to the sliding side door, yanking at it with the urgency borne of impending death.

The door was jammed, twisted out of alignment by the impact, and he reached for his suitcase instead. Bullets thudded into the right hand side panels as he slammed the suitcase against the windows opposite, smashing the door window with his third strike. He shoved the case through the opening to clear as much of the glass as possible before reaching back for Eva.

She had blood running from a cut to her forehead but was moving.

'Out!'

He helped her out the window, shoving her head first and letting her drop to the ground. He turned towards the heavy in the back, shouting at him to move.

His eyes were open but not focussing. One look told him the guy was out of the game. He'd taken at least one round through the chest and was splayed across his seat, leaking blood. His carotid pulse was visibly pumping in his neck. Hopefully they could get through this and get him medical attention, quick smart. Without urgent help he was a goner.

Archer left him and scuttled towards the door window to follow Eva. As he did so he saw that the BMW had skidded to a halt near them and the rear passenger had alighted with his SMG in his hands. He was changing mags as he moved towards the stricken MPV. He was dressed in jeans and a casual jacket, and had a shaggy mop of hair hanging from beneath a black balaclava.

The designated hitter, sent to finish off the occupants.

Throwing a quick look behind them, Archer could see the white VW, now blowing steam from beneath a crumpled bonnet, was stopped further back. Two guys from it were blocking the road, weapons raised, both also wearing balaclavas and casual kit.

Archer poked his head out the window, seeing Eva crouching in the ditch, now mud-spattered to go with her bloodied face. 'Move round the back!' he hissed. 'Guy with a gun!'

She moved quickly and he stayed low in the back of the vehicle, seeing the gunman approaching the right hand side. He searched desperately for a weapon on the floor, anything that might help him right now. He knew that if he didn't do something, they were all fucked.

His fingers played over tiny fragments of glass, a discarded napkin from a café, searching for something more substantial. As the footsteps approached he found it. A piece of glass about the size of his thumb, jagged on both sides and tapering to a point of sorts.

The gunman paused to check the driver then moved to the shattered window behind him to check the rear. He poked his head in the opening, scanning with his eyes, the SMG staying outside the vehicle.

And that was his mistake.

Archer reached up from beneath the shattered window, grabbing a handful of the guy's jacket collar with one hand. Archer's other hand stabbed into the man's face with the shard of glass. He made contact with his cheek through the fabric, opening it up and producing a scream, then shifted his aim, ramming it at the guy's eye instead, holding onto his collar for dear life.

The glass missed the eye but sliced across his temple instead, bringing another scream and a shout from the direction of the BMW.

Archer knew it was only seconds before the gunman's back-up arrived. He yanked on the guy's head, raising himself to his knees now and twisting the head to expose his vulnerable points. The man clicked to what was happening and fought against it, dropping his chin to protect his throat.

It didn't matter – Archer was all over him now, slashing with the shard of glass and ignoring the pain in his own hand as the weapon dug into his flesh, slicing at any exposed surface he could see. The guy twisted backwards, letting his weapon drop on its sling and trying to scrabble for Archer's face behind him.

Wrenching back on the guy's head, Archer drove the glass into his right eye and rammed it in. There was a blood-curdling scream and the guy grabbed at his face as he dropped forward. Archer was dragged half out the window by the dead weight, snatching for the submachine gun.

Two guys from the BMW were jogging towards them, both with pistols in their hands but holding their fire for now, maybe wary of hitting their own man.

Archer couldn't reach the SMG and felt the guy's body begin to slip from his grasp. One of the approaching men raised his pistol, seeing the opportunity open up.

At the last second Archer spotted the butt of a pistol protruding from the guy's waistband and grabbed at it, yanking it free as the man dropped fully to the road surface. He didn't know if he was dead yet or not, but it didn't matter right now.

He dropped the safety with his thumb and triggered a shot towards the two enemy as he fell head first from the window. The shot went skywards but the two guys separated, their guns coming up on line.

Hitting the deck in an awkward roll, Archer twisted round to his knees and got the pistol up in a two-handed grip. One of the other guys was already firing, his rounds pinging off the bodywork of the Mercedes, standing in a front-on Isosceles stance with his gun in both hands.

Archer dropped him with a double tap to the centre mass and he went down like a sack of spuds, screaming and holding his guts.

The other guy was more skilled and had dropped to a prone position, giving Archer the smallest target possible. They exchanged shots, each sending rounds skimming off the tarmac near the other man.

'Behind you!' a voice screamed in his ear, and Archer jumped with fright, seeing Eva right behind him as if she had appeared from nowhere.

He sent another shot towards the other gunner and the slide locked open. He dropped the pistol and scrabbled for the submachine gun beneath the guy he'd stabbed in the eye.

The other man was pushing up, seeing an opportunity to press home their advantage, and another two guys were coming forward from the VW, their pistols flashing.

Archer was almost deaf now but was well aware of what was happening, all his other senses screaming at full noise. He wrenched the SMG free of the body and raised it, mechanically recognising it as a Heckler and Koch MP7. It fired the 4.6x30mm round from a 30-shot magazine, and was used by the German Army.

The safety was already off and he stroked the trigger, putting a burst past the approaching BMW gunman. The guy spun on his heel and raced back towards the car, firing a wild shot behind him as he ran.

Turning towards the other two, Archer stayed in a crouch and fired a short burst. One of the guys stayed and fired back but his mate started backing up, shouting at him.

Archer gave them another burst, his vision blurring as sweat ran into his eyes. He was aware of Eva by his side, tucking in closer to the side of the Mercedes and covering her ears. He flicked a quick look to the left, seeing that the retreating gunman had come back for his fallen mate. He was trying to drag him by one hand back towards the BMW, shakily waving his pistol in Archer's general direction with the other.

The HK kicked in Archer's hands as he sent another burst their way, missing but close enough to scare the guy into dropping his mate and legging it towards the car.

The other two had made it back to the VW by the time he swung back their way, and the crippled car was hauling round in a tight turn. Cars were banked up behind it, motorists gawping at the chaos before them. Some had phones out, either calling the emergency services or recording the incident for social media.

Archer held his fire, knowing the chances of hitting an innocent bystander were catastrophically high. The two gunmen had no such fear and both hung out their car windows, unleashing a last volley of shots as the VW forced its way the wrong direction back down the autobahn.

He swivelled back to the left, rising to his feet now, the BMW taking off with the tyres smoking, the nearest rear door swinging open, the gunman's feet disappearing from view as he scrambled into the backseat.

He had a clear line of sight past the BMW and used it to good effect, emptying the magazine on the HK in short bursts into the vehicle as it roared away. He could see bullets puncturing the bodywork, pieces of plastic and metal exploding off the vehicle, the rear number plate coming loose and cartwheeling along the road surface.

The bolt locked open and blue smoke curled from the empty breech and barrel as Archer lowered the weapon, watching the BMW disappear into the distance.

Sirens were sounding in the background as Archer approached the man he'd shot. He lay flat on his back, his torso a mass of blood. His face was still covered by a black balaclava. The rest of his clothes looked cheap and serviceable. His pistol was discarded to the side. Archer recognised it as another German Army weapon, a HK P8.

Standing over the guy, Archer could see his eyes were still open. He reached down and peeled the balaclava back. The guy stared up at him, blinking to focus. His lips were thin bloodless lines in a waxy face. He was Caucasian, maybe early forties, with a short brown beard. He didn't have long to go in this world.

'Who are you working for?' Archer demanded. He leaned down over the guy, knowing he had only a couple of minutes if he was lucky. 'Who are you?'

The guy coughed weakly, blood flecking his lips. He managed the tiniest of smirks but stayed silent.

'Who sent you?' Archer barked. He was tempted to push the point home, but there were too many watching eyes. Instead, he dropped to a knee and leaned over the guy properly, putting the HK aside and his hands to the man's chest. To any onlookers it would look like he was attempting to give first aid. 'Without me you're going to die right here,' he hissed. 'I can help you.'

The guy coughed again. His eyes were slipping, failing to focus, but despite his situation he hadn't lost any attitude.

'F...fuck...you,' he wheezed.

Archer pressed down on his chest, just enough to make him gasp. He was leaking blood outwardly and probably even more internally, and Archer could smell fecal matter. The guy gasped with the pressure and his eyes widened.

'Don't die on me, buddy,' Archer said loudly, for the benefit of anyone listening, before dropping his voice again. 'Tell me who sent you and I will save you.'

The guy wheezed some more, a trickle of blood escaping his lips and dribbling down his cheek towards his sweaty neck.

'Dead…any…way…' he gasped. His voice was barely audible. 'F…fu…'

He never got to finish the sentence before his eyes glazed over and stopped moving.

Archer lowered his head to check the breathing, but he was gone. He turned to see the first police car arriving from the direction of the airport, lights and sirens still blaring as it skidded to a halt on the other side of the autobahn.

He stood up and put his hands in the air, not wanting to give any nervous cops an excuse to drop him. He saw Eva doing the same, thankfully not waving her ID around. He doubted it would make any difference right now, not with a dead man at his feet, a wrecked car and bullet casings everywhere.

He felt an adrenal tremor go through him as kept his hands high. *No threat here, officer*. The exhilaration of the fight had to be tempered now by common sense. No point in doing something stupid and getting himself shot.

No, he decided, as the two cops approached them cautiously, pistols raised and orders being shouted in German, all-in-all today was probably not such a great day at the office.

# 26

The holding cell they had put Archer in was small and airless, with a thin nylon-sheathed mattress on a cold concrete slab and a stainless steel toilet that reeked of piss.

He had walked a few laps of the cell, concentrating on his breathing, oxygenating his blood and getting his head together. Who knew what was coming next? Probably nothing good. He assessed himself as he slowly paced, checking himself for injuries. There were several minor nicks and scrapes from glass, a decent bump on his left knee that was starting to ache now the adrenaline was wearing off, and his ears were still ringing and made everything sound like he was underwater.

There was no stress reaction this time. At least, not yet.

He ran through the incident in his mind, over and over again. A few things stood out to him. They had been an organised hit team, well equipped and well informed. Experienced but not expert. A single man shouldn't have been able to fight them off, especially starting off unarmed. Five guys – or seven, counting the drivers – with weapons should have been easily able to take out four unarmed, unprepared and unsuspecting opponents. One guy should have been enough.

Archer stopped pacing and sat on the side of the cell bed. He wondered how it would have panned out had he not been there. A slaughter, no doubt. Or would they have taken a prisoner, a hostage? He doubted it. These guys had been playing for keeps.

He looked up as footsteps sounded outside. There was an electronic buzz, a rattle and the door slid open. A burly police officer looked in at him, then turned and spoke to somebody over his shoulder.

A nurse entered the cell and a second burly cop joined the other one in the doorway. They stood guard while the nurse tended to Archer's wounds, cleaning and patching the cuts to his hand where he'd cut himself on the makeshift dagger. He had other minor glass nicks which only required cleaning.

The nurse worked with silent efficiency, never making eye contact, and left as soon as she was done. One of the cops accompanied her out of the cells, while the other one stood and waited, looking down the corridor. Archer sat on the cot and waited. There was no point trying to engage with these guys. Finally, the big cop turned and gestured for Archer to get up.

'Come,' he said.

Archer followed him, his bare feet cold on the concrete floor. Another pair of cops waited there, both in dark suits, blank faces. Detectives, maybe. Here to interview the murderer. He gave them a courteous nod, and was surprised when they both nodded politely back.

They led him down the corridor, through another secure door, along another corridor and through another door. A short elevator ride down a couple of floors before the doors opened into a basement parking garage. A plain white van waited there with the engine running, the rear doors open to reveal dual cages for prisoners.

Archer was directed into the left cage where he sat on a steel bench against the internal wall with his knees pressing against the matching bench opposite.

The cage door was closed, then the rear doors, and the van moved off immediately, pausing for a gate to rattle open then moving up a ramp onto a street that sounded busy with vehicles.

He had no idea where he was going or with whom, and right now, it didn't seem like anyone was bothered to tell him. He couldn't make anything out through the tinted window in the rear door. He sat back and rested as best he could. It was maybe half an hour of driving through city traffic before he was aware of the van slowing, pausing, the rattle of a gate, then the van moved forward again and he sensed they were in another underground car park.

The van came to a stop and the engine died, and he heard muffled conversation through the wall. The door opened, then the cage, and two more men faced him. Both wore nondescript casuals and had the aura of soldiers about them.

He followed their silent directions, climbing down from the van to find himself in a sally port such as was found at police stations and prisons. He had the feeling this was neither. They took him to a pedestrian door in the corner, buzzed through and entered a long corridor with no windows or doors. He walked between them, their boots squeaking on the polished floor, to a door at the far end.

That led them into a lift lobby with doors off it. Eva stood holding one of the doors open, and Archer was escorted past her into a meeting room. He noted she had a small dressing over the cut to her forehead. Four people stood waiting at the front of the room, conversing in hushed tones.

They stopped and looked up when Archer entered.

Rawlins and Jessika, looking like they'd just stepped off a plane. Two men in dark suits, one late forties, the other a few years older, both tidy and unremarkable. Spooks.

'Come in,' the younger man said in accented English. 'Please, close the door Eva.'

She did as she was told and accompanied Archer to meet the small group. Introductions were made all round. The younger German, who was obviously in charge, was named Dieter. His older colleague was Ulrich.

Archer shook their hands and gave a nod to both Rawlins and

Jessika. She gave him a frosty glare and Rawlins ignored him. He mentally shrugged. It wasn't like they wouldn't have done the same in his shoes. He noticed the surreptitious look that Jessika gave Eva, sussing her out as the only other female in the room.

'Please, let us sit.' Dieter indicated for them to sit at the table.

Archer took the closest seat and found himself alone. The two Americans sat opposite him, Dieter took the head of the table with Ulrich to his right, and Eva moved around behind them to sit on his left. Archer rubbed his feet on the woollen carpet beneath the table. It was thick and warm against his bare skin.

'So,' Dieter began, 'I think we should begin by discussing the events of today...'

'With all due respect, Dieter,' Rawlins interrupted, leaning forward to jab a finger across the table at Archer. 'I think we should begin by finding out exactly how our friend here managed to turn up in your country – *without authority*, I might add – and ends up in a shootout on a major road, which is now all over the fucking,' he glanced at the two women – 'excuse my language, ladies, but which is now all over the fucking media. *That* is what I think we should be discussing, first and foremost.'

He sat back with his hands clasped in front of him, his point made. A vein was pounding in his forehead and his face was blotchy red.

Dieter smiled and nodded. 'Yes, thank you for those thoughts, Mr Rawlins. And that is certainly one of the points we will be discussing shortly. I think, however, it is important to remember, with *all due respect* my friend,' he smiled, smooth and comfortable, 'that this is a BfV debrief, not a CIA debrief, and we are in Berlin, not Langley. So we will all get our opportunity to speak, and we will all get our opportunity to listen. And right now, I am speaking.' He nodded again, his own point made.

Rawlins' jaw clamped shut and his face stayed blotchy. Archer couldn't help but admire the German. He certainly had some balls to speak to a senior Agency man like that. He himself didn't dare make eye contact with either of the Americans just yet.

Dieter turned towards Archer now.

'Just so we are all clear, Mr Archer, I am the head of Division 5 at the BfV. As such, I oversee all investigations into foreign operatives and terrorists. This has, in the last couple of years or so, included the actions of one Viktor Kozlowski. He is an American citizen and former member of the American military, who since his dishonourable discharge from the US Rangers has marketed himself in the private sector, what they call the security circuit. You know what I speak about?'

'I do.' He figured Dieter probably knew that already he'd spent time on the Circuit himself, and kept his mouth shut. He may like the German spook, but here was no point flapping his gums just yet.

'Yes.' Dieter nodded and smiled. 'I thought perhaps you would. So Viktor Kozlowski has worked in respectable private security roles, some less respectable paramilitary roles, and has been found in many not so nice parts of the world over the last twenty years or thereabouts.'

The room was silent while Dieter paused to gather his thoughts for a moment. Archer wondered if he could get a drink any time soon. His mouth tasted stale and sticky. A shower wouldn't have gone astray either.

'We also have reliable intelligence that he has been involved in arms dealing on a small to medium scale in various places to a diverse range of customers. Small arms mostly, supplying militant groups such as the Chechens, some African groups, you know the sort.'

Dieter made a steeple of his fingers and tapped the thumbs thoughtfully against his chin. He could have passed for a banker or a lawyer, Archer thought. His dark hair was brushed over and conservative, and his hands had probably never been near manual labour. Still, he had the aura of a powerful man.

'Of late we have been made aware that he has been involved with Islamic terrorists, both in training and in a sort of...' he struggled for the right word, and Eva jumped in.

'Mentoring, sir,' she said.

'Thank you, Eva. Yes, a sort of mentoring role.'

'None of this is exactly news, Dieter,' Rawlins interrupted. 'We are well aware of Kozlowski's affiliations.'

'And I appreciate that you are,' Dieter replied, looking across at his American compatriot with a cool expression, 'however, obviously, Mr Archer is not.'

'Does he need to be?' Rawlins retorted. 'He's not a part of this operation, and surely you'll be putting him on a plane the hell back to Australia quick smart, right?'

'I don't know if Australia would want him,' Ulrich interjected, his voice deep and gravelly.

'Well we sure as hell don't,' Rawlins grunted.

'Considering he is from New Zealand,' Ulrich finished, his hard gaze on Rawlins now.

The CIA man flinched as he realised his mistake and Archer smiled to himself. *How do you like them apples?*

'And geographical issues aside, I think that Mr Archer has actually made a very valuable contribution to this operation,' Dieter continued. 'His actions today undoubtedly saved the lives of two of our officers, for which we are of course extremely grateful.'

He paused to give Archer a solemn half-bow to convey his personal thanks.

'You will be pleased to know that Wagener is undergoing surgery, but is stable and his prognosis is good.'

Archer nodded. 'Pleased to hear it.'

'Look, we're all pleased your man is okay,' Rawlins said gruffly, 'but he wouldn't be where he is right now if Archer here hadn't been operating in your country without official sanction, right?'

'That is one way to look at it, yes,' Dieter agreed. He glanced down at the tablet in front of him, swiped it, and tapped something. The wall at the far end lit up and a head and shoulders passport-type photo appeared, filling the centre of the wall. 'Or we could look at it like this.'

Rawlins looked at him inquisitively. Archer focussed on the face, feeling a prickle of recognition. High back and sides and a few years younger, but he was a dead ringer for the guy Archer had shot earlier in the day.

'This is former US Army Ranger Brendan O'Keefe,' Dieter announced. 'Born and raised in Minnesota, he joined the Army from high school and served eight years before being dishonourably discharged. The reasons for that are not explicit, however given his activities since then, I believe it is safe to say he had criminal tendencies.'

Across the table from Archer, Rawlins and Jessika glanced quickly at each other. He sensed they could see what was coming as well as he could.

'He is the man killed by Mr Archer today near the airport,' Dieter stated, then raised a hand in apology. 'I meant to say, one of the men. He was the man who was shot. This is the other man, the one who was stabbed.' He brought a second image, this time of a younger man, also with a high and tight cut. He had sandy hair and an overbite. 'Former US Army Ranger Keith Thomson. Born and raised in Oregon. He served four years before leaving the Army. As I understand it he was charged with rape but was acquitted at trial.'

'Let me guess,' Archer said, feeling his heart thumping in his chest, 'they were both private contractors for Black Star.'

Dieter gave an appreciative nod and smile. 'Correct. Both currently on the payroll of Black Star International Security.'

Archer felt the familiar flutter in his gut at the mention of that company. Black Star contractors had killed a good friend of his back in Iraq. He had had his revenge some years later when he crossed paths with their crew in London, but the fire still burned.

Dieter didn't bat an eyelid. 'I understand you have had dealings with this organisation before, Mr Archer?'

Archer gave a curt nod, his gaze fixed on the two Americans opposite him. 'I have,' he grated. 'Tell me Rawlins, aren't Black Star one of the preferred contractors for the CIA? Are they still the thugs you hire to do your dirty work for you, the deniable work that's too dirty even for your own deniable operators?'

He could see Rawlins' complexion had paled significantly

beneath the blotchiness, and he was gulping like a man starved of oxygen.

'Even after the human rights abuses, and the myriad of other allegations from reputable sources?' He could see a sheen of sweat had broken out on Rawlins' forehead now. Jessika was giving him daggers across the table. He ignored her and pressed harder. 'Are they still in a commercial relationship with your agency, Rawlins, or are we missing something here?'

He sat back now and waited. The ball was firmly in Rawlins' court and everybody knew it. And it was going to have to be a hell of a return volley to save this match.

Rawlins shook his head weakly. All his bluster was now gone and he was struggling to stay afloat.

'I had no idea, honest to God, man,' he managed, '*we* had no idea.' He looked to his colleague for support, desperate for a hand. 'The Agency does have a relationship with various private contractors, just as many other agencies do, including both of yours... but... as to whether that's a current relationship, I'd have to get back to you...'

'Cut the bullshit, Rawlins,' Archer snapped. 'You're high enough up the food chain to know whose boots you're putting on the ground these days. Don't try the old "I can neither confirm nor deny" bollocks. I'll bet the house on Black Star still being one of those outfits. The real question is, what were they doing here in Germany and what did the CIA know about that?'

Rawlins was squirming and Archer almost felt sorry for him. Almost.

There was a tense silence as Rawlins scrabbled for answers. You could almost hear the cogs ticking in his brain, and the vein was fit to explode in his forehead. Finally Jessika came to his rescue.

'Gentlemen,' she said smoothly, looking between Archer and Dieter, 'perhaps we could stop the finger pointing and get to the heart of the matter together. There's no point in us having a pissing contest about this now, is there? The important thing is that we're all on the same side here. We can work through this to a resolution that suits all parties. Am I right?'

Archer flicked a glance to Dieter, Ulrich and Eva. All three of them were watching her with stony expressions. The Germans did a good poker face. He looked back to Jessika, who had her eyes on him with a conciliatory – almost pleading – look. No doubt she thought she could work him because of their recent history together. Well, he decided, she was going to have to work for it. She hadn't been that earth-shattering.

'Of course,' he said, 'that will require a fair shot of honesty. "I don't know" just doesn't cut it.'

'Naturally,' she agreed. She gave a sly smile, and for the first time he noticed her teeth, small and sharp in a smile that lacked any real warmth or humour. 'That will require honesty on all parts, won't it Mr Archer? So perhaps you could start with explaining why you were operating in Germany without authority?'

Fair call, he figured. She had him there. He smiled in return, maintaining his composure and appearing unruffled.

'Obviously I was chasing a lead on our hijackers. As we all do from time to time, I flew under the radar, so to speak, and perhaps that is something that could have been handled better. For that, I apologise to my friends at the BfV.'

Dieter nodded appreciatively. '*Danke schon.*'

'So that's my end.' Archer cocked his head inquisitively. 'But I'm still interested to know about Black Star.'

Jessika had clearly taken the reins from her boss for now, and she didn't bat an eyelid.

'The CIA had no knowledge of that organisation operating in Germany, nor did we authorise them, or anyone else, to act against any members of either of your agencies.' She looked pointedly from Archer to Dieter. 'Are we clear on that now? Can we move on?'

His instincts told him not to believe her, but there seemed little point in pushing the issue right now. Besides, it was Dieter's show and he could make the call on that. Dieter did, smoothly moving on.

'I think our focus right now needs to be on how this group of mercenaries got into Germany, where they are now, and who sent them.' He turned to Ulrich. 'We have no further updates on the whereabouts of the other gunmen, yes?'

Ulrich shook his head. 'None,' he said. 'Both cars were abandoned nearby, managing to avoid police patrols, and were set fire to. They are being examined, however I have much doubt as to what we may find from them. They were both found to be stolen.'

'I propose that we conclude this meeting,' Dieter said, 'and we convene perhaps tomorrow morning, unless something urgent requires us to meet in the meantime.'

'Just before we do,' Archer interjected, 'have you got a picture of this Kozlowski character handy?'

Rawlins and Jessika paused, half out of their seats already, and Jessika gave a look of displeasure. 'Can't we move on from that?' she said irritably. 'There's been enough finger pointing for one day already.'

'It is no problem.' Dieter tapped at his tablet. 'My apologies, Mr Archer, I forget you are somewhat, how do you say...behind the eight ball?'

'Thank you.' Archer nodded his appreciation and glanced round to the screen.

The photo was a surveillance shot, probably from a covert camera, outside some kind of a café or restaurant. The shot was front on from the waist up. The man was tall and lean, dark hair swept back, a cigarette half way to his mouth.

It was the same man he'd seen in Croatia, the one whose photo he'd got from Semenov.

So this was Viktor Kozlowski. The mastermind, the terrorist.

Archer looked away, knowing he would not forget the image and knowing he was right. He met Dieter's gaze. The German was looking at him blandly, giving nothing away. He could feel Rawlins' and Jessika's eyes on him, but he ignored them. He felt no inclination at all to share with them right now.

'Thanks,' Archer said.

Dieter gave a short nod and killed the screen. The room was

silent. Dieter nodded to himself, as if mulling something over in his head. 'Yes,' he murmured, 'interesting.'

He glanced to Ulrich, who produced three cell phones from his jacket pocket. 'We would very much like to keep in touch with you during your stay here in Berlin, so please keep your phone on you at all times.' He smiled warmly. 'This is a fast-moving situation and we must be on top of our game like the true professionals we are, yes?'

Ulrich slid a phone across the table to each of the visitors. They were cheap pay-as-you-go handsets and Archer had no doubt they were also fitted with tracking devices. He dropped the phone into his pocket.

'I take it that I'm no longer a guest of the *Landespolizei*?' he enquired.

'Of course, of course. That was merely a precaution until we could establish what had taken place.' Dieter gave the warm smile again. He really was a disarming character, but Archer was not fooled. He had no doubt the man was as ruthless and smart as they came. 'We have made arrangements for your temporary accommodation at a nearby hotel, and Eva will take you there shortly.'

Eva caught his eye. 'Perhaps we could buy some new shoes on the way?' she suggested pointedly.

## 27

The HIO Berlin Ku'damm hotel was right next to an underground station and handy to a main shopping area.

A Superior Loft had been reserved for Archer, and he was checked in quickly and efficiently by staff who spoke excellent English. He appreciated the quality of the accommodation, which seemed typical of the courtesy the Germans were extending to him, and wondered how long he would be staying in the city.

As soon as he had dropped his bag in his suite he stripped off his clothes and stepped into a hot shower. As he stood under the jets and let the goodness soak into his tired muscles, his mind turned to Viktor Kozlowski. He had no doubt that he was the man from Croatia, the Boss. He also now knew that the Americans had known all along who he was, so the question was; *why didn't they tell us*? Ingoe or one of his boffins had circulated the photo Archer had recovered from Semenov, presumable at least to the Five Eyes partners if not wider still, yet nothing had come back. Maybe it was simply a time delay issue and nothing more. Maybe he was just tired and wound tight and needed to stop seeing conspiracies where there were none.

Twenty minutes of soaking and scrubbing had his skin glowing pink and he took the time to have a shave and brush his teeth, before removing the plastic bag from the small waste bin and bundling all his dirtied clothes into it.

He dressed in jeans, casual shoes and a loose shirt, pocketed his wallet, iPhone and burn phone – the BfV had taken his passport – and made his way down to the lobby. He exited onto a busy street and joined the evening hustle of workers making their way home, late shoppers and the dining out crowd.

He didn't spot any watchers as he made his way to a nearby restaurant, but had no doubt they were there. Even though he would be tracked by the burn phone, it made sense to keep eyes on any known foreign intelligence officers, regardless of whether they were friend or foe. It would be easy enough to ditch the phone or slip it to an unsuspecting passer-by and send the BfV on an electronic wild goose chase.

Selecting an eatery at random, Archer took a seat at a window table and ordered a stein of pilsner, leaving it to the waiter to pick a brew. To his mind it didn't matter – German beer was a cut above the rest of the world, so whatever he got would be good. With his back to the wall he had a clear view of the street in one direction and scanned the people going by, assessing body language more so than actual faces.

He didn't expect to actually recognise anyone, but often the body language or behaviour of a watcher or threat gave them away before anything else. The hesitation or over-confidence, an unnatural way of moving, unnecessary stiffness or exaggerated casualness; all these things were clues to the observer that someone may not be who they purported to be.

Archer made no attempt to hide his interest in the world going by. Any watchers would expect it anyway, and to the casual observer he was simply a tourist on his own, people-watching as people on their own often did.

He had touched base with Ingoe earlier via his iPhone, and was expecting an update from him later. For now, he was a free agent with money in his pocket and an empty stomach.

His beer arrived, a hefty frosted stein with a decent head, and the waiter carefully placed it on a coaster before him.

'*Danke*,' he said, sliding it closer and accepting a dinner menu from the man.

'Make that two, *bitte*,' Jessika interjected as she appeared from behind the waiter.

Archer cocked an eyebrow as he raised the stein to his lips. It was cold and strong and he savoured the first draught.

'Surprised to see me?' Jessika smirked as she took the chair opposite him.

'Not at all,' he replied coolly, 'just that it took you so long.'

'So is this your usual?' she enquired, lifting the menu for an assessment.

Archer smiled to himself. *She thinks I have ties to Berlin. The CIA want to know why the Germans seem to be favouring me.*

'Not really,' he said, remaining non-committal. He took another pull on his beer. 'I do like their pilsner though.'

The waiter brought her drink and she clinked steins with Archer before taking a long, appreciative drink.

'Ahh,' she purred, putting the stein down. 'Fantastic.' She licked her lips and glanced back to the menu. 'So, what're we having?'

'Well, I *was* going to have a quiet meal and go to bed early,' he replied, pointedly enough to make her pull a sad face.

'Ohh, am I interrupting your quiet time?' she mocked him. 'I'm sorry, how rude of me. I thought you would like some company after your hard day at the office.'

Archer frowned. He didn't like being mocked, and he didn't appreciate her attitude. He was tired and hungry and had a million thoughts buzzing through his head. The last thing he wanted right now was someone else digging for information from him.

'It's not been what I would call a standard day at the office,' he said stiffly, sounding more pissed off than he had intended.

Jessika grinned wickedly. 'Well, you could still get to bed early if you wanted,' she said, with a glint in her eye. He noticed again the greenness of her eyes; they were unnaturally light, so pale they were almost grey, as if she were wearing coloured contacts. It was unsettling to hold her gaze for too long.

Archer smiled tiredly. 'Thanks,' he said, 'but I really just want to unwind and get my head down.'

There was an awkward silence and he could tell she was offended.

'How's your boss feeling now?' he said, trying for a distraction. 'He got a bit bruised today, didn't he?'

Jessika pursed her lips. 'Rawlins? He's fine. He's had worse from better than those guys.' Her eyes met his. 'Our kraut friends certainly seem to like you though, Craig. Especially that little bit of fluff. She's got her eye on you, I know it.'

Archer gave a dismissive snort and picked up his stein. 'I doubt it,' he said. 'They're too busy for any of that sort of carry-on, I'd suggest.'

'So what about you, Craig?' She fixed him with a direct gaze, challenging.

'What about me?'

'Would you?'

He frowned. 'Would I what?'

'The little bit of kraut fluff. Would you?'

His frown turned to a scowl. 'Would I bed her?' he said irritably. 'It's none of your damn business if I would or not, Jessika.'

'No no no.' She leaned forward, her eyes still locked intensely on his. 'Not would you bed her.' She leaned closer still, lowering her voice. 'Would you fuck her, Craig? Would you fuck her hard like you fucked me? Would you fuck that little kraut bitch, Craig?'

Archer was far from being a prude, but he was reviled by her crassness. He sat back to distance himself from her, his mind whirring. The only conclusion he could come to was that she had been drinking before she ever got to the restaurant.

'I've had enough of this,' he said firmly. 'I don't appreciate your comments, and I don't have to explain myself to you. This is over.'

He went to stand but she beat him to it.

'So that's it?' Jessika pouted, raising her voice. 'Am I getting the brush-off now? So it was okay when you wanted something from me, and now I'm yesterday's news?'

A few of the diners turned to look, and Archer felt his cheeks begin to burn. He was too tired for games and he resented her even being there. The waiter started to come towards them.

'Well fuck you, buddy.' Jessika snatched her stein off the table and hurled the contents of it at him.

Archer was too stunned to react in time and took the full load front-on. Cold beer ran down his face and he could taste it on his lips.

'See how you like that, asshole.' Jessika banged the heavy stein back onto the table and stormed out, crashing through the door and out to the footpath. He watched her stride away, barging past other pedestrians.

'Sir?' The waiter was hovering nervously nearby.

Archer turned to him, grabbing a napkin to wipe his face. 'Sorry about that mate.' He dug out his wallet and produced enough notes to cover the drinks plus a decent tip.

'*Danke*, sir.'

Archer gave him a rueful smile and wiped at his shirtfront. '*Frauleins*, huh? Crazy.'

The waiter laughed nervously. '*Ja, ja*. Crazy.'

Archer made for the door. He had no idea what had set her off so suddenly, and didn't really care. His hair and clothes were soaked. He needed to shower and change, and it would have to be room service for dinner instead.

*So much for a quiet night.*

# 28

The hotel restaurant was busy with guests tucking in before checking out, but Archer managed to find himself a small table in the corner. From there he could watch the door and it was also handy to the beverages.

He filled a bowl with fruit and muesli, topped it with milk and yoghurt, poured himself a strong coffee and headed back to his table. His sleep had been broken, constantly interrupted by dreams of Jessika and her performance last night. The whole thing confused him and there was a constant prickle at the back of his mind. Something was there, niggling him like a faint itch that wouldn't go away.

He shook his head and decided to focus on fuelling the engine for now. He'd worked out in his room this morning, a hard half hour of body-weight exercises and stretches that had left his heart pumping and his senses singing, and now his body was craving fuel.

As he started to sit he became aware of someone approaching the table. He paused, mentally bracing himself for another crazy onslaught from Jessika, but the new arrival was an entirely different proposal altogether.

Eva was wearing a sombre charcoal business suit over a snow-white blouse. The ruffled front opened just enough to hint at what lay beneath. She gave him a knowing smile as she slid into the other chair and put her bag down beside her. 'Don't worry,' she said, 'I will keep my drinks to myself.'

Archer smiled ruefully, not surprised that he'd been watched. He took the time to load his spoon before speaking. 'All part of the service?' he inquired. He took a mouthful of muesli, chewing slowly.

'We like to ensure our guests are safe.' Eva caught the eye of a lurking waitress and asked for a coffee.

'Well, it was nothing a shower and a change of clothes couldn't fix.' He set his spoon down and waited while her coffee was delivered.

'*Danke*.' The waitress moved off again and Eva took a tentative sip. It seemed to meet with her approval, and she took a decent shot.

The wound dressing on her forehead had been replaced by well-applied concealer, leaving no hint of the injury she had received in the highway gunfight.

Archer noticed how her nose crinkled when she drank. She was certainly an attractive woman, and he wondered if this visit was purely business, or whether he wasn't just kidding himself. A girl like this would have men fawning all over her. He sipped his own coffee. Best he keep things professional. For all he knew, the Increment guys had blabbed about his relationship with Sarah, and he would have questions to answer once this was all over.

'So what's the plan today then?' he asked.

Eva put her cup down and considered her response. 'You will need to come to a briefing,' she said. 'This morning. There have been some developments which you need to be aware of.'

'Okay.' Archer finished his bowl and pushed it aside. 'What time?'

'Now.' Eva checked her watch. 'You will have time to return to your room and freshen up. I will wait for you in the lobby and take you there.'

Archer downed his coffee, the hot liquid shocking his teeth after the cold cereal. He glanced at her as he set the cup down. She looked amused.

'What? Do I have food on my face?'

'No, not at all. Have you had enough to eat? We can have a few minutes if you like.'

He paused, and she let out a short laugh. He felt his cheeks flush as she quickly suppressed her laugh.

'I am sorry,' she chuckled. 'I was only kidding, but you were serious. You actually thought about it.'

Archer didn't think it was that funny, but her amusement at her own joke appealed to him and he felt himself smiling. 'Eating's a serious business,' he said. 'I'm not here to fuck ducks.'

Eva paused mid-chortle and her brow creased quizzically. She looked at him with genuine confusion. 'Why would you do that to a duck?'

He grinned self-consciously. 'Sorry, it's a colloquialism. It means you're not here to muck around, to waste time.'

'Oh.' She nodded slowly, staring at him as if not quite convinced by the explanation. 'So you don't...you know...have...'

'No,' he said. 'Absolutely not. Well...' he paused, deadpan. 'Not for a while.'

Eva hesitated, unsure whether to laugh or not. Archer grinned and stood. 'I'll see you in the lobby shortly.'

She let out a chuckle again and shook her head as she got out her phone. 'You are a very unusual man, Mr Archer,' she said.

'You just need to get to know me.'

Eva arched an eyebrow at him. 'Perhaps I do,' she said.

Archer wondered if he should reconsider his earlier stance on professional relationships. Right now, it was time to get ready for another exciting day of briefings.

Archer and Eva were the last to arrive at the briefing, and he sensed an atmosphere as soon as he walked in.

Rawlins was in the same seat he'd had previously, but the chair beside him was empty. The next two on that side of the table were filled by the two SOG guys he'd met at LAX – EJ and Rico. Dieter and Ulrich were at the head of the table. All three intelligence men looked as if they were preparing for a funeral.

Eva shut the door and took a seat at Dieter's end of the table.

Archer exchanged nods with the two operators as he sat down across from them. They were still in casual hiking gear, tanned and bearded. It never seemed to bother the Yanks how obvious they looked. He wondered if they even knew.

'Good morning everybody,' Dieter began, 'and thank you all for coming. We have some matters of extremely high importance to discuss today, and I fear the issues facing us are potentially... upsetting for some.'

Archer noted Rawlins' look of distaste. His two sidekicks remained as impassive as ever.

'The first point we need to acknowledge is that our friend Jessika is no longer with us,' Dieter continued, looking at each of them in turn. 'She has returned to the United States at, ahhh, short notice.'

There was a pregnant pause and Archer noted that the Germans all looked to Rawlins, as if expecting him to fill the void. He didn't, and after a moment, Dieter moved on smoothly.

'And so, I appreciate that time is important to all of us, so let us get straight to the point of our meeting today.' He glanced down at his tablet and swiped up a head shot onto the big screen. It was another shot of Viktor Kozlowski, but an earlier image than the one Archer had previously seen. This was a US military ID photo, showing Kozlowski maybe twenty-odd years ago. He looked young, eager and hard. He had the dead eyes of a cold-blooded killer.

Dieter opened his mouth to speak, but Rawlins cut in.

'Let me just jump in there, Dieter,' he said. 'The point of us meeting today is to lay some facts on the table. Facts already known to my organisation, facts you have just recently become aware of, and which I'm guessing you want to share with the group.' His tone was harsh and patronising, and he clearly intended to bulldoze over whatever was coming. 'I don't believe this information needs to be spread any further than it already has been, and I take great issue with being ambushed like this.'

Dieter's tone was calm and even, but carried with it an icy authority that left no room for misunderstandings.

'Mr Rawlins, I appreciate your position, however this is not a matter for negotiation.' Rawlins went to cut in again and Dieter held up a hand, silencing him like a child. 'I will thank you to not interrupt. This intelligence is of extreme importance to the matter we are currently dealing with, and our colleagues need to know. If that causes inconvenience for you or your organisation, then I must apologise, however that is a side issue I cannot help with.'

Order restored, Rawlins looked like a dog that had been kicked. Archer could see he was raging inside but now knew better than to push it with the little German. He made eye contact across the table with EJ, who stared back at him blankly. It was impossible to tell whether he was smiling beneath the beard.

'So, let's continue. We know Viktor Kozlowski has been a mercenary, arms supplier and trainer to various target groups over a long period of time. What we have only just learned, however, is that he has been, and I believe still is – please correct me if I am wrong, Mr Rawlins – a covert source for the CIA, also for a long period of time.'

Dieter paused and a stunned silence fell over the room. Archer bit his lip to prevent his mouth from falling open. Eva looked from Dieter to Rawlins to Archer, and he could see the shock in her eyes. This was as much news to her as it was to him.

Archer slowly turned and looked across at Rawlins. The CIA man stared back belligerently. A vein was pounding in his forehead.

'A source,' Archer said quietly.

Rawlins glared. 'What?' he barked. 'You want me to apologise? Ain't gonna happen, Archer. This had the highest clearance, way above your paygrade.'

'I'm not looking for an apology,' Archer replied evenly, 'and I couldn't care less who authorised it. That horse has bolted. The question is, what are you gunna do about it now?'

'I don't have to answer to you, son.' Rawlins had obviously decided that the best form of defence right now was to bully his way out. 'This has nothing to do with you.'

'Nothing to do with me?' Archer fought the urge to reach over and slap him. 'I think it has everything to do with me, actually. Considering it was me and my team that prevented a hijacked plane being crashed into LAX and killing thousands, yeah, I think it has everything to do with me.'

He glanced sideways, registering the surprise on the Germans' faces.

'Yeah, don't believe the spin from these clowns,' he continued. 'While they were busy funding and enabling the mastermind, we were busy saving lives for them. Of course, they were happy to take the credit afterwards.'

'Time to step back, Archer,' Rawlins snarled. 'Hey, I admit Kozlowski appears to have gone off the reservation right now, but we can get him back. He's been an extremely valuable source for us, and he will continue to be. The list of arms dealers and terrorists he's helped us take down is more impressive than anything you'll ever do in your goddamn life, son.' He leaned forward so there was no misunderstanding. 'So back the fuck off.'

Rawlins sat back again and looked to Dieter.

'I apologise for that, Dieter, but some things need to be said. *We* will get this situation back under control by the end of the day, I can assure you of that.'

'Where is your colleague Jessika?' Ulrich rumbled, his hands folded in front of him as if he were praying. Perhaps he was. Divine intervention would have been quite welcome right about now.

'She's returned to the States, as the man said,' Rawlins replied, indicating towards Dieter.

'Why?' Ulrich's voice was deep and emotionless.

Rawlins didn't bat an eyelid. 'Operational requirements,' he said.

'She's his handler, isn't she?' Archer interrupted. 'You've sent her off to try and get a lead back on the dog.'

'What my staff do is no concern of yours, Archer,' Rawlins retorted. 'But if it makes you feel any better, she happens to be one of the best agent handlers in the business.'

'I'm sure,' Eva interjected. 'She's done a great job so far.'

Rawlins visibly held back, fighting to retain some semblance of control. 'Like I say, the list of targets he has fed us is extremely impressive, and that's all down to her good work.'

Archer shook his head in amazement and Rawlins looked at him, ready to flare up again. Archer didn't keep him waiting; he wanted this all out in the open. The lying and secret-keeping was doing his head in.

'Don't you get it? He's played you. You thought you were calling the shots, but you were never in control. He manipulated you guys from the start, pulling your strings and making you dance like a bunch of puppets. Everything he gave you was something he was happy to give up – this was never about patriotism for him; it was business. Plain and simple economics. You took out his competition for him.'

'Of course we did,' Rawlins growled, his face dark, 'that's a pretty standard motivation for sources, Archer.' He gave a derisive snort. 'Maybe if you spent more time in the intelligence scene and less time playing fuckin' soldiers, you'd know these things.'

Archer eyed him coldly. 'And maybe if you'd spent less time with your head up your arse, Rawlins, you'd see he's fucked you over. You guys have helped create one of the biggest terrorists in the world. I can't believe you don't see that.'

Rawlins fixed him with a steely glare. 'Everything we do, son, is for the greater good. The intelligence that source has given us has helped take down bad guys the world over. You get me? Sometimes, you gotta lie down with dogs to get the job done.'

'Yeah?' Archer replied. 'Well mate, you're waking up with fuckin' fleas. Clearly I'm not going to change your mind, so you do what you do, and I'll go do the right thing.' He stood and turned towards the door. 'Thanks for the invite, Dieter, but I don't think we're going to get anywhere here.' His hand was on the door handle when Rawlins stopped him.

'The right thing?' the CIA man said. 'And what exactly is that, son?'

Archer turned and fixed him with a steely glare. 'It's what needs to be done with every rabid dog,' he replied. 'You put the bastard down.'

# 29

Jed Ingoe wasn't known for looking chirpy at the best of times, but today was a bad day even for him. His face was drawn and tired, and Archer wondered how much sleep he'd had in the last few days.

He didn't ask – Ingoe would just tell him sleep was for babies and retired folk.

They were Facetiming while Archer paced the footpaths, his ear buds in to keep the conversation at least semi-confidential. After the earlier revelation, he strongly suspected the CIA would have his hotel room wired up.

'We got that heads-up just before your briefing,' Ingoe said, 'didn't have time to get hold of you before you went in.'

'From the Germans?' Archer turned down a side street.

'No, from Five.' Ingoe smirked. 'In fact, it was from your friend there.'

'Which one would that be?' Archer tried for innocent but failed.

'The most recent one. They'd apparently just got the word from a US agency – not Langley.'

Archer raised his eyebrows but said nothing. It wasn't unusual for the American agencies to bicker among themselves, and obviously somebody had decided to let this particular cat out of the bag. His money was on the FBI or DIA, but it could have even been an internal leak.

'And obviously the good ol' boys didn't want us to know. Who told the Germans?'

'Don't know. Sarah didn't know either, she's going to do some digging on that. But in the meantime, she's come up with something else of interest.' Ingoe's tone lost any hint of joviality – not that he'd been rolling in it to start with. 'Apparently Jessika never turned up back Stateside.'

Archer frowned, pausing outside an ugly brown stone building with an iron fence around it. He leaned against the fence while he talked. 'As in she's lost in transit or...'

'She never got on her flight. Five have confirmed through Six that she was booked, using her own passport, but she never turned up.'

Archer mulled that over for a moment. 'So the Yanks've redirected her somewhere, and just don't want to tell us, or what?'

'Nope. Apparently the shit's hit the fan and they're like a bunch of headless chooks right now. They believe she's been snatched and they're pulling in resources to find her.'

'Nice of them to share the love,' Archer mused. 'So they think Kozlowski's grabbed her, some kind of revenge thing?'

'It would seem he's the obvious candidate, yeah.' Ingoe's attention was attracted by somebody off screen, and he nodded before looking back to the camera. 'Sounds like something's happening. Gotta go, I'll be in touch.'

Ingoe killed the connection and the screen went blank. Archer unplugged his ears and tucked everything into his pocket. He pushed off the iron railings and rubbed his face. So much was going on that his head hurt. He didn't know who or what to believe right now, so the best thing to do was get a coffee.

He glanced at the building he'd stopped outside, recognising it from his tour. It was a former Stasi base, used for interrogating and torturing enemies of the state. He smiled wryly to himself. Somehow it seemed appropriate.

WITH NOTHING else to do right now, Archer returned to his hotel. He tried calling Eva on the burn phone, to no avail.

There was a small article in the news about a violent street fight in Prague that had left one man dead and two badly injured. Police were investigating possible organised crime links to this, and speculated that it was a drug deal gone sour.

There was no mention of the dead body of a Russian man being found in his apartment, but knowing who he was, they would be keeping that one under wraps. There would be little chance, and probably even less will, to solve that particular incident.

He hated this part of a mission, waiting around for something to happen. He had nothing to work on himself right now, no persons of interest to hunt down, no surveillance to carry out, not even some tedious CCTV to review. What he wouldn't give for something to do other than pace his room.

Finally, bored with his own company after an hour of stewing, Archer went downstairs to the bar and ate lunch by himself at a corner table. He chased a hefty piece of steak and kidney pie and vegetables with a large schooner of ice-cold pilsner. *Fuck it* – if he had to wait around, he may as well dull the pain.

The beer was gone before he knew it, and he thought hard about another one before common sense got the better of him. It wouldn't be a good look to be dispatched by Ingoe to a task when he was half cut.

He charged the meal to his room and had just arrived back there when his burn phone bleeped with an incoming message.

*We have a task. Pick you up in the lobby in five minutes. Eva.*

Archer replied with a thumbs up before deleting the messages. He took a few minutes to brush his teeth and wash his face, running his fingers through his hair as he thought about the German intelligence officer.

He couldn't deny an attraction there, and he pondered whether he'd be able to make something out of it once this job was over. His luck with women had not been memorable lately, even though he wasn't looking for anything serious. He wondered what it would be like to come to home to the same face every night. Was it something he could stand, or would it bore him into an early grave? He didn't know, and maybe that was the problem. He just didn't know what he wanted.

It was a dilemma when dealing with foreign agencies. How far did you take it? There were plenty of desirable women out there, and he had no doubt that the age-old "honey trap" was still in use, much as he had used on Jessika back in LA.

Perhaps Eva was playing that game as well. He had no idea, but he couldn't deny there was interest there, and it seemed to be mutual.

Putting that thought aside, he focussed back on the task at hand. What exactly the hell had happened to Jessika, anyway? If she'd been snatched by Kozlowski, what was the end game for that move? Death? Interrogation? Negotiation?

There were plenty of options, and a spook from one of the big agencies would always fetch top dollar on the open market, but it was also a hell of a big move. He had no doubt that the place would be buzzing with activity by now. Intelligence officers and black-ops guys would be all over it like flies on shit. This wasn't Baghdad or Kabul; there were limited places you could hide a kidnap victim without attracting attention.

Despite his misgivings about her personally, he sincerely hoped she wouldn't be the star of an orange jumpsuit decapitation video. Nobody deserved that. Hopefully there would soon be a ransom demand of some sort, and they would have something to work with.

Either that, or she turned up after being on a bender and ending up in the wrong bed.

He was still mulling that over while he waited for the lift.

The doors slid open and he stepped in, clocking the presence of a uniformed porter with a tall baggage trolley. A couple of garment bags hung from the rack and on the bottom tray was what appeared to be a large empty sack of some sort.

Archer stepped inside, squeezing against the wall around the trolley and gave the porter a quick glance. He was tall and athletic, and was already hitting the button for Basement.

'Ground, please,' Archer said.

The porter ignored him but turned quickly as the doors slid shut. He brought a pistol up in his right hand and fired from the hip before Archer even realised what was happening.

The dart hit him in the left thigh and he felt an immediate burst of pain. The luggage trolley was rammed against his shins, locking him against the wall as he tried to fight back, but it was so difficult.

His limbs felt heavy and uncoordinated, his vision was shifting like he'd sunk too many pints, and the porter was moving from side to side, joined by a friend, then another and another. Archer tried to lurch forward and grab him but his knees buckled and he fell face-first onto the tray of the trolley. He felt soft material against his cheek and could hear his own breathing in his ears, heavy and laboured. He knew he was in serious trouble here but all he wanted to do was go to sleep, so that's what he did.

The porter tucked away the tranquillizer gun, hit the Stop button on the control panel, and set to work. Within a minute he had Archer's limp form bundled into the sack, wrists and ankles secured, zipped up and lying on the tray like a piece of luggage.

He hit Stop again and the lift began its descent. The doors opened at Basement and two men stood there waiting. Unlike him they were clad in black utility kit. A plain white box truck idled nearby, the decals on the side panels identifying it as a fleet vehicle for a local delivery service.

The back was up and it took the two men in black another minute to lift Archer up and into the truck. They climbed up and manhandled him further into the cargo space, leaving him lying near a second similar package.

The porter abandoned his uniform jacket and the luggage trolley, and got behind the wheel of the truck. The other two men jumped down and secured the roller door before one of them banged on the back of the cab with a fist.

The truck moved towards the exit.

# 30

When Archer came to, the first thing he became aware of was an overwhelming urge to vomit.

He was rolling with the movement of the truck, every bump and sway impacting straight through the hard wooden floor. He was in darkness, like he was rolled up in a sleeping bag with the hood pulled down, and it was stiflingly claustrophobic.

His stomach was churning and he could feel it rising, pushing up through his diaphragm, his throat getting tighter with every short breath he took. He immediately regretted the large schooner with lunch.

His wrists and ankles were bound tight and he could feel cable ties biting into the flesh. He swallowed hard, forcing himself to get control. Things had obviously gone very bad and he needed to grip it fast.

He swallowed again, licking his parched lips with a tongue made of steel wool. He slowed his breathing, calming himself and trying to tune into his surroundings. His head was thumping like a bad Saturday morning.

He heard muffled sounds from somewhere beside him, to his front. He listened harder. Definitely a person, very muffled though, so presumably another prisoner who was also cuffed and stuffed. He lifted his knees and pushed out with his feet, finding a soft form right beside him. His touch met with a grunt and he pushed again, trying to provoke a reaction of some sort. It would be handy to know who else was there – friend or foe.

The reaction he got was a savage burst of swearing in German that he barely understand, accompanied by a furious thrashing. There was no mistaking the intent of the words though, or the voice.

'Hello?' he tried. He swallowed, trying to wet his scratchy throat before trying again. 'Eva?'

The other figure stopped thrashing and went silent.

'Are you okay?'

Her response was unintelligible. He wriggled over closer, bumping his head against hers and making her squeal with pain.

'Sorry. Are you hurt?'

'Aside from you head butting me?' she retorted sharply. 'I think I am okay, yes.' There was a pause. 'I was drugged with a hypodermic needle.'

'Same here. Who are they?'

'I don't know. I never saw a face.'

It occurred to Archer that they may well have a guard silently watching them, but he couldn't hear or sense anyone else in the back of the truck. It sounded echoic, as if the cargo hold was empty aside from them.

'Can you move at all?'

'No. I have tried. I have plastic cuffs on my hands and feet.'

Archer strained against his bonds, but all he managed to do was cut into his flesh even deeper. He knew that if these were proper nylon restraints as utilised by military and police, there was little chance of him breaking them. Had they been the standard plastic ties used by gardeners all over the world to guide their prize roses, he would have been free in minutes.

He relaxed his arms and shoulders and lay on his side, his head nudging against Eva's. He could smell her perfume, a pleasant counter to the musty bag over his head.

'What are we going to do?' Eva whispered. He could hear the undercurrent of fear in her voice.

'No point busting a gut right now,' he replied. 'We need to wait and see where we end up.'

'We will end up in a hole in the ground, I think.'

'Not if we can help it.' He angled his head, trying to get closer to her ear. 'Conserve your strength and get your head space right. These bastards aren't going to win, Eva. We will get through this, right?'

'Of course.' She sounded more determined now. 'We are the good guys. We must win.'

He smiled to himself. 'That's right. And if things kick off, just stay close to me and follow my lead.'

'Of course.' She paused. 'You certainly have some strange sayings where you come from. "Bust a gut." "Fuck a duck." I have not heard these sayings before.'

Archer chuckled. 'It's an isolation thing,' he said. 'Living down the arse-end of the world makes you a bit different.'

They settled into a comfortable silence, rocking with the movement of the truck, their heads nudging together. Archer estimated it was another half hour before the truck slowed right down, turned to his left and began up a bumpy track.

It stopped again shortly and he heard voices outside, too muffled to make anything out. The truck swung around and stopped, the engine cutting out.

Wherever they were, they had reached their destination.

THE REAR DOOR of the truck rolled up and Archer heard and felt someone climb into the cargo area.

There was no talking, just hands grabbing him roughly and dragging him by the feet to the back. Without pause, he was dumped unceremoniously off the back of the truck and landed with a thump on an unforgiving patch of bare dirt.

He was still trying to catch his breath when there was another thump beside him and he heard a squeal of pain.

Hands grabbed him and dragged him by his feet across dirt onto gravel. He was face down and tried to keep his head up off the ground. The gravel was sharp and rough through the bag and his shirtfront, grazing at the skin beneath. They reached a doorstep which he was dragged over, his chin bouncing off the ground, then it was down a hallway of some sort. He could feel rough bare boards beneath him.

Finally they stopped and dropped him to the floor. The bag was unzipped and the next thing he saw was the muzzle of a pistol in his face. It was so close he couldn't focus on the face behind it.

'You're going to untie and move. Any stupid moves and I shoot you fuckin' kneecaps. Un'stand?' The voice was harsh and had some kind of African accent.

'Uh-huh.'

The gun stayed in his face while he was rolled on his side and a knife sliced his bonds. He was hauled to his feet, with the pistol tracking him constantly. Two guys handled him while another two stood over Eva, waiting their turn.

They re-secured Archer's hands in front of him, the plastic cables tight enough to cut off the circulation. At least things were a bit more civilised if they were going to keep him tied to the front, he reasoned.

His relief was short lived however, when one of the men stepped over to the wall and lowered a pulley from the ceiling. A large karabiner was attached to the end of a rope that ran through a bolt in the ceiling and over to a hook on the wall. The karabiner was clipped through Archer's wrist ties and his arms were quickly jerked up above his head.

It was then that he realised that the room had a high stud, and as the two guys hauled on the rope he was lifted off his feet until he dangled half a metre or so from the floor. His wrists felt like they were being sliced open with his entire body weight hanging off them.

Archer hung there, struggling to position his hands for the least amount of strain, while Eva was similarly strung up from a matching pulley maybe a metre away.

He took the time to assess their surroundings.

The room was bare aside from a plain wooden chair that faced them. A door beyond that opened into a hallway and he could see that it led outside, presumably the way they had entered. An internal door to the right was closed. Windows to the left allowed a view of grassy paddocks and fences. The ceiling above them was cracked and broken and gave glimpses of an equally decrepit roof in places.

As far as he could tell, they were in a farmhouse somewhere, hanging from the ceiling like two sides of beef about to get butchered, guarded by five armed men.

Things could have been better, he figured.

The men huddled together for a minute in a hushed conference, then there were nods all round and three of them headed off through the internal door, closing it behind them again.

The two men that remained stood separately, one near the door to the hall, the other against the wall. The one against the wall was obviously the number two in this grouping, tasked with watching the prisoners. He was a skinny Arab with a bushy beard and a weathered complexion, and he moved with the confidence of a man with some training. Archer pegged him as an Afghan. Like the leader, he wore casual jeans and a loose shirt, and was somewhere in his late twenties.

Archer turned his attention back to the leader. He was a wiry African, probably Somalian, his skin so black it was almost blue, with a fluffy goatee. His hair was shaved at the sides and exploded above that in a crazy-looking bubble of black fuzz. It gave him an almost comical look, but that was where the humour ended.

His face was pock-marked with scars and his eyeballs were almost yellow. The confidence that he exuded had probably come from surviving to adulthood in one of the worst environments in the world.

Archer hung there, swinging slightly as he tried to anticipate the next move. Whatever it was going to be, it wouldn't be good. There was a sense of expectation in the air as if they were all waiting for something to happen.

When it did, Archer wasn't disappointed.

He heard a vehicle approaching, and the crunch of gravel beneath tyres as it came up the driveway. He caught a glimpse of a black SUV as it turned at the front of the house and came to a stop.

Doors opened and closed, and at least two sets of footsteps entered the hallway. Looking down from his raised position, Archer saw a pair of legs in black trousers appear, hands in the pockets, followed by a black suit jacket and ultimately the lean, drawn face of Viktor Kozlowski.

The terrorist leader removed his black sunglasses as he entered the barren room and tucked them into a pocket. His face was expressionless as he came to a stop near the sole chair and surveyed the two prisoners before him.

He was closely followed by Jessika and the man Archer had dubbed Number Two. They stopped a respectful distance behind Kozlowski.

Archer nodded to himself as the pieces fell into place. Far from being kidnapped, Jessika was moving freely, not bound like a prisoner would be, and when their eyes met, she couldn't resist a smug smirk.

'So, Mr Archer, Ms Graf,' Kozlowski said, 'finally we meet.' His accent was almost neutral and he spoke in measured tones, clipped and business-like. 'You have caused me much aggravation, Mr Archer. Believe me, there were plenty before you who thought they could match me, but clearly they didn't.' He allowed himself a cold smile. 'Just like them, you have now come to realise that the efforts of the American government and her allies are in vain.'

He rocked on his heels as he gazed at them. Nobody else made a sound. There was no doubt at all about who was in charge.

'I must give you your dues though, Mr Archer. You could have had me in Croatia. Nobody else had ever found me there. I take it you witnessed my, ah, little meeting?'

Archer eyed him as he composed his reply, trying to take a

measure of the man. It was like trying to gauge the depth of a black hole. The bastard gave nothing away.

'Your HR practices are a bit different to the norm,' he said.

Kozlowski gave a flicker of a smile. 'That's true,' he agreed. 'But I find them to be effective. It is important that people know I am not a man to be crossed, Mr Archer. If you let one client rip you off, you will let them all. You let one business associate double-cross you to the opposition, you will let them all. You may as well shut up shop and go home.'

Archer listened, keen to glean as much intel while he could. Whether he ever got to use any of it was another matter, but it couldn't hurt to know. Obviously the incident in Split had been a double-cross gone wrong, rather than an official operation. Poor old Kojak had been trying to line his pocket by leaking info to an opposing arms dealer or some other kind of criminal. Who it was didn't matter as much as the fact that he'd been caught.

'I take it he won't be making that mistake again.'

Kozlowski looked at him coolly. 'No. He won't. Dead men tell no tales, Mr Archer. His loving wife, however, did receive a farewell gift from me.' He paused, holding Archer's gaze for a long moment. 'I sent her his heart, beautifully packaged and kept on ice. I thought it was appropriate that whatever he felt for her in his heart, she would be able to hold onto.' A ghostly smile crossed his face. 'Rather touching, don't you think?'

Revulsion for the man tightened Archer's gut as the black eyes bore into his skull. This was not a man at all; this was a monster. Archer knew that right now he was face to face with a truly evil being. He had met bad guys before, brutal sadistic killers who thought nothing of beheading a victim or sending a brainwashed kid on a suicide mission.

But Kozlowski was something else altogether.

'I take it from your silence that you do not share my romantic vision, Mr Archer.' Kozlowski gave a shrug. 'Never mind. Perhaps that's why I'm a successful businessman and you are a spy who is about to die.'

Archer heard a snort of disgust from Eva, and Kozlowski turned to her.

'Something you would like to share with the group, Ms Graf?' he enquired. 'You disagree with my assessment?'

'You are nothing but a criminal,' she retorted hotly. 'A terrorist who kills for personal gain. You are no better than a criminal off the street.'

Kozlowski nodded thoughtfully. 'Interesting assessment,' he said. 'So what makes me any different from your friend here, Mr Archer? He kills people for his government, he gets paid for it. Surely that's also killing for personal gain?' He took a couple of slow steps towards her, appearing to be deep in thought. 'In fact, in Croatia alone, he killed four of my men. He killed one business associate of mine, and permanently crippled another. He killed the girlfriend of one of them.'

Archer frowned. 'I didn't kill the girl. She was hit by your guys' car.'

'Best we don't split hairs,' Kozlowski replied calmly. 'My point is, you are a paid killer. How is that any different to what I do in my business?'

'The people he kills are bad people that know nothing else,' Eva hissed, 'you...you don't care who you hurt. What you do kills and maims innocent people.'

Kozloswki nodded slowly, absorbing her words. 'So it becomes an ideological argument, doesn't it? I was once a soldier serving my country, following the orders of men a long way from the battlefield, men who never tasted the fear, never smelt the blood, never heard the screams of their friends as they died. Men who sent young men to hell and gorged themselves in their mansions on the hill, who built their wealth while their young men died in hellholes nobody had ever heard of or ever cared about.' He stepped up closer to Eva, looking up into her face. 'And because I disagree with that, I'm the bad guy? I'm the terrorist? I'm the criminal?' He shook his head sadly. 'No. No, Ms Graf, I'm just a businessman. I do exactly the same things that the leaders of my former country do; I just do it for myself.'

'No, you're just a fuckin' traitor,' Archer spat, fed up with the man's self-aggrandisement.

Kozlowski gave a start and half turned towards him. 'A traitor? I'm a traitor? No, Mr Archer, I'm a realist. Nobody cares for you but yourself. I bled for my country on the battlefield. I sold my soul for them. And what did they do for me when I came home?'

He stepped away from Eva and faced Archer again. 'They had me examined by men in white coats who had never seen what I saw, never did the things I did. They declared me mentally unfit for service and tossed me aside like yesterday's rubbish.' For the first time Archer saw some hint of emotion in the man's face. His lips were pursed and his jaw tight. The black eyes were as hard as marble. His next words were forced out between clenched teeth. 'I gave everything for my country, Archer, and they gave me nothing. Nothing!'

Kozlowski paused, visibly seething now. He stared at Archer, rage emanating off him. He finally swallowed hard and forced a smile to his face. 'So now, I work for myself. And a wonderful benefit of that, is that I have the opportunity to hurt my former country. You may have foiled the hijacking, Mr Archer, but it is only a temporary reprieve. Such a shame. I've never liked LAX as an airport. But never mind, the next target will be bigger and better again.'

'What about Germany?' Eva asked. 'Why are you here? What has Germany ever done to deserve to be attacked?'

Kozlowski cocked his head and looked at her curiously. 'Germany is an ally of the United States, Ms Graf. A friend of theirs is no friend of mine. But don't worry, Germany is not alone. The good old USA has many friends, and they will all feel their own pain. Don't you worry about that.' He gave a slight shrug, as if remembering something. 'Not that you will have time to worry about it anyway, I guess.'

'So what's the plan, Kozlowski?' Archer decided to push it while he had the chance. Like all egomaniacs, Kozlowski seemed to love the sound of his own voice. 'A good old fashioned suicide bomber in a crowd? A car bomb? Gunmen in a shopping mall?'

Kozlowski didn't bat an eyelid. He may have been a psychopath, but he was no fool. 'Plans are best kept secure, Mr Archer, you know that.'

'So what about you, Jessika?' Archer turned his attention to the female agent who had remained silent so far. 'What brought you to the party? Tired of serving your government as well?'

The woman looked to Kozlowski as if seeking permission. He gestured for her to go ahead.

'Maybe a little,' she replied. 'In the beginning, at least.' She looked to Kozlowski again and smiled warmly, her eyes dancing. 'But then it became so much more.'

'You fell in love with the source you were supposed to be running.' Archer could see it all now, and in that moment of clarity, it all seemed so blindingly obvious. 'You fell for him, you fed him intel he could use, he gave you intel that would take out his competition.' He shook his head in amazement. 'And all the while your agency thought you were doing a great job, running big bad Viktor Kozlowski.'

'They were fools,' Jessika said, her tone dismissive. 'A bunch of old men who thought they knew best. Career men, all divorced – most more than once – married to the agency. While they were patting each other on the back and getting blowjobs from impressionable young agents, the world moved on.'

'Was that you, Jessika?' Archer prodded. 'Were you that impressionable young agent?'

Her cheeks flushed and he expected a backhander from Kozlowski, but nothing came. She huffed and puffed, looking from her lover to her tormentor, seemingly impotent to respond.

'I thought so.'

'Traitorous whore,' Eva snapped. 'You are a disgrace to your agency.'

Jessika was almost at her, her hand raised, before Kozlowski got between them. 'Relax,' he said easily. 'She'll get hers, don't you worry.' He held her by the arms and gave her a reassuring smile. 'They are just playing with your mind, my dear. This is what they do.'

'Of course,' she murmured, 'you are right, Viktor. We must not get carried away and lose sight of the plan.'

She resumed her place and Kozlowski turned to face the two prisoners again.

'Anyway,' he said, 'we have talked enough. It is time to move forward. We have somewhere to be, and you two...well,' he shrugged, 'you two have to die. So.' He clapped his hands and looked to the Somalian and the Afghani, who had stood silently in the wings all this time. 'Gentlemen, I will leave you to deal with our guests. Thank you.' He turned back to Archer and Eva, and threw them each a mock salute. 'I bid you farewell Mr Archer, Ms Graf. We will not meet again.'

He turned to go, Jessika and his wing man following suit. Archer stopped them mid-step.

'So you haven't guessed then?'

Kozlowski stopped but didn't turn. 'Guessed what, Mr Archer?'

'How we got onto you? Croatia? Germany? You're very good at covering your tracks, Kozlowski, so how did we get onto you?'

Kozlowski half turned his head, curious, but unwilling to completely play into Archer's hands. 'You have something to say, Mr Archer, and time is running out. I suggest you just say it.'

Archer paused, wondering how far he could push it. He wanted to instil some paranoia in the man. Paranoia led to fear, which could potentially derail a plan. Given the situation, Archer figured the best he could do was disrupt.

'Who do you trust, Viktor? Who is always in the know?' There was a long pause. 'You can control yourself. You can control your men.' He paused again. The room was dead silent. Kozlowski was all ears, not moving a muscle. Jessika's eyes were on Archer, narrowed with suspicion, a look of horrible realisation creeping into her face. 'There's always a weak link, Viktor. What's yours?'

Kozlowski raised his head ever so slightly, looking to Jessika just a metre or so away. She stared back, fear in her eyes now, trying to fight it down with a weak smile.

'Pillow talk, Viktor. It gets 'em every time.'

'Don't believe him, Viktor,' Jessika said quietly, her voice fragile. 'It's not true.' She reached out for Kozlowski's arm and he yanked it away sharply.

Archer almost felt sorry for her. Almost.

'You know about us in LA,' he continued, determined to drive the knife in. Any disruption had to be a good thing. 'But I bet you don't know about Berlin. And Berlin again. She's quite the firecracker, I have to say.' He managed to inject a sneer into his voice, even though his throat was parched dry. 'I've had better, but it served a purpose. We got what we needed.'

'Viktor, it's not true, I promise you...' Jessika's voice cracked and her eyes were welling with tears. Her hands were clasped in front of her as if she were praying.

Kozlowski remained in profile to Archer, but even at the angle his rage was obvious. He gave a short nod to Number Two, standing behind Jessika.

The thug took one step forward, reached around Jessika's face from behind and seized her head firmly in both hands. There was a shriek of terror from the girl, a vicious yank, and her neck snapped audibly.

The man dropped the corpse to the floor and waited, his face expressionless. Kozlowski said nothing, just turned and walked to the front door. In a second he was gone. Number Two followed and moments later the black SUV was heading down the drive.

Jessika's body lay crumpled in a heap, discarded like unwanted trash.

'Jesus Christ,' Eva whispered.

Archer realised he was holding his breath. He let it out suddenly. The sudden brutality of the murder shocked him.

If that was how Kozlowski treated those closest to him, it didn't bode well for him, or Eva.

# 31

The internal door opened and the three other men emerged. They were all dressed in casual clothes now and had discarded their guns. Archer could see tell-tale bulges under their clothes, but much slimmer bulges than pistols gave. Knives, he guessed.

They huddled with the Somalian, talking between themselves in hushed tones. Archer could make out enough to realise the Somalian was praying with each of them in turn, bidding them farewell to do Allah's work.

There was a definite peace about the four men, a very focussed calm, and Archer realised he was witnessing three suicide killers about to depart on their final mission to gain acceptance into paradise.

It was an unnerving scene to watch.

The Somalian hugged each of the three men and they hurried out the front door. Archer heard a vehicle start up, doors slam, then the sound of a vehicle heading towards the road.

Silence fell on the abandoned farmhouse. Archer thought he could hear crickets chirping outside, but it was hardly idyllic.

The leader turned to face them, sliding the pistol into his waistband. His cohort stood off to the side, out of harm's way, with an old Beretta Model 12 submachine gun hanging off his shoulder. He leaned against the wall, confident enough to relax with the two prisoners strung up.

The leader smiled, exposing some gaps in his teeth. The teeth that remained were crooked and stained. Obviously dentists were in short supply in the Mog.

'You have made a mistake,' the leader sneered. 'You poke your nose in where it no needed. And now,' he leered at them, slowly drawing a long-bladed dagger from the back of his belt. He held it up for them to see, turning the blade slowly while enjoying the looks on their faces. 'Now, I cut your nose off so you not poke it anywhere again.'

Archer felt his gut tighten. He had no doubt at all that this bastard would do as he said. Archer's nose had been broken before and he'd never considered it his best feature, but neither did he have any interest in being parted from it. He glanced sideways at Eva, catching her eye. She had a look of absolute terror on her face, but he sensed resolve there as well. It was strange how the mind worked; the presence of imminent death or dismemberment brought an incredible clarity to any situation.

Archer knew there was no way of talking their way out of this. Two people were going to die shortly, period. He determined it wasn't going to be him and Eva.

The leader took his time, looking between the two of them, hanging there like sides of beef while the butcher sized them up.

Archer blocked out the discomfort and took a moment to consider their two captors. The leader was obviously Somalian, which meant he was most likely a member of Al-Shabaab, the Al-Qaeda-affiliated group from East Africa.

The Afghani was presumably either AQ or ISIS, but given the jihadists seemed to readily switch allegiances these days, he was just as likely to be an AS bandit as well. Or both could just be old-fashioned AQ or ISIS killers. Whatever they were, they were bad news.

He twisted his body again to look at Eva.

'Don't worry Eva,' he said, 'we've got these pricks right where we want them.'

She managed the tiniest of smiles and he hoped she was strong enough to follow his lead. He wasn't quite sure yet what that would be, but anything had to be worth a shot.

'I see who is the funny man,' the leader grinned. 'You think you will win today, Mr Archer? I don't. You will never win. I think all you will do today is die.'

Archer wasn't surprised that the guy knew who he was. It made sense. Whoever they were up against here obviously had good intel, which made them a dangerous foe in anyone's book. Not just any idiot could effect the capture of two intelligence officers. It obviously helped to have a CIA officer on the payroll.

'What are you, Al-Shabaab?' Archer played for time.

'My allegiance is not concern for you,' the leader replied, continuing to twirl his blade. 'I ask questions, not you.'

'Oh, I see. So you were kicked out of the Hubba-Bubbas.' Archer's tone was one of disdain. 'I'm not surprised.'

A look of anger crossed the leader's face and he stopped twirling the blade. 'What is Hubba-Bubbas? You make fun of me? You do not make fun of Al-Shabaab! You are white dog and I will kill you! You do not disrespect Allah and the jihad!'

The leader flicked the blade into his left hand and stepped forward, lashing out with a right fist to Archer's gut. He took the hit and swung backwards on his hook, absorbing the impact. As he swung forward again the leader delivered a much more effective strike to his groin and starbursts of pain exploded behind Archer's eyes.

The leader and his sidekick laughed that one up, loving it, and Archer shut his eyes, trying to breathe through the pain. He reflected that it would be nice if bad guys could leave his bollocks alone for once. Maybe he needed to invest in a cricket box for his next mission – if he lived through this one.

*Fuck them – they're not going to win.*

'Craig!' Eva's voice cut through his self-examination. 'Are you okay?'

He sucked in a breath and opened his eyes. He nodded carefully, not sure if he could speak yet.

'Never better,' he croaked.

'What he say?' The leader turned to his sidekick for assistance. The skinny Afghani shrugged, unsure.

'So you are Al-Shabaab then,' Archer managed, 'I think we can agree on that.' He tossed his chin towards the Afghani against the wall. 'What about Abdul there? What's his gang?'

'His name not Abdul,' the leader snapped angrily, 'you show no respect!' He stepped forward. 'I show you a lesson!'

He drew the pistol from his belt and whipped it across Archer's face, cracking him a solid hit to the left temple then a matching back-hander to the right side. Archer rolled with it, completely defenceless, and gritted his teeth against the pain. His head pounded with the dual blows and he tried to shake it out.

He raised his head just in time to see the next swing coming and pulled back, the pistol glancing off his chin instead of cracking his cheekbone. The leader punched it forward into his gut next, the hard steel barrel itself burying itself deep enough to take the wind from his sails.

Archer hung there, desperate to bend double but unable to, gasping for breath. He became aware of the leader laughing it up, his mate chipping in as well, as he coughed and tried to get his lungs working again. The leader obviously had other ideas, giving him another crack across the side of the skull. This time Archer felt blood begin to leak into his hair.

He sucked in air and tried to compose himself, focussing on a spot on the wall instead of his pain. His eyes drifted to the Afghani, who had a smirk on his face as he enjoyed the show. In that moment, Archer determined that he would kill the man before the day was out.

He shifted his gaze back to the leader, who was chuckling to himself as he surveyed his handiwork. With his ridiculous haircut and the bloodlust in his yellowed eyes, he looked even crazier than before.

'Laugh it up, fucker,' Archer croaked.

'Say what?'

'You won't be laughing,' Archer wheezed, 'when I get my hands on you.'

The leader threw his head back and roared with laughter, waving the pistol in his hand like a baby's rattle.

'You no get your hands on me, Mr Archer,' he chortled. 'You just a dead man hanging out with his friend.'

Both of them roared at that one, and Archer used the seconds to get his breath back.

'So what's the plan then?' he said. 'You're going to kill us anyway, so you may as well tell us why we're going to die.'

The leader abruptly stopped laughing and his face went stony. 'Dead man don't need to know our plans,' he retorted. 'It bigger than you can ever imagine.'

'Thought so.' Archer nodded as if his suspicions had been confirmed. 'So big they didn't even tell you, right? Why would they trust a two-bit pirate hustler like you?'

'Two-bit?' The leader may have been confused, but he knew he was being insulted. 'You talk too much.'

He grabbed Archer by the front of his shirt to hold him steady and raised the knife to his face. The blade was cold against Archer's upper lip. The leader's breath was rancid in his face, even though the guy's head only came up to his mid-chest.

The tip of the blade slid up, into his left nostril and with a quick flick it sliced through the outside of his nose.

Warm blood immediately began to leak down Archer's face, over his lips to his chin, dripping down to his shirt as he braced himself against the searing pain. The leader stepped back, grinning. Archer let out a guttural snarl and spat blood, his nostril feeling as if it was on fire.

The leader lifted the blade and watched a drop of blood edging its way down the tip. He licked the drop carefully off the blade and grinned. Archer sucked in air through his mouth, tasting blood on his teeth. He rolled his tongue and spat a string of blood. It clung to his lip and hung there like a spider's web.

'Is that all you've got?' he panted.

'Fuck you, assholes!' Eva suddenly blurted, her eyes wild as she looked from one to the other. 'You come to my country and behave like savages! Who do you think you are? You are just cheap black market bandits, you filthy animals!'

Archer was as surprised as their captors at her outburst, and although he admired her courage, he had no doubt she was about to pay for it.

The leader turned his attention to her, his dark eyes glittering as he sized her up. 'You...filthy...German...whore,' he grated. 'Your country will suffer for its allegiance to the American infidels.' His grin was pure evil. 'But first...you will suffer more.'

He moved towards her and she lashed out, kicking wildly at him. He dodged one foot but the second caught him on the shoulder and he grunted. He grabbed at her and the Afghani came to help him. The Afghani grabbed her round the waist and held her steady, while the leader stepped up closer, raising his knife.

*Good girl.*

'Your filthy whore mouth will no longer defile the world of Allah,' the leader said, 'when I cut out your tongue.'

She writhed on the hook, doing her best to pull away from him, but both men held her tightly. The Afghani moved with her swinging and ended up with his back to Archer, bracing his feet to hold her still. The leader was to the Afghani's left, face-on to Eva.

Both men were totally absorbed in their task.

The first they knew of impending danger was a creak of chain link as Archer swung towards them. His right foot smashed into the back of the Afghani's skull, slamming him forwards against Eva's hip. Together they swung hard and the leader lashed out at her with the knife as he was thrown off-balance.

The blade sliced across her face and he twisted, turning to confront Archer and ignoring Eva as he did so.

He slashed out at Archer's legs with the blade, connecting with his left thigh but forgetting about the woman beside him.

Eva's legs swung up and over his shoulders, locking around his head from behind and pulling him in close as if she were sitting on his shoulders. She clamped her thighs together and locked her ankles, bracing him in a smothering lock.

The Afghani staggered groggily, trying to gather his wits as he turned towards Archer. His hands were fumbling for the Beretta over his shoulder.

Archer smashed him in the throat with his next swing, his heel going straight into the man's Adam's apple with full force. The Afghani forgot all about the submachine gun and clutched at his throat, gasping like a fish on a wharf. He stumbled to the side, his eyes bugging, and hit the wall, sliding down to a sitting position.

The leader was going hell for leather, thrashing and heaving against Eva's grasp. He flailed at her legs with his knife but she held fast, her face screwed up in pain as he connected with the blade. She let out a scream as the blade entered her thigh and he bucked again, both of them twisting in a macabre death dance.

Archer got a good swing on and kicked out, his heel striking the leader above the eye and opening up a gash. The leader jabbed at him with the knife, narrowly missing before Archer kicked him again, going low this time and driving his toe into the leader's gut. He swung back and came in again, booting the leader between the legs.

*Fair's fair.*

The leader squealed and Eva screamed again as the blade sliced across her thigh, the twin peals piercing in the unfurnished room.

Archer brought his right foot up again and connected with the leader's temple, slamming his head sideways in Eva's weakening grasp. He pulled back and repeated the action, putting all his weight behind the sideways stomp and driving through the guy's head like it was a speed bag.

The leader's head bounced and his eyes rolled up, his body going limp.

'Hold him,' Archer panted, swinging back and lining up another shot.

Eva's eyes were still screwed shut but she was clinging on desperately, both of them knowing they couldn't afford to let this guy go.

The last blow was a brutal heel to the eye socket, Archer's boot smashing the orbital bone as the head was snapped sideways.

The leader was completely out now and Eva could no longer hold his dead weight, letting him drop to the floor in a heap.

Eva let loose a burst of anger and pain that contained every German swear word Archer knew and many he didn't. He took a moment to catch his breath. She was bleeding from a cut below the left eye, and her pants were darkened and torn in at least two places on the right leg.

Archer could feel blood still running down his face and a stinging across the side of his left thigh where he guessed he'd been cut. No time to worry about that just now; they were still alive and still in danger.

He eyed the ceiling above him. He doubted he'd be able to disengage himself from the pulley's karabiner from below, which left only one option. Thanking a lifetime of fitness training, Archer worked himself into a swing, throwing his weight back and forth until he was almost hitting the wall behind him. His feet brushed the ceiling on the upswing and he flung himself back again, using his legs for momentum and arcing upwards.

One boot went through the brittle ceiling panel then another and he fell backwards, his shoulders feeling like they were going to tear free. The next swing was weaker and he quickly worked himself into a rhythm of one low swing to build momentum followed by one good swing that allowed him to break away more of the ceiling.

The floor was soon littered with broken pieces of rotten ply and Archer was coated in sweat, his arms, shoulders, core and lungs all screaming at him. But after a minute or so a beam was exposed, close enough for him to be able to hook a foot over with any luck. His first attempt was just an inch too low and he took another couple of swings to get refocussed and go hard at it.

He got his left foot up to the ceiling, through it, and felt his ankle catch over the beam. He pulled, his entire body working at holding on, knowing that he couldn't keep trying all day. This was it. The clarity he'd gained earlier had never left; if he failed, they died.

He strained at it, clawing his way up the rope towards the bolt at the top. He could see blood on his wrists now where the flexi-cuffs had broken the skin. He grasped the bolt and the karabiner with slippery hands, completely horizontal to the ground now. He thumbed open the gate on the karabiner, worked it around with his fingers until the plastic cuffs slid free, and dropped the karabiner again.

Archer unhooked his foot, let his body weight fall and dropped to the floor with a loud crash. He lay there for a few seconds, his body a mass of pain, before he realised the Afghani was stirring. He forced himself to his knees, shuffled forward to the chair, and pushed himself up.

The Afghani's eyes were on him now, his face a blotchy red-blue, shallow breaths coming in rasping wheezes, as if he was breathing through a straw. The guy was making no effort to move, seemingly focussed solely on getting oxygen down a badly damaged throat.

Getting to his feet, Archer moved over to the leader, pausing to pick up the guy's knife. He awkwardly sliced through his flexi cuffs before anything else, then bent over the Somalian terrorist and made to check for vital signs. The head lolled back loosely as soon as he touched it, hanging off a broken neck.

No need to check for a pulse on that one.

Archer moved over to the Afghani, picked up his Beretta M12, and slung it over his own shoulder. He worked the bolt, caught the ejected round and dropped the magazine. The action worked smoothly, so he replaced the top round and reloaded the weapon, chambering a round again and applying the safety.

Satisfied that he could now defend them, he shifted his attention to his partner.

Eva had opened her eyes by the time he got to her, and was breathing through clenched teeth, obviously in great pain. Archer wasted no time in releasing her pulley and lowering her to the ground where he quickly freed her. She collapsed to the floor, pressing her hands to the wounds on her legs.

Archer stripped the Afghani of his belt, checked him for other weapons, and used the belt as a tourniquet on Eva's right thigh. He slit the pants leg open with the Somalian's knife and inspected her wounds. The two slashes were both long and shallow, and the puncture wound itself was deeper and messy looking.

He ripped her pants leg and wadded it against the stab wound, pressing down firmly enough to make her cry out. He grabbed her hand and placed it over the makeshift dressing.

'Keep it there,' he said, 'keep the pressure on. The other two are okay, they'll just bleed a bit.' He inspected the cut to her face, which was still trickling blood. 'That's not too bad, nothing a bit of plaster won't fix up.' He gave her what he hoped was a reassuring smile. 'Just where we want them, eh?'

She grimaced. 'You have a very strange sense of humour, Craig Archer.'

'The good guys've always got to win,' he told her, forcing himself to his feet. 'It's the rules.'

He made his way over to the leader's dead body and frisked it. He came up with a burn phone, a set of keys and a Heckler and Koch USP 9mm semi auto. He checked the load – a full 15 rounds.

Archer pocketed the phone and keys and slid the pistol into his waistband. He crossed to the Afghani, slumped against the wall, wheezing like an old man with emphysema. His eyes followed Archer as he crouched down.

'You speak English?'

The man gave the slightest shrug, so Archer switched to Farsi.

'Name.'

The Afghani wheezed, his lips moving weakly but nothing coming out.

'Where have they gone?'

Another tiny shrug. The guy's eyes were losing focus and Archer knew he was on the way out.

'Where have they gone?' Archer demanded, giving the guy a shake. 'What's their target?'

The Afghani's eyes rolled and his head slumped to the side. The wheezing stopped. Archer checked his pockets, finding another burn phone and a crumpled packet of cheap Turkish cigarettes. A vicious-looking flick knife was tucked into the guy's sock.

'Fuck it,' Archer muttered, straightening up. He moved back over to Eva and rechecked her wounds. The bleeding was easing back but she definitely needed stitches and proper medical attention. If she carried on bleeding she would end up in shock and could die.

He crab-walked over to the dead leader and used the knife to cut his shirt to pieces. He wadded some into makeshift dressings and tied them over Eva's cuts.

'We need to move.' He helped her to her feet and they made their way past Jessika's discarded corpse to the front door they had originally been dragged through.

Archer was about to open it when they heard the sound of a car approaching. He quickly checked the window to the side of the door. A white panel van was pulling up outside the house.

'Shit!' he growled. He grabbed Eva by the arm and hustled her into a side room off the entranceway. There was a dirty-looking sleeping bag on the floor and an open bag of clothes. Obviously somebody had been staying there; presumably whoever had just arrived back.

'Stay down and out of sight.'

He moved quietly back to the door and waited, the Beretta in his hands. He heard at least two voices as the door began to open.

## 32

The first man through the door had his head down and was chuckling at something the guy behind him had said. He walked into the hallway oblivious to the impending threat, and Archer let him keep coming.

The second guy was mid-sentence when Archer appeared in the doorway, the Beretta submachine gun braced against his hip, and the guy's jaw dropped open.

Both men were Middle Eastern of some sort, with tidy short beards and curly hair. They were in casual jackets and jeans and looked like students, aside from the pistol in each of their waistbands.

Archer wasted no time with niceties.

The stubby chopper snarled out a short burst, rounds ripping into the torso of the closest man. He let out a grunt and crashed into the wall, clutching at his shredded gut.

The second guy reacted quickly, scrambling backwards while he ripped his pistol free and unleashed a fast shot in Archer's general direction.

Archer's second burst was wide as the guy reached the door, throwing another wild shot behind him as he shouted a warning to someone unseen to Archer. Archer unleashed a third burst and nailed him in the back and side as the guy turned to run. The rounds threw him sideways to the ground and he triggered another wild shot as he fell.

Archer went after him, realising there was a third guy there when the van started up. The guy on the ground was trying to crawl away, his pistol still in his hand, dragging himself with his other arm. The van was starting to back up and he saw a glint of sunlight as the driver's window was lowered.

He hunched over and sent a short burst towards the van then swivelled and put another into the lower body of the guy on the ground, raking his legs and lower back with several rounds. The guy screamed and bucked, and Archer booted his weapon away as he moved past, eyes on the van.

The driver had his arm out the window with a pistol, throwing shots all over the place as he tried to reverse at speed.

Archer put a burst into the front grille of the van as he moved fast across the gravel turning area, careful to maintain his footing. There were overgrown empty paddocks on both sides and a road about a hundred metres distant. The driveway was gravel and dirt and bordered by spindly trees and scrub.

The van's engine was starting to whine and pick up speed. Archer followed, the Beretta up at shoulder height so he could sight properly. The driver was still putting shots down but may as well have saved his ammo.

Archer pumped a burst at the windscreen, seeing the rounds strike and ricochet due to the angle and distance. He gave it another burst and the windscreen cracked.

The driver jerked the wheel in fright, sideswiping the undergrowth on the right. Archer's last burst stitched across the windscreen and caused it to spider web.

The van jerked again and went backwards into the scrub, the engine still whining as the Beretta's bolt locked back on an empty chamber.

Archer let the SMG fall on its sling and drew the HK from his waistband, racing forward in a crouch. He needed to get up on this guy before he had time to react.

The van bunny-hopped backwards and stalled, and the driver's door started to open. Archer sent a double tap his way and got to the front left of the van, leaping onto the bonnet and pumping two more rounds through the broken windscreen, seeing both bullets impact the driver's torso.

The multiple rounds had blown a decent hole in the glass and he could see the driver clearly now. Like his mates he looked more like an international student than a terrorist. The guy still had his pistol in his hand and his eyes were on Archer, so he put a round into the guy's face before jumping off the bonnet and racing to the door.

The driver was dead, his forehead split by a 9mm bullet, blood leaking down into his bushy eyebrows.

Archer turned the ignition off and searched him, finding only a spare magazine to his pistol. It was another Heckler and Koch USP. Archer pocketed the mag and the van keys, tucked the spare pistol into his belt and headed back to the farmhouse.

He became aware then of the guy on the ground outside screaming his head off. He was writhing and clutching at his side, his movements clumsy.

As Archer got closer he could see the guy's legs were ripped to bits and leaking blood in a steadily-spreading pool. It seemed unusual that, despite, the open fleshy wounds in his legs, he seemed more concerned about the less messy wounds to his side. Archer noticed the guy's legs weren't moving and he seemed to be frozen from the waist down.

Suddenly it clicked.

The guy's spinal column must have been severed by the bullets, rendering him paralysed from the waist down. Even though his legs were in bits and he was bleeding out, the poor fucker had no idea.

*Poor fucker? No, not a poor fucker. Just a terrorist fucker who got some of his own medicine.*

Archer stopped to frisk him on the way past, finding no more weapons, and left him to scream while he went back inside to check on Eva and the first guy.

She had come out of the room and was covering the guy with his own pistol. He was slumped in a large pool of blood and his face was slack and waxy looking. He was trying to hold his guts in with one hand, which was covered in blood.

Eva looked at Archer with wide eyes, and he gave her a reassuring look.

'You okay?' he asked.

She nodded tentatively. 'I think so. What happened out there?'

'Two bad guys down.' He glanced back at the guy at their feet. The terrorist's eyes were fixed in a vacant stare at the wall and his hand had fallen away from his wounds. 'No need to worry about him anymore.' He moved back into what he guessed was the lounge, where the bodies of the Somalian and the Afghani lay. No need to check them. He turned and looked down at Jessika. She lay on her side, her head lolling at an unnatural angle. No matter what he thought of traitors, the suddenness of her killing had shocked him.

'Are you okay?' Eva touched his arm. 'Craig?'

He sniffed and gave a short nod. 'The bitch is dead,' he said coldly. 'She got what she deserved.'

He turned on his heel and led the way outside to where the second guy lay in the dust. His screaming had diminished to a constant whimper, and he had managed to half roll onto his side. He looked up at them as they approached.

'Allahu Akbar,' he panted. 'Allahu Akbar.'

'He may be, but he's no use to you now.' Archer stood over him. The sun was up and he felt his head and shoulders getting warm. 'Where have they gone?'

'Allahu Akbar!'

Archer switched to Arabic. 'Where have they gone?'

'I will tell you nothing, infidel dog! Their blood will be on your hands and we will live forever in paradise!'

'Where did they go? What are they going to bomb?'

'Allahu Akbar! Jihadi will never betray Allah!'

'Unless you get help you've got about two minutes before you bleed to death. I'm a medic. Tell me what the plan is and I can save you.' Archer shrugged. 'If not, you can bleed out here like a dog.'

He could feel Eva's eyes on him. He ignored her and kept his attention on the dying terrorist. He didn't have time to fuck about with this guy.

'I will tell you nothing! They will all die! We must teach the Western dogs a lesson for their decadent ways!'

Archer took a step closer and crouched down. 'Here's the deal. We're too late to prevent this anyway; just let us know where to go to pick up the pieces. You do that and I'll give you a gun and let you send yourself to paradise right here.'

The guy's eyes flickered as he processed the proposal. Archer waited, conscious that the pool of blood was spreading around the guy. It was slowly edging its way around his boot.

'I will meet my saviour and live in paradise,' the guy wheezed. He coughed wetly, blood flecking his lips. 'Allah is my saviour.' His focus wandered and Archer could tell he was on the way out. 'I am cold... today...judgement will come...to...the decadent...infidels... West... Allah will meet me...at the gates...' His face seemed to draw in on itself and he started to smile. 'The gate...will be...truly the gate...to paradise...' His eyes glazed and he relaxed into the dust and gravel. 'Allahu...'

With that he was gone and Archer pushed himself up. He looked to Eva. 'We need to move.'

'What did he say?'

He frowned for a moment until he realised she didn't speak Arabic. 'He wouldn't tell me, but right at the end he started talking about the gates to paradise, and the gate truly being the gate to paradise.'

'*Brandenburger Tor*,' she replied softly, and he nodded.

'That's right,' he said, 'I think they're going to hit the Brandenburg Gate.'

## 33

The wind whistling through the shattered windscreen and bullet holes in the van made it hard to hear even with the phone on speaker.

Archer was driving, belting the white panel van along the country roads as fast as he dared, while Eva made contact with her HQ. They had recovered their own belongings from the farmhouse, along with some extras left behind by the terrorists, and were blasting towards Berlin as fast as possible.

The BfV were screaming into action and GSG9 had been mobilised.

The Brandenburg Gate was the venue today for a large anti-immigration rally. Archer realised he'd been aware of it during his time in the city, without actually giving it too much thought. When he did now, the realisation made his blood run cold.

The sight of Middle Eastern terrorists running amok in Berlin, attacking unarmed civilians, would only serve to incite further violence by an already-militant sector of the community. The likely outcome was widespread street violence, rioting, looting, firebombs and death on both sides of the divide. It would destabilise the Berlin community and potentially the entire German society, which was already a powder keg of immigration issues.

The violence would spread like wildfire. Channelling resources into fighting it would leave the Germans vulnerable to attack in other areas. It could be a cyber-attack, a power station getting bombed, poisoning of water resources; any number of options could open up from a single day of street violence, and it would quickly become a feeding frenzy.

Archer concentrated on driving, leaving Eva to make the necessary arrangements.

All he could guess so far was that it would be a knife attack similar to that perpetrated at Tower Bridge in London earlier in the year. Such an attack was extremely difficult to prevent, and caused massive panic which resulted in more injuries than the attackers' blades themselves.

The GPS put the farmhouse near Wandlitz, about 30 klicks north of Berlin. They had been on the road nearly ten minutes now and were on the 109 highway, overtaking anything that got in their way.

Local police had been warned to be on the lookout, and it didn't take long for a BMW patrol car to come flying the other way, throw a U-turn and get in behind them.

Archer pulled over and they got out, hands in the air, while the two Brandenburg State *Landespolizei* officers approached them cautiously, hands on their holstered weapons. Eva handed the phone over to the senior cop who listened intently for a few seconds before handing the phone back to her.

'*Jawohl*,' he said, '*kom*.'

Archer turned the van off and grabbed their gear from it before hurrying to the patrol car, both cops raising their eyebrows as they saw the folding stock AK47, the Beretta submachine gun, the two Heckler and Koch USP pistols and the bag of spare magazines he'd scrounged from the farmhouse.

He was still buckling himself in when the driver gassed it, bells and whistles all go, and he was pushed back into his seat.

Eva continued on the phone while Archer busied himself with

the weapons. He saw the two cops looking at each other incredulously, and the driver was watching him in the rear view mirror.

'It's okay,' he told them, 'nothing to worry about.'

They looked even more surprised at his use of German. The driver swerved around a truck with a blast on the horn, muttering under his breath.

Eva disconnected the phone and accepted the pistol he handed her. 'Take us straight to the Brandenburg Gate,' she told the cops, 'I'll give you more specific details when we get closer.'

'Yes ma'am.'

Archer checked the safety on the AK and held the weapon across his lap. He took a moment to catch his breath. Things were moving at lightning speed and he needed to get his head clear.

They were belting towards what they believed to be Ground Zero of a terrorist attack, already behind the eight ball, and the enormity of it all threatened to be overwhelming. What they had just been through, the situation they were now heading into and the potentially catastrophic outcome if they failed to stop it certainly made it one of the bigger days he'd had in the office.

The stakes were astronomical.

But despite it all, he was buzzing. The adrenaline was pumping, his senses were all peaking, and he could see everything with perfect clarity. This was what men like Archer lived for, and no matter how many times he'd been in such a situation, it never got old.

Eva was on the phone again, having to shout to be heard over the noise of the siren, talking so fast he could barely make out a thing.

When she hung up she issued the driver directions then put her phone away and sat back again.

'This is it,' she told Archer. 'GSG9 are on the ground in plain clothes. My people are there. Everybody is ready.'

He nodded. 'Are you?'

She looked at him sharply. 'Of course. These bastards must be stopped.'

She set about checking the HK USP he'd given her. Even though they both knew it was loaded and actioned, it was always good to check. He guessed that, like most intelligence officers, she would have had some basic weapons training. He'd trained some officers back home, making sure they had enough skills to defend themselves in the unlikely event that things went really pear-shaped. Well, today was that day for Eva.

'It's okay,' she said, giving him a sideways glance. 'I know what I'm doing.'

'I didn't say anything.'

'You didn't need to. You gave me that look.'

'I have a look?'

'All men have a look.' She frowned at him, her brow creasing. She was still beautiful when she was pissed off. 'That look about the little woman handling a gun.'

'Sorry, I...'

'I was in the Army for three years before the BfV,' she continued, ignoring his attempt at an apology. 'So don't worry that I will accidentally shoot you in the foot.' She tucked the pistol under her thigh and gave him a deadpan look. 'Not accidentally, anyway.'

Berlin city centre was busier than normal, with streams of pedestrians making their way towards the rally point, disregarding the vehicular traffic.

They quickly found themselves crawling at a snail's pace. Despite the bells and whistles forcing vehicles aside, they were unable to push their way through the foot traffic without causing more issues.

A group of skinheads in windbreakers and jeans cut across in front of them, thumping their fists on the bonnet of the police car and shouting obscenities before disappearing back into the crowd, laughing and hollering at the inability of the police to stop them.

The agreed RV point was in a side street near the Brandenburg Gate itself, and Archer realised they would never get there in time.

'We need to go,' he told Eva brusquely, slipping the AK47 between the front seats and following it with the Beretta submachine gun. 'Thanks for the ride fellas. Look after these for us.'

He forced the door open and got out, using the door to push aside passing pedestrians so they could both alight. Some grumbled and swore, jostling him, and he could feel the animosity in the crowd. It was shaping up to be an ugly day, and the sooner they were away from the police car, the better.

He grabbed Eva's hand and kept her close, pushing across the stream of the flow, making it to a footpath and hugging walls as they cut away from the hordes towards the RV.

'The rally starts in ten minutes,' Eva said. 'Cut through here.' She took the lead now, pushing her way through a door, across a building lobby and out the other side into a different street. 'There they are.'

Dieter and Ulrich were huddled beside a van with the side door open, with a man and a woman in black coveralls sitting at a workstation in the rear of the van. The vehicle was kitted out as a mobile base, with radio and camera equipment set up and a fold-down table for the troops to use.

Both BfV men looked up and nodded as they arrived, both doing a double-take at the physical state of the newcomers. Archer guessed they must look a right state, with cuts and bloodstained clothing.

'This is the GSG9 commander,' Dieter said, 'his men are stationed around the rally. They are looking for the perpetrators, but there are so many people there it is like looking for the proverbial needle in the haystack.'

'Tell them to focus on the fringes,' Archer said urgently. 'These are Middle Eastern guys; they'll stand out in this crowd, and they won't want to be noticed until they're ready to go.'

Ulrich relayed the message to the commander, who studied Archer for a second before turning away and jabbering into his mic.

'There is a general alert out for Kozlowski and his associates,' Dieter said. 'So far no sightings.'

Archer wasn't surprised. Kozlowski had survived this long; there was no reason to think he couldn't do it again.

Ulrich looked back at Eva. 'Are you okay, Eva?'

'Fine, thank you sir.' She smiled. 'We are alive; they are not.'

'You did well.' He nodded sombrely, looking like a big bulldog with his heavy jowls and tired eyes. 'I am pleased.' He turned his attention to Archer. 'Thank you for what you have done, Herr Archer.'

Archer was about to reply when he saw a group of people hurrying across the road towards them. It was the CIA man, Rawlins, flanked by three other suits. None of them looked happy.

'What the fuck is going on, Archer?' Rawlins demanded before he'd even reached the footpath. 'I just took a call from your pal Ingoe, telling me that one of my agents has been killed by one of his agents, and I wanna know why, and if you can't gimme some goddamn answers I'll be hauling your sorry ass the fuck outta here to someplace you don't wanna go and you'll gimme the goddamn answers whether you like it or not!'

He was right up on them now, veins bulging in his neck, his face a blotchy purple and red, dry spittle flecking his lips. His three guys hung back at a safe distance.

Archer held his ground, eyeballing the other man but remaining silent. It didn't take long for Rawlins to lose his patience.

'Well what?' he exploded. 'You lost your goddamn tongue, Archer? You better start talking or I'll...'

'Yeah yeah, I heard you,' Archer replied. 'Scary place, goddamn everything, make me talk. I get it.'

Dieter stepped forward now, his normally relaxed demeanour gone, replaced by a solemn air that was all business. 'Stop talking, both of you,' he said. His tone was quiet but firm. 'Mr Rawlins, unfortunately your agent was a traitor. As you Americans would say, she was in cahoots with Viktor Kozlowski, who had one of his men kill her. It was not Mr Archer or Ms Graf who was responsible for that. She is dead and that is that. An investigation will undoubtedly follow, but right now, we have a terrorist attack to prevent. So if it is okay with you and your agency, I would like to carry on with that.' He looked from one to the other then gave a short nod. Archer wasn't sure, but he had the impression the man even clicked his heels. 'I thank you.'

With that the enigmatic German turned back to the GSG9 commander and left them to stare at each other. Archer could see the blotchiness in Rawlins' face starting to fade ever so slightly, but the veins in his neck still looked fit to burst.

'This ain't over, Archer,' the CIA man hissed through clenched teeth. 'I need details.'

Archer shrugged. 'No problem,' he said. 'Later.' He glanced over Rawlins' shoulder, recognising two of the three suits now. It was EJ and Rico, the two SOG boys. The third guy was clearly a spook, more awkward-seeming than the two operators, slicker and softer-looking. He gave them a toss of the chin and they nodded back in unison.

The commander spun on his chair and spoke in urgent tones to Dieter and Ulrich. 'We may have a sighting,' he said. 'Three Arab-looking men together.'

'Where?' All eyes were on the man in black as Dieter pressed for details.

'Just near the Starbucks. One of my men is observing them, but he is unsure of them. He says they are together and appear nervous.'

Archer ran over the ground from memory. 'That's just the other side of here? Looking out to the *Pariser Platz*?'

Eva nodded excitedly. '*Ja, ja*.'

The RV was on a side street across from a parking garage, the garage being part of a large building complex that formed the north-eastern corner of the plaza. They were less than a hundred yards from the coffee shop.

'We can ID them,' Archer told the commander. 'Tell your man we will be coming. We'll update Dieter by phone.' He glanced to Eva. 'Come on.'

As they started to move, he saw Ulrich place a big hand on the GSG9 commander's shoulder. 'Don't let your men get trigger-happy and cause a panic,' he rumbled, his jowls flapping. 'This will be a false alarm.'

Archer wasn't sure he agreed.

# 34

They set off at a run, Eva already hitting speed dial on her phone as she kept pace with him.

Archer was aware of Rico and EJ falling in behind them as well. They turned the corner of the building and could see the towering gateway ahead of them, at the far end of the *Pariser Platz*. In the past it had been the centre stage for all manner of major events, hosting world leaders and rallies of all sorts, from the dark days of the Nazi regime to more recent times when peace became the goal.

Today was different, however, with the normal-looking civilians attending the rally heavily interspersed with more anarchic types. Shaved heads and black jeans were easily seen, with some of the placards in the crowd displaying slogans that encouraged a return to the dark days. "*Germany for Germans*", "*Germany Is Not An Islamic State*", and even "*Peace Through Superior Firepower*" were on display.

A temporary stage of some sort had been set up beneath the famous arches, and he could see a small group of rally leaders up there with megaphones.

Archer shut out the chanting and hustle, concentrating on getting to the Starbucks, still forty metres away. The crowd was thick and it was heavy going, trying not to bring attention to themselves but still move quickly.

Suddenly he heard screaming up ahead, shouts, and the crowd started to move. A shot sounded, followed by more screaming, and he felt himself caught in a wave as the crowd surged in all directions.

Already he saw a woman with blood on her shirt up ahead, a young Arab in a hoody visible now in an opening in the crowd, charging towards people as they tried to get away, slashing wildly with his knife.

'Man down!' Eva shouted in his ear.

Archer took that in and pushed harder, moving against the tide, going towards the fight rather than away from it. All around him were terrified faces. Another shot sounded, very close now. Suddenly he burst free, open space about him, finding himself in a clear space with the attacker just a few metres away, slashing at a man who was trying to fight him off.

Another guy lay on the ground, bleeding onto the concrete, a radio discarded near him and a pistol in his hand. Presumably the GSG9 operator. Archer guessed he'd been attacked and got a couple of shots off. A third guy was staggering backwards away from him, a knife in one hand, blood soaking the front of his hoody.

There was no sign of the third attacker that should have been in the cell.

Archer ignored the two wounded men and went after the active bad guy, leaving the pistol in his waistband for now. With the number of people around, any missed or through-and-through shot would take out a civilian.

He darted towards the attacker, the guy turning to see him coming, his eyes widening with shock when he recognised the new arrival before him.

'Surprise, motherfucker.' Archer confronted him, hands out, ready. 'Let's do it.'

The guy was young, maybe twenty, with a scruffy bum-fluff attempt at a beard. He looked like he was high on something, but Archer guessed it was probably just jihadist fervour. He jabbed at

Archer with the knife, muttering under his breath as if he was trying to gee himself up to do it.

Archer closed in further, barely outside striking range now, his hands still empty. 'Stop fucking about and have a go,' he snarled. 'Come on, princess!'

The guy lunged forward with a rapier thrust. Archer stepped left, grabbed the wrist in his right hand, twisted hard, smashed a left jab to the side of the guy's neck, and pulled him in. Twisting the knife hand up and around, Archer heard a snap as something gave way. He used his left hand to hold the guy in close, screeching now, and felt the knife drop to the ground.

He let go of the wounded wrist and used his right to smash the guy straight in the Adam's apple. The guy gasped and heaved and all the fight left him.

'*Polizei! Polizei!*'

A pair of plain clothed GSG9 operators raced up, guns drawn, and Archer shoved the attacker to the ground, putting his hands up so they were clear on who the bad guy was.

They leapt on the guy immediately and Archer stepped back, scanning the area as he moved away from the GSG9 guys and their prisoner.

He could see Eva crouching by the wounded operator, another cop with her. Sirens sounded. People were still screaming and stampeding, but fortunately away from him. He could see a few injured people dotted around, some trying to hide, some trying to get up and run.

The other attacker who had been shot by the GSG9 operator was backed up against a wall outside the Starbucks, still waving his knife despite being confronted by two operators with their guns drawn, Rico and EJ backing them up, all of them shouting at the guy.

As Archer watched he knew it was the end for that guy. A split second later the guy lunged forward and a volley of shots rang out. As the guy crumpled to the ground Archer was hit from behind, the full body weight of a running man slamming into him and throwing him forwards, unable to stop himself.

The runner came with him, and for a moment Archer guessed it was some panicked civilian trying to get away. But as he went down with the person still clinging to him, he realised this was no accident. The concrete rushed up and he slammed into it, the air exploding from his lungs. At the same time as he hit it he felt a jab in his side as if he'd been punched.

The guy rolled off him, got to his knees, and Archer tried to move. He couldn't breathe and the guy was holding him down with a knee on his lower back. He twisted his head and made eye contact with his attacker.

It was the guy he'd dubbed Number Two, Kozlowski's right-hand man. The guy was grinning as he raised a knife, ready to plunge down.

'You should've stayed dead,' the guy said, and drove the knife into Archer's side.

It felt like a hard punch and Archer wondered abstractedly if the guy had somehow missed. Another one followed before the guy pushed up, shoving Archer away as he did so. Rolling half onto his side, Archer dropped his hand to the USP in his waistband.

He felt his leaden fingers close over it, pull it free and lift it. Number Two looked surprised, stepped forward and lifted his foot to kick the gun away.

Archer's thumb swiped the safety off and he pressed the trigger once, twice, three, four times. The first shot blasted through the raised foot and took his assailant in the thigh, the second in the groin as he started to drop, the third in the centre chest as he fell. The fourth round took him on the point of the chin and smashed it to pieces before travelling through into the skull.

The guy was dead before he hit the ground. Archer's fifth and sixth shots punched the sky before he realised he had no target anymore and he flopped onto his back, his gun hand falling back. He tried to breathe but it felt wet and heavy, and he could taste copper in his throat.

He craned his neck to check himself. His torso was a mass of blood. He was pretty sure he'd been stabbed, and now he thought that, it hurt like a bastard. His eyes moved further down and he saw jets of blood spurting from his right thigh. It looked bizarre, solid bursts of red jetting out like a fountain. It clicked in his brain that he had a severed artery and was losing blood fast, but it made no sense. He didn't think he'd even been hit in the leg. He pushed the thought aside; no point trying to figure that out just now.

His medical training told him he needed help urgently or he would die. It seemed like an abstract thought, as if he were looking at someone else and assessing their situation, not himself.

He could faintly hear voices, far off, urgent sounding. Eva, maybe? He tried to look around for her. People were standing around, some distance away, watching. One of them was a tall man, all in black. He stood at the front of the crowd, staring straight at Archer.

*Kozlowski.*

Archer knew it. He tried to lift his gun but his arm was refusing to co-operate. He tried to shout but all he managed was a gurgle that made him gasp for air.

Eva appeared over him, looking concerned, asking him if he could hear her. He could, but when he tried to talk all he could taste was blood and he felt it trickling down his cheek.

*The fucker was going to get away!*

Eva was shouting, pulling his head onto her lap at the same time, other people were shouting too, and there was chaos all around. A pair of paramedics in orange and black uniforms appeared and took over. They seemed to know what they were doing, but Archer didn't care. He would happily bleed to death if someone would just turn and see their quarry standing only metres away, watching, lapping it up. His plan had been foiled so the next best thing was to watch Archer die.

Bucking against Eva and the paramedics, Archer tried desperately to speak. He grabbed Eva's arm with both hands and got eye to eye with her, his lips moving but no words coming out. Blood filled his throat and welled up, over his teeth and down his chin.

Eva was pushed aside by a medic who roughly grabbed Archer

and held him down. He could feel hands on his leg, probing and jabbing, and a jolt of pain shot through him like an electrical current.

He tried to scream but it felt like he was underwater, slipping down into the abyss, his vision blurring as he went deeper beneath the surface, the people around him, the sun overhead, the buildings, the famous arches themselves, all staying on the surface, floating, watching him go under.

He looked around desperately for someone to help him, and laid eyes on the tall man with swept-back hair, standing some distance off, watching him and smiling. It wasn't a nice smile. It was the smile of the devil, cold and sadistic, taking pleasure in watching him die.

It was the last thing Archer saw before the blackness of the abyss sucked him right down.

## 35

The ceiling and walls of the room were a soft off-white. The blinds were lowered over the window and the small TV on the wall bracket was switched off. The sheets on his bed were crisp and the pillow beneath his head was soft and inviting. The bed was raised to a 45-degree angle. His torso felt tight and achy, and his right leg was heavy.

Archer wondered how long he'd been asleep. The lights were low and cast shadows in the room, but he could make out someone in an armchair in the left hand corner. Sitting, watching him silently. It was a man, average sized and compact, all hard angles.

He jerked upwards, feeling pain jolt through his chest, panic rising. He needed to defend himself before this guy killed him.

'Sshhh, Herr Ascot, it is okay,' a soothing voice said in his ear. He jerked his head around to see the smiling face of a pretty brunette nurse beside him. He had a drip hooked up on that side, attached to a lure in his right hand. She checked a monitor that was also attached to him, wires running to a clip on his finger, then smiled again and ran a soft hand down his cheek. 'You just woke up and got a fright. It's okay. You're doing well. Go back to sleep.'

He felt her gently easing him back onto his pillow, and a warm heaviness was sliding over him.

*Who was Ascot?*

As she stroked his cheek again he noticed that the top button of her sharp white uniform was open and the swell of a significant cleavage was asking to be let free. He thought she should do that. He smiled to himself as sleep took him down; it was a good idea.

As he succumbed to sleep again, Archer realised he'd forgotten to ask Nurse Cleavage about the man in the corner.

THE BLINDS WERE UP, filling the room with light, when Eva and Ingoe arrived.

Archer was sitting up in bed, having just finished a proper meal. He felt a million dollars better with some food inside him, despite the tube hanging out the side of his chest.

Eva's face lit up when she saw he was awake, and she threw her arms around him, hugging him tight enough to make his side hurt. He didn't mind; she smelled wonderful and felt soft and womanly in his arms. He inhaled her, letting her finally break away so she could look at him. Her blue eyes, normally so cool, were now damp and concerned.

'I thought you were going to die,' she whispered, her bottom lip quivering.

'I'm okay.' He hoped his smile was reassuring. 'It's just a graze.'

Ingoe grunted behind her and settled himself in the corner armchair. Archer suddenly clicked that it had been Ingoe sitting with him that night – last night, he thought, maybe the day before? It was typical of the man. One of his boys was down for the count, so of course he would be there, watching over him.

'Just a graze, he says,' Ingoe mocked him. 'I don't think you realise how lucky you are, Arch. Your femoral artery was nicked, almost right through. You weren't far off bleeding out from that alone. The collapsed lung was the least of your concerns, but it was bad enough. Want to know how much blood you lost?'

Archer shrugged, patting Eva's hand as she parked her perfect derrière on his bed. She was wearing tight jeans and a short bomber jacket. Her hair was loose.

'Not really,' he replied. Eva held his hand between both of hers, angled to face him rather than Ingoe.

'Well let's just say that the clean-up crew at *Parisier Platz* were a busy little crew.'

Archer nodded, feeling his chest tighten. He wanted to know the answer to just one question, but was also dreading it, fearing he knew the answer. Ingoe read his mind.

'No,' he said bluntly. 'He got away.'

Archer felt the weight of defeat crush down on him. Eva squeezed his hand sympathetically.

'But we saved so many lives,' she said reassuringly. 'We stopped the attack before it really got started.'

'How many?' Archer asked, feeling detached. He didn't really care; all that mattered was that they'd failed to capture or kill Kozlowski.

'One dead,' Ingoe said, 'five injured, none critical. All three attackers were taken down, only one of them survived, plus the other guy who stabbed you.'

'Is the prisoner talking?'

Eva nodded. 'A lot, but he doesn't really know much. He was just a small player. A lamb, not the shepherd.'

'How did Kozlowski get away?'

'Lost in the crowd in all the confusion. We've got him on CCTV and tracked his movements for some distance until he was picked up by a car and driven away. No record of him leaving the country, but no surprise there.' Ingoe's face was hard. 'The man's like a goddamn ghost.'

Archer felt his fists clenching. He couldn't believe they'd failed. To be so close and have the target slip through their fingers was more than he could bear.

'It's nothing you need to worry about right now, Craig,' Eva told him. 'You only need to concentrate on getting better, *ja*?'

It wasn't much consolation, but Archer knew she was right. 'How long have I been here?' he asked.

'Three days,' Eva replied. 'You've been asleep most of that time. And when you were conscious, you were away with the goblins.'

'Fairies,' he automatically corrected her.

'Hobbits,' she retorted, her cheeks creasing.

Archer smiled, feeling his spirits lift. He squeezed her hand. 'And how long am I in here for?'

'They've said you will take up to a month or so to recover, then rehab on top of that,' Ingoe told him. 'So as soon as you're well enough to fly, you'll be heading back to Auckland.'

'No.' Archer's tone was sharper than he'd intended. 'I need to carry on here. We need to find Kozlowski.'

'No,' Ingoe said firmly. 'He's the BfV's problem now. As far as we know he's still on the run somewhere in Germany, or at least Europe. He has no connection to New Zealand, so he's no longer our problem.'

Archer opened his mouth to protest but saw the steely look in his boss' eye and knew better than to argue. *Fuck it*, he decided. He'd have to find another way to continue the hunt.

THE NEXT FEW days were like Groundhog Day, a continual cycle of the same things over and over again. He made steady progress, the chest drain came out, and he was up and about faster than the doctors had anticipated.

They credited his high levels of fitness with aiding such a rapid recovery. Archer didn't care what caused it – he just wanted to get back in the game. It felt like every day he was laid up was a day lost in the hunt for Kozlowski.

Even the presence of Nurse Cleavage and her sisters in arms was not enough to keep his mind from the job. Besides, he felt himself growing closer and closer to Eva with every minute they spent together. Not only was she beautiful and compassionate, but she was smart, brave and had a quirky wit about her that Archer found enchanting. In the quiet moments when he managed to push aside thoughts of the hunt for Kozlowski, he found himself dreaming of spending more time with her. An extended holiday. Maybe even a future – whatever that entailed.

Travis, Brad and Susie Q had been sent to guard him, and he bugged them incessantly for updates until Travis finally snapped one morning.

'If you don't shut up, he growled, 'I'll put you back in Intensive Care. Now fuck up and just do your rehab.'

Archer took the hint but simply moved his attention to Eva and Ingoe. Eva had also been out of action for a few days with the injuries she'd suffered, and Ingoe soon tired of being badgered.

'I've got you booked on a private flight to England,' he told Archer. 'You'll have a couple of weeks or so there before heading home.'

Dieter was also there, paying his second visit of the week. Ulrich had been in every day, sitting and talking with Archer, spending hours debriefing him very subtly, digging out any little nugget of intelligence he could. With his hangdog appearance and deep voice, he was like a big bloodhound, a cuddly favourite uncle.

Archer wasn't fooled. He knew that beneath that disarming exterior lay a razor-sharp mind and a hard streak.

The two German men nodded their agreement with Ingoe's decision.

'It is a good idea,' Dieter said. 'There is nothing you can do here, Mr Archer.'

'I will miss our little chats,' Ulrich rumbled. 'But you have done enough. Leave this man to us now. We will get him.'

'Besides,' Dieter said, a twinkle of merriment in his eye, 'perhaps Ms Graf would like to travel with you to, ah, continue your debrief?'

Archer felt his cheeks begin to colour, much to the amusement of Ingoe and Ulrich.

'In the interests of inter-agency cooperation, of course,' Dieter finished.

Archer figured the man would have made a great poker player.

# 36

The next morning was bright and sunny, perfect conditions for the short flight to London City airport.

Archer and Eva were escorted to a private hangar at Berlin Tegel, where the BfV crew left them. As the Mercedes MPV cruised off, Archer heard footsteps approach them from within the hangar, and a man appeared with a clipboard in his hand.

He was somewhere in his forties, serious-looking, with short clipped hair and the trace of a South African accent. He checked their passports against his notes and walked them across the tarmac apron to where a sleek silver and white Cessna Citation sat waiting, the props turning slowly.

'The pilot is aboard already,' the man told them. 'You are the only passengers today so as soon as you board you will be away.' He smiled flatly. 'Have a pleasant journey.'

He watched them climb aboard before turning away. The cabin was lined with four seats on each side, each side having two pairs of facing chairs. The door to the flight deck was closed.

'First class,' Archer muttered to himself, settling into the closest pod with his back to the flight deck. He wasn't used to such luxury. In his Cat boots, jeans and loose chambray shirt, he felt out of place in such an aircraft. Naturally, Eva fit right in in her casual chic. The dressing was off her face, leaving a distinct pink scar on the left cheek.

She sank into the opposite seat and Archer watched her as she adjusted her belt and buckled up. When he'd first laid eyes on her back in that Berlin café he had known she was very attractive, but somehow, in the days they'd spent together since then, she seemed to have become even more so. She had a beauty that he couldn't describe; it seemed to draw you in like an intoxicating scent.

As he had gotten to know her he realised that, like all truly beautiful people, her beauty radiated from within. She was a good soul beneath the outstanding physical surface, and that made her so much more appealing than the superficial beauties he had tended to spend his time with.

Archer realised he was staring when she laughed at him, and he blushed self-consciously. Her sharp blue eyes met his and he smiled.

'Something on your mind, Craig?' she asked.

'No.' He shook his head. 'Just daydreaming.'

She leaned forward, reached out and took his hand in hers. Her hand was warm and soft and strong and felt good in his. He squeezed it and she smiled. He was vaguely aware of the sound of someone climbing aboard behind him and sealing the door. Footsteps then the flight deck door opened and closed.

None of that mattered to him when Eva was so close, her eyes two deep pools of blue as they searched his, her scent filling his senses, the touch of her hand on his.

Archer was aware of nothing else but her presence, right here, right now. With him. *Being* with him. He knew how much he wanted to be with her. It was funny, he mused to himself. Nothing had actually happened between them, no kissing and certainly nothing more, but he knew, and he knew she knew, that there was something strong between them.

Something almost tangible, a bond from their shared experiences that could never be broken, and yet it was more than even that. It was more than just beating death; it was the desire to live. To share that life with not just any person, but this person. This fantastic girl who was gazing at him with a dreamy expression, holding his hand. He felt like a schoolboy again, and Archer knew then, knew for sure right at that very moment, that he was falling in love with this girl.

Eva Graf of the *Bundesamt für Verfassungsschutz.* Thirty-four years old, never married. One brother. Parents still alive. A very capable foreign intelligence officer. There had been many women in Archer's life, but he knew without a doubt that nobody had ever consumed him like her. She was the real deal.

Eva's eyes sparkled as she smiled at him. 'I haven't spent much time in England,' she said, interrupting his thoughts. 'You'll have to show me the sights of London.'

'I was thinking more of a cosy B&B in the Cotswolds,' Archer confessed. 'An open fire, pub meals, rambling in the countryside.'

'I hope there would be time for some...other activities,' she teased.

'I don't know if I'm up to it,' Archer replied. 'I'm pretty banged up.'

She pretended to pout. 'Well I think I'd rather see a show then...'

She was cut off by the sound of the engines winding up, and they sat back and buckled up as the plane began to taxi. They were soon in the air and continued making their plans for the stop in England. Ingoe hadn't been too specific on how much time off Archer was allowed, but he knew the leash wouldn't be too long before he was expected to front up to the Director for a formal debrief.

But for now the time was his own, and he could think of no better way to spend it than with the beguiling Eva Graf.

They had levelled out and must've been somewhere over Holland, when Eva remarked, 'There's obviously no in-flight service. I wonder what you must do to get a drink around here?'

'The pilots haven't said boo, either,' Archer mused.

'Why would they say "boo"?' Eva asked, her brow creasing as she tried to decipher his latest weird saying.

At that moment the door to the flight deck opened Archer heard someone approach them. He saw Eva's eyes widen with surprise when she looked up, and he immediately swivelled, sensing danger. Ulrich stood before them, his pilot's uniform tight across his belly.

The compact Walther PPK stainless in his hand was pointed at them. The underpowered .380ACP round made it a lady's gun, not something Archer would ever select himself, but it was perfect for this situation. As long as Ulrich hit one of them in the torso, it was highly unlikely to damage the skin of the aircraft. A loose shot, of course, was a different story.

'Ulrich, what are you doing?' Eva demanded. 'Have you gone mad?'

'On the contrary, dear Eva,' he rumbled, 'I know exactly what I am doing. I have known this for a long time.'

'You're on Kozlowski's payroll,' Archer murmured. The realisation hit him hard. Not only had they had been betrayed by Jessika, but also by Ulrich. Two people of influence in completely separate intelligence agencies. 'You're a traitor as well.'

'I prefer to think of myself as a realist, Herr Archer,' Ulrich responded. 'I have two ex-wives and five children – do you think I can afford to keep them on what I earn working for the government? A government that lies down with the Americans and does their bidding for them? That opens the borders to all the gypsy scum of Eastern Europe and the Middle East, to come and poison my beloved Deutschland? No, Herr Archer.' He shook his head, his jowls wobbling. 'That is not the life I choose. I will instead retire somewhere warm, take a new identity and live the rest of my days in comfort.'

'You traitorous, murdering bastard,' Eva hissed, her eyes blazing. 'You trained me. *I trusted you*. I looked up to you, Ulrich!'

'And I must say, dear Eva, that I did a good job. You are an excellent asset to the BfV. However, I am not, and you will never see things my way.'

'You're right,' she agreed. 'I never will. Because I love my country and I would never betray it to lie down with the dogs like you.'

Ulrich shrugged his big shoulders indifferently. 'Many people in our country don't see it that way, Eva. There are many who feel betrayed, who want a return to a more...traditional way of life.'

'Fascism.' She spat the word out with disdain. 'A return to a history that failed. What kind of future is that for our country – for your *children*?'

Archer could see the despair in her face. The rug had been well and truly pulled from beneath her.

'So you've been working against us this whole time?' he interjected. 'We've been hunting terrorists while you've been helping them.'

'One man's terrorist is another man's freedom fighter, as they say,' Ulrich retorted. 'I see a freedom for my country which will never be recognised in today's political climate, and I have the strong heart to fight for that.'

'By helping a madman kill innocent people,' Archer snapped back. He eyed the Walther, trying to gauge whether he could get to it before Ulrich fired. It would be a close call, but it may be the only one he could make.

'I hope you burn in hell,' Eva spat, 'you are nothing to me!'

'Easy there, *fraulein*,' came a new voice from the rear of the cabin.

Viktor Kozlowski stepped into the aisle, appearing from the storage area at the rear. He was dressed in a black jumpsuit and had a parachute strapped to his back. A pair of goggles was pushed up on his head.

He grinned at their shock.

'Surprised to see me? It's been a while. I wondered if we'd ever get this chance, but as fate would have it, here we are.' He leaned casually against the back of a seat at the next pod. 'Congratulations on your speedy recovery, both of you. Shame it's gonna go to waste.'

'So what's the plan, Viktor?' Archer said. 'The plane goes down with us on board while you jump to freedom? A tragic accident, pilot error?'

Kozlowski nodded. 'Something like that. Right now we're flying on auto-pilot, am I correct on that, Ulrich?'

The big German nodded. '*Ja*. The pilot has unfortunately suffered a heart attack while flying, and very shortly he will crash into the Eastern Alps.'

'Bavaria,' Archer said. 'So you're heading where – Switzerland?

Austria? There used to be a good cobbler in Vienna apparently. I heard his business might have gone bust though.'

'I thought that was probably your work,' Kozlowski said. 'Shame. He did good work.' He hiked his shoulders and gave an icy smirk. 'Saved me a job, anyways.'

'See how he treats his friends, Ulrich?' Archer prodded. 'You want to watch yourself, mate.'

Kozlowski gave a derisive snort. 'Stop talking horse shit, Archer. He's just tryin' to mess with your head Ulrich, don't listen to him.'

'It's true, Ulrich.' Archer held the German's gaze. 'Look around you – not many of his friends remaining, are there?'

Ulrich shifted uneasily and looked at his boss, who was glaring at Archer.

'Don't worry about him, pal. He's in a bind and he knows it. They'll both be dead soon enough.'

'While you two disappear like a pair of ghosts to start again.'

'That's right. The plane goes down with you on board,' Kozlowski smiled, his black eyes gleaming at his ingenuity. 'The pilot's real, not one of my guys. If there's even anything left of this crate, there'll be no trace of us on board. As the big man here said, we get away and start afresh, completely under the radar.' He smile disappeared. 'You already disrupted one plan, Mr Archer, but there are plenty more where that came from, I can assure you.'

'I've no doubt there's all sorts of evil shit crawling round in your crazy head, Kozlowski,' Archer growled.

Kozlowski shrugged casually. 'The world's an evil place, buddy. Plenty of people willing to pay good money for bad things to happen.'

'So this was all just a paid job?' Eva said incredulously. 'You weren't doing this for any idealistic goal, were you?'

Kozlowski gave a short laugh. 'Don't be ridiculous,' he said. 'The opportunity to get back at my former employers by blowing up LAX? Yeah, sure, that was a nice opportunity, but I still got paid for it. Or I would have done, if your boyfriend here hadn't got in the way. That cost me dear. Meant I had to take the Berlin job at short notice and a reduced rate.' His face darkened. 'And because that was only a limited success, I gotta get away for a while 'til things cool down a bit. There's more than one outfit with a price on my head right now, thanks to you.'

'Good.' Archer's jaw was set tight. 'I hope they flay you alive. It's more than you deserve.'

A matching stainless Walther appeared in Kozlowski's hand and he held it at his hip, aimed at Archer's chest.

'No doubt they would agree,' he said, 'but it ain't gonna happen. This is it, pal. I get the last laugh.'

'The guys you used?' Archer prodded. 'Black Star?'

Kozlowski nodded. 'And some guys from overseas thrown in for good measure.'

It made sense to Archer. The attackers on the airliner and at the Brandenburg Gate – probably their captors at the farmhouse, too – had been genuine jihadists, chasing their cause, but the man pulling the strings behind the scenes had been a simple mercenary.

A terrorist for hire, conspiring all the while with traitors from two different intelligence agencies. It took real cunning and determination to pull off such a performance.

And now the evil bastard was going to get away with it.

Ulrich and Kozlowski edged past them, back towards the flight deck door, the twin Walther muzzles never leaving them.

Kozlowski covered them while Ulrich removed a parachute from a storage locker and began to step into it. As he got himself sorted, Archer caught Eva's eye. She was pale and tense.

'Wait for it,' Archer mouthed to her. He knew what Kozlowski was going to do – it was the obvious cover up.

Ulrich opened the flight deck door and they could see the pilot slumped forward in his seat. He fiddled with the controls and they felt the nose of the Cessna begin to dip.

As his cohort returned to the cabin, Kozlowski unlocked the side door and swung it open. Archer grabbed his armrests instinctively and Kozlowski laughed at him.

'Don't worry, Mr Archer,' he chuckled, 'we're not high enough for you get sucked out of here. All I'm doing is getting ready to exit the stage.'

'So am I,' Ulrich rumbled, joining in with a hearty chuckle.

'Unfortunately, no.' Kozlowski told him. He turned and aimed his Walther at Ulrich's expansive gut. 'I need you for something else.'

'What?' Ulrich looked confused. 'What do you mean, Viktor?'

'I need you to be the bad guy,' Kozlowski told him with a cruel smile. 'See, you're gonna shoot these two and in the struggle, you'll also be fatally wounded. You'll all go down with the plane, while I walk away.'

'You're double-crossing me?' Ulrich looked aghast. 'But...but...'

'No buts, Ulrich. Archer was right about one thing. This is how it's gotta be.'

Ulrich grunted and lifted his pistol, squeezing the trigger. The hammer snapped forward on an empty chamber. He stared at the gun in his hand as if he couldn't believe what was happening, and that was when Kozlowski shot him in the chest.

The big German staggered back, blood blossoming across his shirtfront, and Kozlowski fired again.

Archer pushed up and threw himself forward, the nose-first dropping of the plane helping his momentum as he went for the terrorist. The Walther was coming round and another shot sounded, but Archer got a hand to Kozlowski's jumpsuit.

The Walther crashed against the side of his head and he felt himself going down, his weak leg unable to keep him up. The whine of their descent and the scream of the wind were almost deafening now and the floor had tilted crazily.

Archer clung onto Kozlowski with one hand, trying to fend off his blows with the other. The Walther fired again, close enough to deafen his left ear and singe the hair at his temple. He got a hand to Kozlowski's wrist and let go with his other, lashing out.

Eva came in over the top, punching at Kozlowski's face. The Walther fell free and skittered away. Out the open door, Archer could see the ground coming up incredibly fast. If they didn't move soon they'd be spread across the countryside. He had no idea how to pull the plane out of a death dive, so there was only one option.

He pushed himself up, taking a decent jab to the temple from Kozlowski, and got a hand to the guy's face. They were jammed against the wall now by the force of gravity, and he used it to his advantage, gouging at Kozlowski's eyes while he hammered his other hand into the terrorist's head.

Kozlowski was screaming, Eva was shouting and Archer couldn't hear a damn thing. He grabbed Kozlowski by the hair and slammed his head back against the wall, once, twice, three times.

He felt the man go slack and start to slump. He gave him a solid hook for good measure and let him fall to the floor against the open cockpit door, and Archer turned, looking for Eva. She already had Ulrich half out of his rig and Archer feverishly helped her. They were practically vertical now and he figured they only had seconds to go.

They ripped the harness free from the dead traitor and Archer yanked it over Eva's arms, snapping it closed across the chest and waist. No time for the legs – if they were lucky, it would hold.

Forcing their way to the open door, Archer gave Kozlowski a last glance. The man's eyelids were fluttering and he was struggling to move. Archer wanted to finish him off, but if he wasted time doing that, they were all dead anyway.

He grabbed Eva in a front-on bear hug and locked his hands around her waist. 'As soon as I tell you,' he shouted, 'pull it!'

She nodded as he shuffled her backwards, her eyes wide, and he turned, sitting down with her half on top of him.

He knew the door was very close to the wing, and the engine was attached to the tail higher than the wing, sitting parallel to the body of the cabin. If he played this wrong they'd either smash themselves on the wing as they went out or get sucked straight into the engine. They had to get low enough to go under the wing.

Archer leaned out until his head was in the slipstream.

He took a quick glance to his right and gauged the fall. A quick glance to his left showed a tree covered mountainside screaming towards them.

# 37

There was no time to lose.

*Fuck it. Balls out.*

With that he rolled himself backward, jerking Eva with him and clutching her to him.

It wasn't his most graceful exit ever from a plane but they somehow managed to avoid injury, the wing skimming past the back of Eva's head by a hair's breadth as they plunged into the slipstream.

As soon as the tail flashed past them Archer bellowed at her, 'Pull it! Pull it!'

She yanked the rip cord immediately, the wind tearing at them as the Cessna plunged away.

They were jerked upwards with a loud snap and Archer clung to her for dear life. He hoped like hell she had done some jump training in the Army.

They were in a mountainous area, trees and cliffs seemingly close enough to touch, and in the near distance he heard a massive crash followed by a crumping explosion. Glancing that way, all he saw was a cliff. The plane must have skimmed over the top of it and dropped out of sight. He didn't care; they had bigger things to worry about right now.

He glanced down and saw water, what looked like a mountain lake, racing up to meet them. With the water surface the only thing he could see below them and no way to tell how far away they actually were, he yelled at Eva to flare the chute.

She fumbled with it, their descent slowed slightly then they hit with a thump. As soon as Archer's boots broke the water he let go of Eva and pushed away. The water was shockingly cold and it took his breath away as he went down.

He kicked out as soon as his descent stopped and swam for the surface, his clothes heavy and cumbersome on him. His head broke the surface and he gasped for air, realising now that he'd probably held his breath the whole way down.

The 'chute was nearby but there was no sign of Eva.

'Eva! Eva!'

Still nothing. She should've been up by now. Archer took in a lungful and dived, kicking down hard, seeing her a couple of metres below the surface, thrashing about.

She was struggling with her harness and he could see that something was preventing her from getting free.

She saw him and screamed silently, her face terrified.

Archer dived harder, seeing now that the rigging had got tangled on a submerged tree branch. The length of the tree extended beyond his sight, and had presumably fallen into the water, landing on its side with the branches reaching out like arms.

They must have narrowly missed the branches themselves when they landed, but the long lengths of roping had become tangled and Eva was now trapped, probably only seconds away from a panic reaction that would kill her as certainly as a plane crash.

He reached her, grabbed her arms and held them firmly out of the way. He leaned in, locked his mouth onto hers and forced air into it. At least now she had some air in her lungs and could hopefully last while he tried to free her.

He grabbed the chest clip and unhooked her, and began on the waist clip. It was somehow jammed and he pushed and pulled, manipulating it as best he could. Parachute harnesses didn't have complicated mechanisms, but it was the first time he'd ever tried to undo one in these circumstances. The freezing cold water wasn't helping his dexterity at all.

Eva was flapping properly now, probably out of air and seeing her life flash before her eyes. His own lungs were burning and his body wanted to float up. With Eva's top getting in the way, he couldn't even see what he was doing, but something worked because suddenly the fastening popped open and Eva was kicking hard for the surface.

Archer followed suit, gasping for air as soon as his head was clear of the water.

They trod water until they had caught their breath enough to speak.

'*Der scheisskerl*,' Eva managed, pushing her hair back from her eyes.

Archer wasn't sure whether she was calling Kozlowski or Ulrich a son of a bitch or a motherfucker, but it didn't matter; both were accurate for both men, and he seconded the motion. He reached out and pulled her to him, feeling her arms go round his neck as he kissed her hard on the mouth.

'We need to get to shore,' he told her. 'Come on.'

'*Ja*,' she agreed, kissing him back, her hair plastered to her head and her eyeliner running. Her lips were cold but soft and tender. 'Yes, we do.'

He stole another kiss before she put a hand on his chest and gently edged him back.

'I am freezing to death,' she said, and he relented, knowing there would be time later for more of that.

They struck out together to the nearest bank of the lake – a very narrow strip of pebbly sand several metres away. They were surrounded by thick vegetation with a scarred cliff towering over them. Archer though he could faintly smell burning on the light mountain breeze.

They reached the shore and crawled onto the tiny beach, flopping onto their backs with their legs still in the water. They lay there for what seemed like a long time, exhausted and wringing wet, slowly coming back to their senses. As Archer got his head together, the absurdity of the situation struck him and he began to laugh.

Eva propped herself up on one elbow and looked at him quizzically. 'Have you gone mad?' she asked. 'Did you bang your head?'

'We survived,' he told her, feeling a wave of relief suddenly hit. 'We fell out a goddamn plane that was going down, with one 'chute between us, and nearly drowned. And we survived!'

She frowned at him for a moment before she started chuckling too, the chuckling leading to full-on chest-heaving belly laughs, and the pair of them lay there laughing their heads off, the elation and relief overwhelming them in equal measures.

'I can't believe it,' Eva said between bouts of hysterical laughter. 'This is ridiculous. This is not what I signed up for at all.'

Archer forced himself to his feet and shook himself off. He knew they hadn't fallen terribly far, but it had been a hard enough landing to leave him feeling bruised and battered. He stripped off his shirt and wrung it out, then unlaced his boots and tipped the water out. He saw Eva watching him.

'You need to do the same,' he said. 'We'll be walking some distance, so the more comfortable we are, the better. And hypothermia's not so helpful either.'

She shrugged and stood, shucking off her bomber jacket and dropping it to the ground. He squeezed out his socks as she removed her top, leaving herself exposed in just the flimsiest of ivory lace that had gone completely see-through in the water.

Archer tried not to stare. It didn't work. Eva gave a small smile and wrung out her top.

'I didn't anticipate your first view of me in my underwear being quite like this, Craig,' she said, giving him a coy smile.

'Neither did I,' he admitted, 'but I'm not complaining.' He looked around them. 'Any idea exactly where we are?'

'*Nein*.' Eva upended her shoes. 'But I think if we head downhill we will find someone.' She dug her phone out of her jacket pocket and pulled a face. 'A very expensive paper weight.'

Archer had lost his own phone somewhere in the jump or swim.

He looked around, listening for any sign of approaching danger. Nothing.

He waited, politely looking away while Eva wrung out her jeans and redressed. 'Ready?'

'Ready.' She pushed back her wet hair, looking dishevelled and beautiful at the same time. 'Let's go.'

She took his hand and he led the way.

'As you would expect,' Ingoe said, 'the plane was completely toast. No survivors, three bodies on board.'

'Three?' Archer felt his eyebrows shoot up his forehead. 'Are they sure?'

'Very.' Ingoe nodded. 'Two are confirmed as Ulrich and the kidnapped pilot. The third is being officially confirmed as Viktor Kozlowski.'

'Confirmed how?' Archer pushed himself off the windowsill and crossed the board room to the side cabinet. It was deep mahogany and carried decanters of whiskey, brandy and port, along with the matching glassware. 'DNA?'

'Don't have any for Kozlowski.' Ingoe watched him use silver tongs to drop ice cubes into a tumbler, then pour a good slug of whiskey over the top. 'They're basing the ID on the fact there was no one else on board the aircraft, according to you and the German bird.'

'We didn't say that.' Archer turned, tinkling the ice against the glass. 'We didn't see anyone else; doesn't mean they weren't there.'

They were in the bowels of New Zealand House, the High Commission in London. The lights were dimmed and it was early evening. It was three days after the plane crash, most of which Archer had spent being debriefed and medically treated at a German military base.

He and Eva had spent the better part of a day hiking out of the mountains, battered and bruised, before reaching a farm and making contact with the rescue parties dispatched to the crash. His body still ached and his right leg was weak, but accepting good medical care and drinking more hard liquor than normal had worked wonders.

'I know what you're saying,' Ingoe was telling him, 'but the ground crews found no trace of him in the mountains, and there's been nothing come through other channels either. As far as we can tell, Kozlowski's dead, burned to death in the crash.'

Archer opened his mouth to speak, but Ingoe cut him off with a cold look. 'That's it, Archer. We carry on as normal. If something should come to light to say that he's somehow miraculously alive, then it will be investigated.' His tone took on a hard edge. 'But not by you. Understand?'

Archer took a swallow of whiskey. It was quality Irish liquor, but it did nothing to lighten his mood. 'Understood.'

Ingoe studied him in the half light. The former warrior's face was all sharp angles and weathered lines beneath clipped grey hair. He pursed his lips as he watched Archer take another hit.

'You've got ten days' leave,' Ingoe said. 'Going anywhere nice?'

Archer shrugged, non-committal. 'No plans yet.'

Ingoe was silent for another moment, considering the next step. Years of experience with Archer told him that he'd pushed it far enough just now. Archer would do whatever he was going to do regardless of what Ingoe told him, but at least he'd been warned.

'Enjoy,' he said abruptly, heading for the door. He paused with the door half open and looked over his shoulder at Archer. 'Stay in touch.'

Archer gave a short nod and said nothing.

# 38

*Three months later*
*London*

The desk lamp cast a warm glow, a cone of light in the otherwise darkened office.

The PC screen was live, a half-completed email on it requesting stores. It was yet another mundane chore in a seemingly endless string of mundane chores. It was the lifeblood of an office bore, a lab rat on the 9-5 wheel of life, running, running, running, just waiting for the misery to end.

*To die.*

Archer was convinced it was killing him. Despite continually working out, he felt out of shape. Despite eating healthily and cutting down his alcohol intake, he felt lethargic. He hadn't been on the range since the end of the Berlin op.

It had been a great success, they all told him. A significant terrorist attack stopped, numerous lives saved, the CIA rescued from crippling humiliation. In fact, the CIA had gone so far as to put

Jessika forward for an Intelligence Star. There was no way that dirty little secret would be coming out. Nations were grateful. People thanked him. And yet he felt unsettled about the whole deal. It wasn't finished.

The reported death of Viktor Kozlowski bothered him. He could not have survived that crash, everybody knew that. But without a body, it would always remain unresolved for Archer. If he and Eva had managed to jump clear, maybe he did too.

Archer wanted to get his hands on the bastard himself, to choke the life out of him and be sure he was dead. He needed to see the life leave the traitor's body with his own two eyes.

Sarah had tried calling a couple of times but he never called back, just as he hadn't responded to her single, desperate-seeming email. He felt sorry for her; she was a good lady, and despite her show of being a "big girl," he felt like a cad.

He hadn't seen Eva for a month now but they had three days in Tuscany planned for the following week, and he was hanging out for it. After many failed attempts at romance, things finally seemed to be working out with her. The distance was a pain, but neither of them was rushing anything just yet.

His leave had been spent with Eva, travelling together through Europe. A week with her, dining out and travelling, staying in hotels, talking and laughing, making love and baring their souls, had been cathartic. He hadn't realised how much the op had taken out of him until he began to unwind.

The week had proved to be a turning point for Archer in more ways than one.

Not only had he fallen into something he had no desire to get out of, but he had also begun to believe that maybe, just maybe, Kozlowski actually *was* dead. Despite the efforts of multiple intelligence agencies and police forces, there was no sign of the man anywhere.

Not a trace. Nobody was that good.

He pushed back from the desk and stared out at the night sky. Christmas had been and gone, snow was forecast and the temperature had dropped again. The weather. The bloody, infernal weather. It seemed to dominate conversations here. That and the bloody football.

London was ablaze out there with light and energy, movement and activity everywhere, shows to go to, sights to see, excitement to be had. It was out there.

*Life.*

Yet he felt bored. The Director had given him a secondment to New Zealand House, a "development opportunity." He was to replace Rob Moore, who'd been missing for over a year now. It was a proper intelligence officer role, with secondary responsibilities to Division 5.

It would be good for him, the Director had said. Archer wasn't convinced. Aside from the burgeoning relationship with Eva he felt life slipping away from him. If this was to keep up, he'd tender his resignation and piss off to Iraq, get back on the circuit and have some fun.

The death of Jessika bothered him unreasonably. He tried to convince himself that he felt no remorse for having incited her killing, but he knew he was only fooling himself. His disruption tactic had failed miserably. The Americans had been extremely doubtful about his version of events, but with Eva's backing, he had come through the initial enquiry.

Sod this, he thought to himself, staring out at the night, unseeing. As Eva had said back on the mountainside, this wasn't what he'd signed up for.

The ping of an incoming email stirred him from his malaise. Hopefully it was Eva, finally responding to his last message. He swivelled round in his chair and pulled up to the desk.

He minimised the draft he'd been slaving over. Equipment orders could wait. The Inbox showed an unread message from an email address he didn't recognise; graf.eva.graf@gmail.com. He double-clicked on it without thinking and the message opened up.

The screen went black for a second before a theatre scene materialised from the darkness, lights shining up from below onto a stage where two puppets danced together. Oom-pah music accompanied the bizarre scene. One of the puppets wore a black tuxedo and had a silver fern crest on his collar. The other was an Oktoberfest serving girl with blonde braids.

They danced together, seemingly happy, but as Archer stared at them, he realised they were both crying. Droplets of blood ran from their eyes, dripping onto the stage floor beneath their feet.

In the background, above the curtains of the stage, Archer could see the person holding the puppet strings. One set in each hand, wiggling and waggling them, making the marionettes beneath him dance to his tune.

The puppet master.

Only this puppet master had the face of Viktor Kozlowski, grinning madly, thoroughly enjoying himself as the puppets at his fingertips danced.

A maniacal laugh sounded through the speakers, deep and resonant, a full-bodied belly laugh of evil.

Script began to appear across the screen, roughly drawn as if with a well-used paint brush, the lettering blood red.

*See you real soon*

Archer felt a chill run up his spine as the screen went blank again. The evil bastard was back.

END

The **Division** series continues with *No Second Chance*,
the fifth book in the series.

# BONUS CHAPTERS

# EARLY WARNING SERIES #1

MARTIAL LAW

Some would say I was paranoid, but they'd be wrong.

There's a difference between being paranoid and being smart.

To put it in real terms, if one President with a big red button and an ego problem butts heads with another with the same issues, it's probably a good time to start preparing for the worst. That's what I did, and every step of the way I prayed it would all be for nothing.

I wasn't the only one, but we were still the minority. Nobody wants their worst fears to be proved right, but I also didn't want to be one of the mindless sheeple that relied on someone else to pull their arse from the fire.

This was a country built by pioneers, tough resilient folk who travelled round the world to land on a handful of islands down near the bottom of the South Pacific. They battled adversity every step of the way, creating a national mindset of independence and humility. Shout your name from the rooftops? Expect to get cut down. Nobody round here likes a blowhard.

My name's Mark Dobson. I'm just the guy next door.

I don't care too much what people think of me, but of course there was another very good reason to keep my preparations quiet. If my predictions came true a lot of people would be caught short. Food and fuel would be the big issues. Lack of medicines. Unheated homes. Mental health issues would be exacerbated by the stress. Those that were desperate would steal to feed and clothe their families. The lowlifes would do that and more, whether they needed supplies or not. Violence would break out.

Those that were unprepared would fall victim to the predators. That wouldn't happen to my family, not on my watch.

No fucking way.

## THE SERVICE SERIES #1

WARLOCK

*Village of Magas*
*Drina Valley, North-Eastern Bosnia*
*June 1995*

Death came at dawn.

The sun was creeping over the lip of the valley and the village was starting to come to life. It was a small settlement of simple houses, many already damaged by various attacks over the years and repaired as best they could be.

The main road into the village was rutted and narrow, potted with holes and horseshoe imprints.

The trucks of the short convoy crushed the ruts flat as they rolled down the road from the south, heavy diesel engines throbbing and gear boxes grinding as the drivers struggled to maintain momentum and stability at the same time.

The villagers heard the trucks coming and knew it was not good news. People started to come out of their houses, peering up the road to try and see who it was. Could it possibly be a UN visit? Probably not. Nobody cared enough about these poor peasants to send the UN to them.

A few people started to make haste, rousing their families and getting ready to run. But it was too late.

The first truck rounded the last bend and gunned it straight into the centre of the village, a small town square surrounded by a few basic shops and shuttered buildings. The head elder of the village had been awakened and shuffled out in his coat and hat, his pyjama legs flapping in the light morning breeze.

The first truck ground to a halt and the rear flap opened, discharging a dozen armed soldiers. They quickly spread out across one side of the village square, rifles at the ready and game faces on. They wore the standard Serbian Army uniforms with the shoulder patch of the Red Wolves, the feared elite paratroop unit.

The elder felt his gut go cold as he recognised the men before him, and he knew without a doubt what was about to happen.

More trucks rolled into the town square, a jeep in the middle of the convoy making directly for the elder. It pulled up beside him and the front passenger got out. He was a tall, barrel chested man in an impeccably smart uniform, and with a face like stone. His black eyes bore into those of the elder, who immediately recognised him.

Josef Durakovic, Major. Commanding Officer of the Red Wolves.

The elder felt his bladder loosen and warm urine trickled down his leg.

Durakovic walked slowly towards him as the soldiers kicked in the doors of the houses nearby, dragging the occupants out at gunpoint, women, children, men, old and young alike. Screaming, terrified.

They were bundled into a group in the centre of the square, soldiers surrounding them, rifles raised threateningly. The soldiers were calm and in control, waiting for orders.

Durkavoic halted a metre short of the elder, his eyes never leaving the face of the old man.

'You know who I am?' Durakavic asked softly.

The old man nodded slowly.

Durakovic nodded too.

'Then you know why I am here,' he stated.

The old man nodded again, slowly.

'I know,' he croaked through a mouth dry as tinder. 'You come to kill us.'

Durakovic' thin lips twitched into a smile, fleetingly then gone.

'Yes,' he agreed. 'All Muslim pigs like you. You had your chance to go. You didn't go.'

'We had no chance,' the old man croaked angrily, tears welling at his eyes. 'We are just peasants, we are nothing to you. We don't fight.'

Durakovic nodded again, not smiling now.

'That is correct,' he said. 'You are nothing to us.'

His right hand went to the holster on his hip, and undid the flap. As he started to draw out his pistol, the old man took a step forward and spat as hard as he could. The dry white spittle landed on Durakovic's tunic front and hung there.

'Serbian shit,' the old man snapped hoarsely, and Duracovic's pistol came up.

The single shot made the civilians jump, and the bullet blew a spray of blood and brain matter into the air behind the old man. The body dropped like a stone into a crumpled heap of stick-like limbs and thin tatty clothes.

A woman screamed and her scream echoed around the town square.

Durakovic turned to the sergeant standing nearby, and holstered his pistol.

'Kill them,' he said calmly.

The snarl of automatic fire was deafening as bullets ripped through the throng of people, and within seconds magazines were being rapidly changed as the eager soldiers tried not to be the last one to get a kill.

Silence fell again and the soldiers began to move between the bodies, single shots ringing out now as they administered kill shots to those still twitching.

Durakovic let his eyes wander across the buildings around them, seeing the odd flicker of movement as civilians who had been hiding made a break for freedom. He was happy to let them go; they would spread the word of what had happened here today, and his reputation would spread further.

He turned to his sergeant again and an unspoken warmth passed between the two men.

'Burn it,' Durakovic ordered.

# MESSAGE FROM THE AUTHOR

Thanks for taking the time to read *The Berlin Conspiracy*. I hope you enjoyed this fourth book in the **Division** series. The fifth book in the series is *No Second Chance* - From the tropical Cook Islands to central London, downtown Auckland to the breathtaking Bahamas, this is one mission that will push Archer beyond his limits.

I'd love it if you could please take the time to leave an online review of *The Berlin Conspiracy* with your favourite book retailer.

If you'd like to know about new releases and receive a free book, sign up to my **Hitlist** on Facebook -

https://www.facebook.com/writer-angus-mclean

Cheers,

*Angus McLean*

## ACKNOWLEDGMENTS

Thanks go out to all those readers who keep me inspired.

Most of all, to my family. You are everything to me.

This is a work of fiction, and all errors are the responsibility of the author.

# ABOUT THE AUTHOR

Angus McLean is a South Auckland Police officer.

His experience as a cop and a private investigator give his writing a touch of realism. He believes reading should be escapist entertainment and is inspired by the TV shows he watched as a youngster.

His real identity remains a secret.

www.writerangusmclean.com

www.ingramcontent.com/pod-product-compliance
Ingram Content Group UK Ltd.
Pitfield, Milton Keynes, MK11 3LW, UK
UKHW020425250726
13967UKWH00007B/2819